ABOUT THE
DARK HART COLLECTION

THE DARK HART COLLECTION is a line of novels and novellas curated by me, Sadie Hartmann, aka "Mother Horror," for Dark Matter INK. These stories map new territories in the ever-evolving landscape of the horror genre. I invite you to escape into books written by authors who blur the lines between multiple genres, and who explore the depth and breadth of dark hearts everywhere.

Sincerely,

Sadie Hartmann
Curator, The Dark Hart Collection

PRAISE FOR APPARITIONS

"Horrifying and also deeply human. A heartbreaking look at the way society fails people and the monstrousness that grows in the dark places that we turn away from and refuse to see. A highly addictive read."

—A. C. Wise, author of *The Ghost Sequences*

"A young deaf man escapes years of cruelty and abuse—deprived of love, language, even a name—into the arms of a troubled savior who gives him all three at a terrible cost. *Apparitions* is a gripping, pulse-pounding thriller about desire and terror, faith and revenge, suffused with ever-escalating dread as it hurtles towards its devastating conclusion. Adam Pottle evokes Cormac McCarthy and Jack Ketchum with his taut muscular prose and his wrenching insights into the lonely violent lives of those who are forced into society's margins. An intensely unsettling read that wound its way into my nightmares."

—David Demchuk, author of *The Bone Mother* and *RED X*

"I want to shout from the rooftops about how incredible this book is. Suffice it to say, it's leapt straight onto my Top Reads of 2023 shelf. Unique, compelling, simply breathtaking! If this story doesn't break your heart, then you're nothing but an empty cage of bones."

—Catherine McCarthy, author of *Mosaic*

"*Apparitions* gripped me from the very opening line. Pottle effortlessly weaves a coming-of-age tale that's somehow both devastatingly brutal and exquisite; both tragic and full of hope. His command of story through emotion, language, and character is really unparalleled."

—Steph Nelson, author of *The Vein*

"It's been a long time since I rooted for a character as hard as I did the enigmatic protagonist of *Apparitions*. This short novel packs a whole world into its few pages and signals the arrival of a thrilling new storyteller with much to say."

—John Fram, author of *The Bright Lands*

"Language is both a means of connection and a gateway to horror in Adam Pottle's disturbing and heartbreaking *Apparitions*. It's the kind of novel where you're never quite sure where the true danger lies—which means you read it all the faster to find out."

—Andrew Pyper, author of *The Residence* and *The Demonologist*

APPARITIONS

CONTENT WARNINGS

Ableism, forced institutionalization, religious abuse, child abuse, graphic violence, sexual assault, verbal and physical abuse, references to colonial violence, homophobia, animal violence, family dysfunction, graphic sex, trauma, extreme isolation, imprisonment.

Reader discretion is advised.

Edited by Marissa van Uden
Book Design and Layout by Rob Carroll
Cover Design by Rob Carroll

ISBN 978-1-958598-18-4 (paperback)
ISBN 978-1-958598-50-4 (eBook)
ISBN 978-1-958598-51-1 (audiobook)

darkmatter-ink.com

APPARITIONS

ADAM POTTLE

DARK
MATTER
INK

APPARITIONS

ADAM POTTLE

To my fellow ghosts—

All those who go unseen and unheard—

I see you.

AUTHOR'S NOTE

AMERICAN SIGN LANGUAGE (ASL) does not directly translate into English. Grammatically speaking, ASL is closer to Mandarin. If I wanted to ask, "What is your name?" in ASL, I'd sign "Name you?" Emphasis and tone stem from the vehemence of the signer's expressions, the quickness of their movements, the animation of their eyes and faces. This story is therefore a crude approximation of the original version, which was recorded on video at the Saskatchewan Federal Penitentiary in Prince Albert from October 1987 to June 1988. The narrator, whose real name exists only in Sign, was part of a study produced by a now-defunct non-profit group on how inmates were treated in prison. Due to funding cuts, the study was never finished, so these videotapes formed part of a research archive that sat untouched for thirty years; small clips were used for educational purposes, but the interviews as a whole have not been seen until now.

While I've done my best to capture the narrator's astonishing tale, which he told with a furious and beautiful physicality, the story needed numerous edits for clarity purposes. According to Charity Blanc, who originally interviewed the narrator, the narrator's experiences, and especially the time he spent at his father's house, severely damaged his ability to distinguish between time periods. He experienced everything in the present—nothing else existed for him. As a result, the story offered here is not in the order it was first delivered. Much of it had to be pieced together using different resources as guidelines: newspaper articles, court documents, arrest reports, journal entries, school records, prison records, and psychiatric reports. To help clarify the timeline, and to provide context to the narrator's story, some of these resources have been included in this book.

The narrator completed his prison term in January 2005. He has given me permission to share his story, provided I do not give away his current location or occupation.

I made every effort to contact Felix Jimson's mother, using both private and public channels, but I was unable to reach her.

Felix Jimson's whereabouts remain unknown.

ESCAPE

MAKE A FIST. Tight. Thumb crossed over your fingers, like you want to punch someone. Drag it upward from your gut. Drag it slowly. As your fist nears your heart, arc it outward and open your hand wide like you're spreading something, sharing something. That's my name. Felix gave it to me. I'm not sure how long ago—I have difficulty with numbers. My parents never registered my birth, so I've never been sure of my age. No matter. I'm here. Whatever they tell you my name is here, they're wrong. I don't live on paper; I don't exist on paper.

Neither my mother nor my father taught me language. My mother tried but gave up. She preferred smoking and lying on the couch and watching TV. Her face was always sad, even when she smiled. Her eyes never smiled with her. Whenever I ran through the living room in her house, she spoke to me with a mouthful of smoke. For a few seconds her words were visible. That was as close as I ever came to understanding her.

My father took me from my mother and kept me below ground. Everything was violent at his house. The way the cement floor was broken. The way the cement chips jabbed my small bare feet. The way the walls seemed to sweat like they ached to crush me. The way tiny nails twisted out from the wall around the entire doorframe. The way the door was always locked. The way my father and his people ignored me when I beat on it with my fist. The way the ceiling pushed down on me until my shoulders caved and my head hung. The way the light was always on.

I had to learn to live with that light pressing on my eyelids. Each night I turned over on my mattress and faced the corner. I learned to create my own darkness. Time meant nothing. All that mattered was what my father and his people did. All I knew was what I clutched in my hands or had ripped into my skin or seared into my eyes.

My first language wasn't Sign. It was violence.

When they spoke to me—when anyone speaks to me—they speak in ghosts. That's what words are. We don't see them, but we feel them. My father and his people spat ghosts at me. They wanted their words to penetrate me, to fill me, to haunt me. But I was protected. The way I am saved me from becoming like my father. Preserved my heart like a steel box. That's what Felix said.

My heart is safe, or at least clear. But my mind is not. All those years swirl and spill into puddles like water from a child's glass. My thoughts drift. I can't hold them still.

I BEGAN TO think I'd die in that basement room. The thought sickened me, emptied me—toward the end I felt my backbone go hollow. No matter what happened, I had no choice.

My father never came to see me. The bigger man and the long-haired man were the ones who took me out of the room to wash me. I'd see my father in the metal building or in the kitchen or outside smoking. The more I saw him, the more I remembered a picture my mother used to have. The man in the picture had longer hair, but it was him. They were smiling, hugging each other. I had no mirror so I couldn't compare our looks. Over time, I sensed in the way he rejected me, and in the way he avoided looking at me, that I was related to him. His anger toward me grew from something deep as blood. That kind of rejection, that kind of hatred, comes only from family.

I don't know why he took me. He didn't want me. Spite maybe, or power. Something to hold over my mother.

One night, I sat on the mattress, fingering the silver tape wrapped around my arm—I'd broken it the last time they'd taken me out—and my father and two other men came in, shoving the red drink in my face. I didn't touch it. The two men held me while my father squeezed my jaws and poured the drink into my mouth. Their grim pink faces leered down at me. One man gripped my arm, which they had pressed a stick against and wrapped tight with the tape. My father's beard clouded his lips as he spit ghosts at me. *Fuggin. Urry. Riddim.* I tried to yell but choked on the drink. The men let me go, and they all left.

I sat on my mattress. Clenched my fists. Waited for the drink to clatter in my blood and stir that familiar outrage that had bubbled up so many times before.

I grew sleepy. Peaceful. I lay on my side and let my hands roll open.

The walls and mattress and clothes blurred. They weren't fully there. My body completely relaxed. Scars cracked across my arms like striations of ice across a frozen puddle. They shone in the light, and I traced them with my finger. They seemed distant, like they belonged to someone else. The world above me soon felt emptied out. This beautiful feeling was all mine, a slow soothing bloom in my brain. Everything was air. Nothing mattered. Total peace.

The two men came back and dragged me out of the room, through the house. My head grazed the ceiling. It didn't used to—I'd been there so long. My bare feet knocked against each stair, my toenails poking at the wood. I still felt my broken arm, but the pain was far away, just a blinking light in the distance.

Outside, I saw blue sky for the first time in a long time, a small sliver just turning to black. Nobody waited by the cage. The men took me around the back of the metal building with the wide sliding doors, past the trucks. There was no light.

The air was cool. I smelled the trees on the other side of the tall fence.

They dragged me between the back of the metal building and the fence, then stopped. Right in front of me, in the very corner of the property, the bigger man was digging a hole. I knew each man by his posture, the shape of his head. In the blackening sky, they were little more than shapes.

My father stood to the left of the hole, his gun at his side. I thought I could see the front gate, about five or six car lengths behind him. My feet sunk a little into the loose earth surrounding the hole. I squeezed it between my toes.

I tried to concentrate. The red drink had trapped me within my body. I felt I should be fighting, running, shouting. I tried to pull my arms away from the men holding me, but I had little strength. In the darkness my father's face was a soft gray oval. He spoke to the bigger man. His mouth moved like a bat's wing. *Urryup.* The bigger man stood waist-deep in the hole, tossing dirt over his shoulder. I slumped. The two men held me up. I knew what was happening, but I couldn't fight it.

The bigger man climbed out of the hole. He hunched over and held his chest. He'd lost so much weight, his shirt sleeves swung off his thin arms furred with gray hair. I smelled his thick sweat mixed with the dirt. The two men holding me dragged me over to the hole. I made a small noise like a moth rising from my throat. My father stood on one side of the hole, the bigger man on the other. Their eyes settled on me like leeches. I wanted to scream but my voice was too heavy for me to lift. I hated that my father had drugged me and wouldn't let me cry. Hated that he'd kept me in that room for so long. He smelled like metal. I tried to reach out for him, but the men held me still. They kicked out the backs of my knees and pushed me to the ground.

I stared into the hole. It pulled on me the way my mattress did at the end of a night of fighting. Another small noise fluttered up my throat. Tickled the roof of my mouth. I didn't want to die. But part of me was tired. Part of me wanted to slip into that hole while I was full of that peaceful lazy feeling.

I wanted to become part of that darkness. A soft nudge circled my mind, something like, Might as well.

My father walked around behind me. He squeezed my shoulder. To wish me well. Or hold me steady. The end of his gun settled on the back of my head. I took a full breath and searched the sky for that last sliver of blue. A click echoed through my skull.

Yellow lights swung toward us from the left. Something splashed onto my face. The bigger man stumbled back against the fence. He stared at my father, blood spurting from his neck. More blood burst from his chest; his arms and legs folded upward as he fell into the hole. My father took his gun away from my head, and the men dropped me. Some ran around the corner into the metal building, while others, including my father, ran back to the house.

Two trucks had driven through the front gate. The gate and the loops of sharp wire lay crumpled beneath their tires. Men stood behind the truck doors, angry yellow flashes obscuring their faces as they fired.

I struggled to stand. My father and the men disappeared. I finally hoisted myself up, but my feet slipped and I almost fell into the hole. More lights surged from behind me. Another truck rammed through the back fence. It stopped just in front of me, its lights burning into my eyes. I tried to amble around the side of the truck, but the door kicked open and knocked me backward, sending pain blaring through my arm. A man with a beard stepped out holding a long gun. He looked at me. He looked past me. He started shooting at the metal building. Holes popped through the silver. I got up and scrambled through the splintered fence.

Flashes from the shots followed me into the trees. I ignored the rocks and needles jabbing into my bare feet. I looked back once. Another man in a hat stood in the back of the truck firing at my father's house, blowing out the windows and sections of the siding. The flash from his gun was bigger and sharper than the others—the force of his shots slapped against my chest. An outraged ghost.

I kept running. I couldn't see the flashes anymore. The sky became completely black. I couldn't see anything. Still, I ran. My toes beat the hard ground and stubbed against rocks and roots.

I stopped. My body shook. The red drink still swam in my blood—my brain was liquid. I felt around me and steadied myself against a tree. I waited for my eyes to adjust. They didn't. I was too used to light. The world tilted beneath my feet, and I held onto the tree with both hands. I didn't trust the ground in the dark.

Standing there gripping the tree, I thought of going back. I knew that place. It had light, food, a mattress, faces I recognized. Death might almost be worth it as long as I could see it coming.

I waited some more, shivering. Then I started walking. My broken arm hung heavy at my side. I tugged at the tape, but it was wrapped too thick. My ear was wet and sticky. The top part was limp, folded down over the hole where sound was supposed to enter. Something had torn it down the middle. The pain crawled and spread through my head.

I sank to the ground and made a noise. I couldn't face the darkness alone. I lay with my chest against the ground, hugging the earth to ensure it would stay beneath me. I rubbed my face against the dirt and the green fur growing up from the ground. My head swirled with their smells and textures. I squeezed twigs and dirt and pebbles. They filled me with beauty. But they were too different. I was too free. I dropped the twigs and dirt and pebbles and clung to the ground and cried.

I never slept. After some time a line of blue appeared in the sky. Up ahead, I saw fields of green fur beyond the trees. I walked toward them.

The cold awakened my skin. My body shuddered as my skin breathed freely. I wore a T-shirt and pants that stopped just below my knees. My feet bled. One of my toenails had snapped off. I smelled green. Fresh growth. As the sun rose, the prairie opened up to me. It stretched all the way to the sky. I squinted—my eyes weren't used to seeing distance.

Soon the whole sky was blue. A field of yellow flowers spread all around. The sun's warmth overwhelmed me. The first truly gentle touch I'd felt in years.

A few steps into the field I felt a breath on my neck, like someone had spoken and their words had brushed against me. I spun around. No one. Nothing. I stared at the trees. Waited. The shadows between them seemed coiled and about to burst forth. I picked up a stick and backed away, then turned and ran deeper into the field.

A white and gold bird circled in the sky. It flew down hard at the ground, carving a straight line on the air, and arose clutching something. A small tail hung from its feet. The thing wiggled in its claws, then fell limp.

The sun rose straight above me, and the yellow flowers ended. I kept looking over my shoulder. I stepped into another field. Wide and green. My tongue was dusty. I had trouble swallowing. I picked some tall green bristles from the earth and put them in my mouth. They tickled the roof of my mouth and I coughed and spit them out. I kept walking. Water formed on my skin. I licked it.

The first time I tripped, I landed on my broken arm and the stick-brace snapped. I cried out. I sat still for a long time holding my arm, waiting for the pain to settle to an ache. I tried flexing my fingers but couldn't push the message through to my hand. I tried digging beneath the tape to remove the stick, but it still wouldn't budge. Splinters from the break dug into my arm.

I peered around. No one was anywhere near, but I sensed something was following me. The green fur on the ground shuddered like something hidden within it had exhaled. I yelled. It was like the sky sucked up my voice. It held everything. Saw everything. It didn't care.

I walked on, keeping my arm close to my body. Each time I tripped after that I made no noise. Just bit my lip.

The field ended and I turned down a dirt road, walking along the side to avoid the rocks. Bugs flew and skipped all over the road. A few of them bit me. I stepped on a few. I couldn't help it; there were so many.

An orange sign with black writing on it blocked the road ahead. Behind it, a deep hole opened in the road. The dirt in the hole was darker than the rest of the road. For a moment I thought my father or the bigger man had made it. I ran, wincing with each step, my feet and broken toenails bleeding into the dust.

I turned down another road. My body filled with the chugs of my own breathing. Running felt so odd. My body wasn't used to stretching, to taking up so much space. My broken arm throbbed, and I stopped to rest. I dug my toes into the warm dirt. Clenched pebbles between my toes. All around me there was nothing but fields. I stuck out like a pimple.

I threw rocks into the fields. I wanted people. It seemed impossible that in all that space, I couldn't see another person. The prairie was hiding them, clutching them.

The sun beat on my back the rest of the day as the field gave way to more fields. Then the sky turned red, and the air cooled. I hurried down the road. I didn't want the sun to leave me. Didn't want to be outside at night again. I was tired and had nothing to eat or drink. My feet thudded on the ground, the impact of each step rattling up my legs into my throbbing arm. I wondered if my mother was close and if she'd want me back. I wondered if my father was still alive and if he was trying to find me. I tried to remember the path my father had taken the night he stole me from my mother. I recognized no landmarks, no swale of land, no arrangement of trees.

I yelled. Punched myself in the head. Hated my own ignorance. I didn't know the path. I didn't know where to find food or water. I didn't know anything that could help me. My father had kept me that way.

The sky grew bruised. Then black. Stars were like tooth holes the dogs punched in my arms.

As I searched for a place to sleep, a heavy raw smell clogged the air. Flies bumped against my face. A large lump rose out of the ground. I stopped hard. Only its outline was visible, something meaty and hairy and swollen with death. I slapped the flies away and ran around the lump into a field. Tall bristles of fur tickled my knees. I kept wincing, expecting someone to hit me. I wasn't used to gentleness.

Eventually I slowed down, holding my arm tight against my body and stroking the thin ridge beneath the tape where the stick had snapped. I'd sweated all day and the tape had loosened a little, but I had no strength to unravel it.

Another breath, another ghost brushed past my shoulder. I winced and slapped the air, my way of telling it to stop. I shouted several times. The prairie offered no answer. I was missing something—my father and his men had understood each other when their mouths moved and their breath plumed up and their words dug into each other. They could find each other, direct each other with their words. I couldn't tell where I was the way they could. I scanned the prairie for light or movement and found none.

On the far edge of the field, a large black shadow squatted in the distance. Blacker than the sky. Neither a tree nor a hill—its edges were too straight. I ran toward it. The shadow slowly grew bigger. My leg snagged on something, and I fell hard onto the ground. My broken arm caught beneath me, the splintered ends of the stick jabbing into my skin.

I reached down and pulled part of a wire fence out of my leg. A long bloody rip zagged up my shin. I got up and limped toward where I thought the shadow was.

I squinted in every direction. I made a sound through my dry throat, forcing my voice up like unwanted food, hoping it would bounce off something. The blackness had thickened, holding me like a womb. I smelled sweat and blood and dirt and green growth. My head filled with churning smoke. I heard nothing. My voice haunted no one. I stood in the center of perfect nothingness. I tried to sense walls. Walls were what I knew. They were built into my skin.

Another warm breath skirted across my neck. In the dark the soil seemed looser, as if the ground would cave in and swallow me with any move I made. The blackness made the entire prairie seem to open up into an enormous hole. More breaths swiped past me, pressing my clothes against my body. I cringed and covered my head. Ghosts seemed to close in from all directions and circle around me, poised to batter against me, dozens of them in the shape of my father and his men, whipping down from the sky and seeping up from the land and aching to worm their way into me, the prairie spouting everything it hid during the day.

I shut my eyes and screamed at the ground, hating my helplessness. I stumbled one way, then another. Every direction felt like a mistake. Blood slipped down my leg and I felt dizzy. I dropped to my knees and felt my way along the ground, yelling into the dirt, the ghosts pawing at my shoulders.

My hand closed on splinters of wood, pieces of glass. The black shadow loomed before me again, and I crawled toward it until the front steps of a house emerged. Gray and unreal in the dark. I scrambled up the steps and pushed through the broken door. It snapped off and fell onto the floor.

The house was even darker inside. I knocked on the wall and called out. I placed my hands on the floor to feel for footsteps. Only my heartbeat echoed up at me. The house smelled like old blood. Cool air blew through the door and the windows, as if the house were speaking to me. I felt my way over to the left-hand wall and stayed close to it as I inched my way along to a doorway. A floorboard snapped upward when I stepped on it.

My hunger dug at me, my stomach a fist grasping at air. I couldn't think straight. My body quaked with fear and the fevered hope of safe rest. A few of the ghosts still clung to me and I tried to quicken my movements as I searched for food and water. In the first room I stumbled on a hole in the floor. Splinters brushed my skin. I punched the wall. In the next room my knee bumped against something solid. My hand sloped down a cool porcelain wall and settled on a metal valve. I tried turning it, but it wouldn't move. None of the light switches worked. I kept moving to the kitchen and tried the faucet in there; it spun loosely, emitting nothing. My foot stubbed against something, a set of stairs. I followed them up slowly, keeping my hand on the wall. The steps were narrow, each one a different height. The darkness was so thick that someone could've been standing in front of me and I wouldn't have known. I kept knocking on the wall in front of me as I climbed. With each step I felt the ghosts sloughing off me.

I reached the top of the stairs and stopped for a moment. If I stood still, I felt like I was floating. I held my broken arm against my chest. I touched my torn ear. My pain seemed diminished in the dark. Less real.

I moved along the wall and entered another room. Hard paper stuck out from the wall in tattered curls. I felt my way over to a window. It was still whole. I kept going until my hand jammed against flat wood, which moved a little. I made a fist, knocked on it, then pushed it—a door swung away from the wall. I moved around it into a new room. I touched my leg. My skin had rolled all the way up to the top of the rip and ended in a small bundle just below my knee. My finger came away slick. I licked it. My tongue loosened a little.

Through my bare feet I felt the vibration of something scrape along the floor ahead of me. I stopped and caught a smell of baked hair. Something was right in front of me. I blinked. My blinks made gray marks on the black air. I waited and took even smaller breaths.

I took a step. Another step. The thing pattered on small feet along the floor. Whatever it was had waited for me to move too. I shouted at it.

Part of me thought it was a dog. Maybe one I'd fought before. I made myself small and huddled by the wall and waited.

Whatever it was didn't move again. I moved further into the room and sensed nothing near me.

The air felt looser. The window in the corner was broken. Something soft greeted my feet. The edge of a rug or blanket. I picked it up and, as soon as I felt how soft and heavy it was, I was tired.

I sat against the wall and pulled the covering up over my legs. Dust rose into my face; I coughed and rubbed my eyes. My head swayed—I'd never been on the second floor of a house before.

The thing pattered again. I searched my imagination for something that might match those small feet, tried to give it shape, but it remained a loose form in the darkness.

I pulled the soft covering tight around me, covering my legs and feet so the thing couldn't bite me.

I knocked on the floor. Shouted. Waited for the thing to move again.

The last of the ghosts slid away, and I fell asleep.

THIS WORKBOOK BELONGS TO:

Felix Jimson

16 MARCH 1973

Ms. Bonney in front of the class told me to put in my hearing aid no I said, Jesus ~~the Deaf~~ healed the Deaf her lips said hearing aids ~~is~~ are proof of his healing touch did I want to ~~Deafy~~ defy Jesus who died for our sins, did I want to defy God who loved me and made me in his image. Her lips moved funny over her teeth and I laughed and asked if ~~Jesuses'~~ Jesus's farts smelled and everyone laughed hahaha she made me stand in front of the class her eyes all angry and she picked up the stick and hit my hands hard smacksmacksmack but I didn't cry. In her drawer I poured her coffee from her yellow smiley mug. Have a nice day. She tattled to the ~~princputt~~ principal and the principal told mom, mom said she was sorry. I was angry, why was she sorry?

17 MARCH 1973

Grandpa today told me what Heaven looks like. his fingers they are old and move slow full of spots and bumps gross, Heaven he said is full of golden light there's no darkness everyone sees each other's true beauty and everyone understands everyone else, everyone who is not heard on Earth God in Heaven hears them. Deaf people are blessed grandpa said, Deaf people are like ghosts on Earth he said, people don't see Deaf people or disabled people they don't listen to us, they pretend we're not here but still we remain he said a

~~my~~ neighbor once tried to heal him by pouring oil in his ear but it didn't work because Deaf people are angels and angels don't need curing, they're full of love and that is Heaven. Do we haunt people I said to grandpa he said nothing I want to haunt I like being a spooky ghost.

ACHING FOR DIRT

TWO PEOPLE CARRIED me through a long white hallway. Maybe three people. The air smelled like it was trying to hide other smells. Made me sick. They sat me up in a white bed. The walls were white. Everyone wore white. Their gloves were white. Even the lights were white. They all stared at me. Tried to talk to me. They showed me words on a piece of paper and pointed at my ear, my arm, my leg. I yelled at them. I didn't like that they were talking about me. I pointed to my mouth. My hunger clawed at my belly. They touched my shoulder, and I pulled away from them. They reached out for me. I punched a woman in the face and tried to run. Many people grabbed me. I elbowed a man in the chin and kicked another in the ribs. Someone stuck a needle into my arm, and I felt some of that floating feeling from when I last drank the red drink.

When I woke up, I was lying beneath a large machine that lowered from the ceiling. Wires looped out of it like stray veins. It narrowed into a large unblinking glass eye. My broken arm was laid out flat on a table beneath the eye. The tape and the stick were gone, but pink marks lined my arm where they used to be. Two men stood near the wall. I pulled my arm away and tried to run for the door. One of the men grabbed me and hauled me down and sat on my back while the other stuck another needle into my arm.

When I woke up again, I lay in a room by myself. My arm was wrapped in something like warm hardened snow—I tried to rap my knuckles against it, but my good hand was bound to the bed with a brown leather strap. I jerked on it. My leg was bandaged. My skin had been washed. I leaned forward just enough to feel my torn ear—it'd been sewn shut. My clothes were gone, and I was wearing a white shirt with no back.

A woman in white came through the door. I pulled on my leather bonds. She held a tray full of food and picked up a plastic fork.

I stopped pulling. I grabbed the food and started eating. Fast. Spilling food on myself, leaning forward and straining against the strap. White meat. Watery potatoes. Gray-green salad. Cookies that crumbled as soon as I tore open the package. A yellow apple that I ate whole, seeds and all. I banged on the tray. I wanted more.

The woman offered me a glass of water. I drank it. She picked up the plastic pitcher to pour me another drink. I strained against my bonds and opened and closed my hand. She gave me the pitcher of water, and I drank it all. She put her hand on my shoulder. Her soft mouth gently opened and closed, forming shapes, forming words. Her teeth were straight and white.

I finished the water and dropped the pitcher on the floor. I sat in my bed shaking. I pulled on my bonds again and made a noise and looked at her. She looked at me like she didn't know what to do. She picked up the pitcher and the tray and walked away.

The floor glinted. The blanket was stiff and fresh. Everyone who passed in the hallway wore perfect white clothes. Their shoes made no tracks. The cleanliness disturbed me. I had lived my life in filth, wearing old clothes either too big or too small, sleeping on a stained mattress with my piss and shit festering in a bucket in the corner. I didn't belong in such a clean place. My skin ached for dirt.

Everything swam together in my belly. The meat knocking into the lettuce. Apple seeds floating in the water. My stomach lurched hard. I tried to clench my body, clamp myself shut, but I threw up over the side of the bed. Chunks of yellow apple and gray lettuce spread on the floor. I stared at them. I grew hungry again.

The same woman who'd brought me the food passed in the hallway and saw the puddle. Her face tightened. I pointed to my mouth. She nodded, waved at me, and began cleaning up the puddle. I had to piss, but I didn't see a bucket. I made a noise and pointed at my thing between my legs. The woman shook her head and walked out of the room. I yelled. Other people passed in the hallway, but no one listened.

I pulled away my white shirt and pissed over the side of the bed right where the vomit had been.

The same woman came back. Her mouth shaped hard words: *Jeezusriest*. She picked up a metal bowl, dropped it on my legs, and jabbed her finger at the bowl. Then she cleaned up my piss from the floor.

At night, the hallway outside my room darkened. Everyone moved slower. I yelled if they passed my room and didn't come back right away. I couldn't stand it when they left my sight.

I didn't sleep. I kept thinking my father would show up. I wanted to ask about my mother. The shape of her face, framed by wispy hair, filled my head, but I couldn't remember the details of her face. It was like her face was made of mud and someone had wiped her eyes and nose and mouth away. I had to see her. Had to fill that shape with details.

I slipped off the side and lowered my feet to the cold floor and stood up straight. My arm twisted. The leather strap held me in place. I pulled. The silver bed rail didn't move. I planted my foot on the edge of the bed and hauled on my bonds. The rail gave a little, slowly separating like a loosening tooth. I took a breath, then pulled again. The rail tilted toward me. A shadow moved at the edge of my eye—someone from the hall coming toward me. I planted my foot and put all my strength into hauling again.

The rail snapped, and I stumbled back against the wall, sending the rail whipping into the person's face. They fell down. I ran past them out into the hall, dragging the rail with me.

Two men coming up the hall grabbed for me. I dodged them. People lying in rooms and sitting in chairs watched me run. I pushed through a door into a hallway with many other doors. I ran straight. A woman walking down the hallway saw me and hesitated. I held up the rail like I would hit her, and she stepped back out of my way. I felt air on my ass. I ran hard and shoved through another door.

The air smelled fresher. One of the doors had a window looking out onto a darkened sidewalk. I headed for it, but someone tackled me from behind. I landed on top of the rail. A few other people landed on top of me. I couldn't move. I felt a small sting in my ass.

When I woke up, I was in a new bed in a new room with a window that had white bars on it. Both my legs and my wrist were bound. I couldn't move. My ear itched.

A woman spooned food into my mouth each day. If I yelled or jerked against my bonds, they injected me. I pissed in my sleep once or twice, and they had to change my sheets. Two large men held me while another man put fresh sheets on my bed. They put a metal bowl under my ass, and it was hard to get comfortable. People in white coats pointed at me. Talked about me. Talked at me. Showed me pieces of paper covered in black writing like neat lines of ant corpses. Stared at me like I was an animal. I slept all the time. Woke up with welts on my good arm from trying to fight in my sleep while the strap dug into my skin. Red lights flashed on the wall at nighttime. They were the only real color I saw.

One time, the woman who fed me put down the spoon and took out a pen. She drew something on the white substance wrapped around my broken arm. She took her time. Drew long loops and tight curls. Filled in the spaces with blue ink. She kept stopping and sitting up straight to look at it. Watching her calmed me.

When she finished, she nodded her head and put her pen down. I turned my arm over and studied the drawing. Circles within a circle. All of them full of arrows and swirls. I'm not sure what it was, but it was beautiful. The lines all came together in unexpected ways. She had filled in all the right spaces. She smiled. I smiled back. She picked up her pen and wrote something at the bottom of the drawing. I cried out. She'd ruined it. I turned my face away when she tried to feed me again. She left my room angry. I searched for her pen so I could draw something—a monster, maybe, like I had in my father's basement—but she had taken it with her.

One day, three men came in. One wore a white coat and held a needle. The other two held me still while he injected me in the arm. Then they tried to shove someone else's shoes onto my feet, but they were too small.

They tossed the shoes aside and undid my bonds. I tried to keep my eyes open. They put me in a seat with wheels on both sides and steered me into the hallway. I think people watched me—all I saw was shadows crowded together.

A door opened, and light fell onto me. I smelled cold water and cigarette smoke. A white van stood in front of me with its back door open. The whole back of the van was a cage. I tried to stand, but I could hardly move. The men lifted me out of the chair, sat me in the back of the van, and strapped me to the wall. The back of the van smelled like armpits.

The cage was blue and spread across all the windows, darkening the van. I squinted to see through the bars. The trees outside looked trapped.

The man in the white coat and the other two men who'd brought me outside walked back into the building. It was light brown on the outside and had many small windows. Now that I saw it, I didn't want to leave. I wanted to peer out each of those windows, see the world from their views, wander in and out of the rooms on my own like I had back at the empty house.

I'd explored every room of that house, searching for food and water, fingers probing the walls, pulling back paper and splintered panels. I'd tried eating leaves off the tree in the back. They were bitter and I spat them out. I thought about leaving but wasn't ready to give up my safety.

One day—I'm not sure how long I'd been there—I saw someone digging a hole in the field in front of the house. I stepped out the front door and shouted and waved at them. The person turned toward me. It was my father. His face and clothes were soaked in blood. He pointed at me, and his eyes flashed through the blood and his teeth gleamed through his beard, and I ducked back inside and ran upstairs, staying away from the windows. I picked up a long piece of wood and hunkered down in the corner of the room I slept in and waited for him to come. Something shifted behind me. I yelled and swung the wood into the wall. Someone had been there, hiding in the wall, breathing onto me. I crouched in the corner by the door, gripping the wood.

The house darkened. I peered out the window toward the field and saw no one. I put down the wood and tugged the mattress I'd found up onto the metal skeleton. Then I pulled the blanket around myself. My good arm ached from the work. I lay on my side, hugging my tightened stomach.

As it got darker, my hunger hardened. I hit myself in the belly to try and silence it. The fist in my stomach kept clawing for food. I wished for a sandwich, a banana, a bite of apple. All my food had been brought to me. Now there was no one to bring me food, and I didn't know where to find it and didn't want to leave the house.

Darkness curdled, black and dense. I strained my eyes but couldn't focus. I couldn't even see my hand in front of my face. I bit down on my knuckles to fend off my hunger, but the ache scratched in my belly.

White lights swung onto the wall. Steady and thick, not flashes. I ducked beneath the blanket and watched the door through a small scratchy hole. My nerves branched out, scanning the air for changes, footsteps, breaths, like I was part of the house.

The lights fixed on the far wall. The long piece of wood was lying on the floor across the room, and I crawled out from under the blanket to go pick it up. I waited for someone to come and point a gun at me or scream at me and shove me down the steps. I took small breaths to hide myself. The lights never changed. I slowly pushed up off the floor and backed up against the wall.

From where I stood, the back end of a truck was visible from the window. Red lights glowed then went dark. Slowly, I crept closer to the window. I still couldn't see who was in the truck, but it might be one of my father's men. The truck's front lights were focused on the house. I tensed, ready to fight.

Both truck doors opened at once, and a woman and a man stepped out. They were young, not much older than me. The woman carried a small bag with a strap hanging from her shoulder. My mom used to carry one like it. They came together in front of the lights and hugged. They smiled, said soft words, then pressed their mouths together. I hadn't seen anyone do that since I saw it on my mother's TV.

Should I show myself? What if they knew my father? They might know someone who knows my father. They might hurt me. But they were young. They might help me. They might have food.

I made a sound. The man went still. He glanced around. The woman pressed her mouth to his cheek. I edged closer to the window and made another sound. The woman's shoulders jolted. They both stared up at the house. I stepped fully into the window frame and waved down at them, making more sounds. The man pointed up at me. *Wuhdefugg*, the woman said. They ran back into the truck and got inside.

The truck backed away from the house. I yelled at them and ran out of the room and down the hall. The lights from the truck scraped along the walls. I stumbled down the stairs, my toe catching on a board. I burst out the front door, my hunger pushing me onward. The tires kicked up dirt and the truck almost drove into the field before it turned sharply and sped away down the path. I ran after it, waving my hand and choking on dust. The truck veered one way, then another, then straightened and sped on. My breath snagged in my chest. My eyes filled with water. The back end of the truck got smaller. Soon all I could see were its red lights, like two glowing eyes in the darkness. The lights turned onto a new road and slid softly across the prairie, then they disappeared.

I stood there breathing hard, focused on the point where the lights disappeared into the fields. Bugs landed on my arms and neck. I swatted them away.

I wiped my eyes. Looked back toward the house—a hard black shape in the shadows. The same black as the hole my father wanted to put me in.

My stomach had hardened into a shell. I limped down the path. I felt the rocks and weeds more now than when I had been running over them. The bugs kept coming, but I'd grown tired of swatting them away. My arms and legs and neck itched.

The moon was a small white dent in the sky, offering no light. The fur on the ground grew claws in the dark. I focused on the path. The more I walked, the less real I felt. Not dead. Just empty. Though it was too dark to tell, I was sure my feet left no prints in the dirt. Like I'd never existed. I kept squeezing my broken arm, reigniting the pain. It reminded me that I was there taking up space. So did the tear in my ear and the empty fist in my stomach. The last time I'd walked so freely, I'd been much younger. I'd seen so little of the world, and the world had seen so little of me. Even in this wide-open place where anything and anyone could be seen from a long way away, no one knew me. No one wanted me.

Something scampered across the path in front of me, snapping the solidity of the darkness. I walked faster. Whatever it was made me think that more living beings may lie ahead.

I came to a gravel road and turned left. When I came to another road made of concrete, I turned right.

Lights arose behind me. I turned and waved at the oncoming car. It passed me. I followed it. Another car passed. White signs with black words and numbers rose from the side of the road. I walked fast to beat the cold out of myself.

An orange glow emerged. I started jogging, and soon small buildings began blooming up from the earth. Houses planted in rows. Orange lights at the top of tall poles. Behind me, the edge of the sky was blue. I shouted. There was no one around. I sank to my knees. I thought I should go to one of the houses and knock on the door.

I lay in the dirt, staring up at one of the tall lights. I shut my eyes and breathed deep, my eyelids a comforting red.

TWO DIFFERENT MEN walked around the van and sat in the front. Both had mustaches. One of them drove while the other read a book. Neither of them looked at me.

As the van turned a corner, I rocked against the cage wall. My hair kept swinging into my eyes, and I kept pushing it aside.

We drove past more buildings and houses and people walking freely. I hadn't seen so many people before. They looked unreal, like puppets. I felt like I could reach out and knock them over with my finger.

The buildings and houses and people soon fell away and the prairie began to roll past us. Flatlands, brown and scruffy like the chest of a dead dog. The sky flat and gray. I kept seeing flashes of my father's house. The basement. The hose. The cage. Felt the breath of the ghosts on my face.

I strained to lift my hand and knocked meekly on the blue cage wall. Neither of the men responded. I lifted my foot and dropped it on the floor. The man reading a book swung his fist backwards and pounded on the cage without looking up.

Outside the window, the ground was moving too fast. Every ridge and pebble and bump in the road rattled up through my body. I became sick and vomited. The toast and juice I'd eaten that day spilled onto the floor and gathered in the narrow runnels in the van's floor.

That woke me up a little. I kicked at the cage, rapped against the windows. The man shut his book and turned to me and pounded on the blue wire of the cage again. His face was red. His fist was thick—the wire trembled when he hit it. I made noises that I hoped asked why he was doing this and told him that I didn't deserve this and wanted out. The men held their hands to their noses as the vomit sloshed along the floor.

The van curled onto a thin dirt road. On both sides, skinny trees chopped up the sky. White clouds heaved up from behind a building at the end of the road. Red brick. Small windows on three levels. Wide doors that looked hungry. As we got closer, the building widened out and seemed more like many buildings spread out and stuck together. I battered the cage. Split my knuckle open on the wire. I kept punching. Both men shook their heads, and their mouths and teeth formed hard shapes.

The van stopped. My vomit washed past the wire into the front. The men quickly stepped outside. Couldn't get out fast enough.

They jerked the back door open, and I swung at them. Behind them, a path rolled out from the building doors like a concrete tongue. A woman with black curly hair and a blue shirt stood by the doors talking to a man in a white coat and glasses. She was wiping her wet eyes and jabbing her finger at the building. The man in the white coat smoothed back his thin white hair and nodded, holding up his hands like he didn't want to listen to her. She bent forward and hurled her voice at the building, her cheeks blooming red. Blue lines jumped out of her neck. The man pushed his glasses further up his nose and showed his teeth in more of a growl than a smile and pointed the woman away. The woman's eyes stretched so wide I thought they'd drop out of her head.

One of the men grabbed my arm and held me tight while the other removed the straps and seized my legs. The men carried me toward the doors. I tried to kick free and hit them with my hardened left arm. A few people looked down on me from the windows above. I called to the woman by the doors. Her hard eyes quickly melted, and she started toward me with her hands spread open, but the man in the suit stood in her way.

When we reached the doors, the man carrying my legs dropped them—my heels smacked on the cement. He pushed a button on the wall, and I peered back at the woman. She was still fighting with the man in the white coat. Still staring at me. Still reaching for me with her long pink fingers.

Above the doors was a sign full of carved words, old fash-
ioned and jagged, like they'd draw blood if you ran your finger
across them. The doors themselves were also carved, showing
people with smiles like hooks and flat eyes that stared out at
the prairie. Their hands reached out and grasped for colorless
flowers. The carvings were stained with dirt and slashed and
dented all over.

One of the doors opened. I smelled dust. A small woman
wearing green stood there. One of the men gave her a piece
of paper. She studied me. Spoke to the men. Shook her head
at me.

Behind us, the man in the white coat was trying to push the
woman with black curly hair away from the door. Whatever
feelings she'd been hurling at the building were now focused
on me. For some reason, her fury was beautiful.

The woman in green stepped aside, and the men carried me
in. The woman with the black curly hair and I reached for each
other, straining until the closing door cut us off.

Two sets of stairs—one on the right, one on the left—led
up to the next level. A man with a beard was sweeping them
with a broom. The two sets came together on the second level,
and on the ground floor between them was a wall bearing an
enormous painting. Not in a frame—the wall itself was the
painting. A golden field lined the bottom of the painting, and
the rest of the wall was blue sky and clouds. A round orange
sun peered out of the top corner like it was shy.

The woman opened another door onto a hallway seething
with people. They all turned their heads—their eyes gripped
onto me like mosquitoes. Some had white hair and cracked
skin. Some had dark hair and oily skin. A few wore suits.
Others wore pants with strings hanging from them. A few
smiled and spoke.

The men shoved me into a small empty room with pink
walls, and the woman pulled the door closed. I turned the
doorknob, but it spun without catching.

In the corner was a small window crisscrossed with metal
bars. It inhaled dull gray light that made the pink walls look

like rotted meat. Outside, I saw a square yard covered in yellowed fur instead of green, with a narrow dirt plot and a small spot of concrete with a metal circle standing atop a pole. A young man was trying to throw a ball into the metal circle. The red brick walls of the building rose on all four sides of the yard. In the dirt plot, a few people were digging small holes and setting plants into them.

I moved to another corner of the room. The pink walls made me want to vomit, but I had nothing left in my stomach. I pictured the people in the hallway crowding outside the room and had a feeling that I'd have to fight them all. This building was another cage, and I'd have to show my strength to stay alive.

The door opened, and the man in the white coat and the woman in green and the two men who drove me all came in together. The two men reached for me, but I swung at one of them with my broken arm. He ducked and tackled me, pushing me into the wall. The other one grabbed my good arm.

The man in the coat held a needle. I yelled. My arm had become bruised for all the previous jabs. His glasses made his eyes look empty. I jumped up and kicked at him, but I missed. I cried. I was so tired.

THIS WORKBOOK BELONGS TO:

Felix Jimson

1 JUNE 1973

Dad works at St. ~~Patricks~~ Patrick's ~~orphenige~~ orphanage cleaning all the rooms with his bucket full of yuck. The other kids they don't have mothers and fathers I try to be like a big brother to them, sometimes mom wants hearing kids to play with me she's hearing too she doesn't see that always the kids make me read their lips saying fuck shit asshole pussy bitch and asking me what did I say. One day I pointed at all of them and called them all bastards they pushed me away. Grandma and mom say dad should work somewhere else and have respect for himself, maybe work in the shoe shop with grandpa. One time I acted out scenes from ~~Frankensteinstein~~ stein holding out my arms and chasing the smaller kids they laughed and they every time now tell me do the same thing, freak they call me freak freak freak.

FELIX

FELIX HAS BEAUTIFUL eyes. Green with blue around the black dot. Long lashes. Sometimes if he gets excited, the black expands and the blue disappears and his eyes swallow you, and you let yourself be swallowed.

His hands are birds. They own the air. They fill every space with grace. Each finger is its own beautiful being. He can make anything make sense, even to me. I understood the world through those hands.

The last time I saw him, he was running away. He ran like he was made of air, his worn shoes skimming over the snow, his bloody hands swinging up and down, the back of his blond head shining blue in the moonlight. I ran after him, his blond head a bobbing blue dot shrinking into the darkness. He ran past the playground—I caught him and shoved him against the car. He kneed me between the legs, then dove into the car and aimed it toward me. I tried to get out of the way, but my foot slipped and the car slammed into my hip and I rolled back onto the icy ground. He drove away. Never looked back.

He never told me why he was in the institution. He didn't seem dangerous at the time. None of the other patients did either. Sometimes they played around or yelled at each other or shoved each other, but they never hurt anyone. Felix told me they were all divine. He said I was his apostle. I asked what an apostle was. He asked me if I wanted to do good. I said yes. Another time he asked if I believed in him. I said yes. He asked if I loved him. I said I didn't know what love was. He kissed me and asked if that felt good. I said yes and asked him what love is. He kissed me again.

9 JUNE 1973

Grandpa died. He went to Heaven to be in the light and grandma is sad. Father Hoff spoke his words blahblah with his bad breath like a green burpcloud over grandpa's body, grandpa ~~tyed~~ ~~tayd~~ lied in front of everyone like a couch or food on tables. I ran from the church and cried and punched a tree and knocked down a trash can grandpa would be angry with a funeral like that with a priest who sucks and says thy and thou and other old words. I want him back. Grandma said God's always watching out for him. I asked grandma if he's still Deaf in Heaven and grandma said Heaven is not Heaven without Deaf people.

JUNE 16, 1973

Mom took me to Stellan's and I got a burger, they put too much mustard again gross. I made stick people out of my fries and made blood stains with ketchup like Dracula. Mom said with her mouth grandpa is at peace and he would want me to be good she said I need to learn hearing things like speaking and listening, no no no I told her Ms. Bonney again and again won't let me sign I don't like speaking with my tongue the other kids laugh at how my voice sounds pointing freak freak freak. I want to go to the Deaf school but Mom said no said teacher knows best. I said I like being a ghost I want to be with other ghosts. Mom said nothing. I said why does the bitch hit me. Mom slapped my face then bought me a ~~sunday~~ sundae, I said I bet the teacher didn't hit you when you ~~was~~ were in school. Mom said again she's sorry because the world is not made for me or dad or grandpa and grandma. Why are we here then I said.

WELCOME

I BECAME AWARE that I was sweating and awoke straining for coolness. I lay in a narrow room where the rotten pink color had been scraped off the walls in many places. Tall barred windows filled the opposite wall and offered a view of weeds and gray sky and scruffy prairie.

A row of beds stretched across the room. I lay in the corner bed farthest from the door. From there, the beds looked like steps leading to nothing. A desk stood near the door, full of papers. I tried to sit up, but my limbs were strapped to the corners of the bed, and a heavy white blanket pinned me down. The blanket came all the way up to my chin.

In the bed next to me, an older man slept. Black stubble coated his cheeks. His limbs were strapped down too. A see-through bag hung on a pole above his bed, and a thin tube curled down from the bag into his arm. A woman slept in the bed closest to the door, her body flattened under the sheet. Her gray hair swayed in and out of her wide-open mouth.

I smelled them both. I smelled all the people who'd been in that room and everything they'd left there, all the sweat and breath and spit and piss. The smell wrapped around me, absorbed me and my smell.

I called out. The man didn't move, but the woman winced and twisted her face away. The man's chest hardly raised. He looked more unconscious than asleep.

My body cooked beneath the blanket. I strained my neck, trying to edge my chin over the top of the blanket to get some cooler air. My breath came in thin drags. The sheets clung to me and pulled me down. Soon, they became another restraint. The more I struggled, the more I sweated, and the more I sweated, the deeper I sank. I tried to shout—my voice skittered up my dry throat. I licked the sweat from my lips and made a louder noise.

No movement. The door stayed closed.

I lay back, trying to breathe more slowly. Licking more sweat off my lips, I peered around, into the corners, under the beds, hoping none of the ghosts I'd left on the prairie had followed me.

A woman in a blue jacket came into the room and stopped at the desk. Her white hat stood on her head at a strange angle, like it was about to fall off. I cried out, but she never looked at me.

She slid a piece of paper into a large black instrument and poked at round keys with her fingers. The paper skidded to the side with each poke, and she pushed it back into place. I yelled at her again. She pulled the paper from the instrument, tucked it into a flat wooden board, and left the room.

I stopped trying to move. My body glowed from the heat.

The gray-haired woman's head rolled over to face the ceiling. Her mouth moved like a rubber band.

The man with the white coat and glasses came in, carrying a needle. When the woman on the bed saw it, she shook her head and spoke to the man. *Nuhmuh, nuhmuh.* The man stuck it into her shoulder, and after a moment her body began shaking and she strained against her straps and gritted her teeth. Then she relaxed and faded back into sleep.

The man in the glasses smiled at me, then left the room.

The sky blackened. The lights in the ceiling hung like empty fruit. I kept sweating—even when I lay perfectly still, something in my body pushed all the water out. I twisted my head back and forth and blew my long hair out of my face. I shouted. My throat crinkled like paper. It was possible no one would see me until the morning, and I wasn't sure I'd last that long. My brain had begun to boil. I could feel it softening and thought it might drain away and leak out my ears.

The light from the hallway sliced into the room through the square window in the door. Shadows crossed it, but no one stopped to look in at us.

My skin chafed. Swallowing was painful—my tongue was a crumpled leaf. I needed water even more now than when I'd been in the empty house. I should've stayed in that house. I'd been free then. Just me and the fields. I wished I could go back to that house and experience again that thick darkness that filled every fiber in the air, that embraced me like water. I had feared that embrace, and I shouldn't have. I had the chance to settle into myself, to know myself without interference from someone else. I didn't have to worry about misunderstanding in the dark—I only had to worry about my own heart and mind. No room for other people's words. That darkness had held me so gently that I became part of it. Not like in my father's basement or in the institution or in here. In that house, I could feel myself dissolve and float around in the darkness. My heartbeat echoed throughout that darkness. I felt the weight of each room, my own heft, the weight of my self or rather the possibility of my self. I was somewhere in that darkness. Light allows us to see, but it also shows us things that we might not want to see. Light singles everything out. It divides us. Everything blends together in darkness.

SUNLIGHT SPLASHED ACROSS the pink walls and slid over the ragged scratches, making them into shiny white wounds. The woman in the blue jacket was cutting my fingernails. She had to angle the small scissors on both sides of my fingers because my nails were so long. The woman, or someone, had removed the blanket. I felt flattened. Ironed down.

My sweat had crusted over—chalky white streaks flaked off at my elbows. My crotch and asshole itched. My teeth creaked against each other like wood. There was new writing on the white wrapping on my arm. Large, sharp letters.

When the woman finished with my nails, she dipped a cloth into a bowl of cool water and wiped my body. I gasped as my skin opened up and began to breathe. The woman gave me a pill and a glass of water, then folded all my fingernails into a white tissue and threw them away.

The man in the bed next to me was gone. Only his soft outline remained. The woman in the far bed was still there, still sleeping. The daylight caught the wrinkles around her eyes and mouth, and she looked much older.

The woman in the blue jacket sat down and spoke to me. Her eyebrows had been drawn onto her face, and they bent at sharp angles, like broken sticks. I tried to understand. Tried to make my eyes as friendly as possible. She picked up a different bowl from the table, this one was full of lumpy gray mush. She held a spoonful out to me. I thought it was mud, but I opened my mouth—and gagged on the mush. I recognized it as something I'd eaten before. Maybe my mother made it once. I moved to spit, but my stomach pawed for food. I choked the mush down.

The woman gave me another spoonful. It went down easier. She spoke to me as she fed me. I shook my head. She pulled the spoon away. I nodded hard and groped for it with my mouth. She gave me another spoonful. I kept my face flat, even when she touched the scars on my arm. Didn't want any more misunderstandings while I ate.

I ate the whole bowl and drank another glass of water. A man in a blue-striped suit came into the room. He had beautiful brown skin that I had never seen before and thick black hair that neatly curled across his forehead with a gentleness that seemed almost impossible. He smiled at me and at the woman. The two of them talked to each other and nodded at me as they talked. He brushed his hair back, and it settled into the exact same spot. His cheeks had wrinkles, yet his eyes were bright and young. I made a noise and pointed at the empty bed next to mine, trying to ask what had happened to the man with black stubble. The man in the suit left the room and the eyebrow woman held up a finger and followed him out carrying the bowl and the glass.

I watched the small square window in the door. Sometimes people stopped to look at me. A few smiled. Most just stared.

My stomach clenched. There was something about this place. Only certain people came here.

The eyebrow woman came back with two men wearing matching white uniforms. I smiled at them. She spoke to them, and the men came over to me, removed the straps, and took me by my arms. They stood me up, and I let my arms sag within their grips. The woman said something. The men let me go. Let me stand on my own. She raised her eyebrows and spoke slowly to me. *Oh-hay*. I nodded. She smiled and handed me a pair of black pants and a red shirt with black writing on it and a pair of blue shoes with white laces. I beamed. I hadn't worn shoes in years.

The shirt dug into my armpits, and its bottom stopped just above my belly button. I fingered a little tuft of brown belly hair. The pants swayed as I walked; they were so loose they felt like a skirt. Both they and the shirt were clean.

The woman helped me tie the shoelaces. The shoes themselves were a bit big, but I loved having the space. For a moment I just stood and enjoyed having my feet wrapped in a warm protective covering. I rolled and wriggled my toes. Watched them poke up at the blue cloth. The soft barrier between my feet and the floor gave me grip. An anchor. Made me feel taller and more stable. I nodded at the others. A golden feeling arose in me—I wanted to thank them. I started to open my arms but then withdrew them as the men stiffened. Best not to do anything drastic. Not even with joy.

I followed the woman and the men down to the floor below, keeping my eyes away from the sleeping woman.

A man waited for us at a set of doors. Black and yellow shirt. Round face and bright eyes that shone even behind his glasses. He offered his hand, and I gave him mine, and he smiled

and shook it and pointed at my broken arm and said something. He swung his arm toward the hallway in a heavy arc. He
wanted us to follow him.

Paintings hung between most of the doors. Faces. Trees.
Landscapes. The walls were a soft green; white pipes curled
out from them. The white floor was streaked with black marks.
A few people in the hallway watched me, their cigarettes glowing orange. The hallway smelled like smoke and old food; the
air had a thickness that settled onto my shoulders. My feet
dragged on the scuffed floor, and I tripped and almost fell—I
wasn't used to wearing shoes. One of the men behind me
touched my shoulder, and I walked more carefully.

The man with the round face spoke the whole time. Even
with his back turned to me, I could see his mouth moving and
his chin jumping up and down. His face was boyish but his
hair was gray. His hands never stopped fidgeting. Sometimes
he nodded or pointed at things. A sign on the wall. A room full
of people sitting in a circle smoking and talking. A painting.
Another room where many women and a few men fed cloth
into machines with silver teeth that punched thread into the
cloth. Small rooms with beds and desks. At the end of the hall,
the man turned toward me, and I saw he was speaking to me.
Maybe he had been the whole time. He stopped speaking and
lifted his thick gray eyebrows.

The others waited, watching me. They expected a response.
I nodded.

They waited still. Nodding wouldn't do. I clenched my fists.
My feet sweated. I had been waiting for them to put me in a
cage or strap me to a bed again, but they had already shown
me more kindness in one day than I'd experienced in many
years, and I didn't know what to do with it. By taking me out of
the restraints and letting me walk around, they were trusting
me. I didn't want to react the wrong way and be put back in
that bed with the heavy blanket and left to cook until my body
dissolved. I looked at the floor and kept my eyes there.

The man said something then held up his hands like a calm-
ing gesture and walked on. I relaxed my fists.

The building was enormous, but it seemed too small for the number of people it housed. People filled almost every room. The smaller rooms all had two beds but three or four people. Everyone looked distinct. No one's face was alike. No one's eyes held the same amount of light. No one moved the same way as another. Each had their own rhythm. A few people waved. A few showed me their middle fingers—the uniformed men did the same to them. Some stared. Some glared. Some spoke to me. Some smiled at me. They were different from the woman and men in white, whose faces had been stiffer, and who all had the same rhythm, the same kind of light.

We came to a large room. All tables and bookshelves. Barred windows full of sky. People, many of them about my age, sat at the tables reading books or playing games or drawing pictures. A few of them watched me pass the door. I dropped my eyes to the floor; my brain had grown heavy with all the new faces.

We carried on down the hall until we reached a small room at the corner of the building. The round-faced man clapped and pointed inside. A window. Two beds. A wooden closet. A table with a lamp. He waved me inside, skipped over to the bed under the window, and slapped it like he was cleaning it off.

I looked at the woman, who pointed at a sign beside the door. All the small rooms had signs like that, each with different writing. I understood. They'd been showing me the building, where everything was. Because I lived here now.

I stepped into the room and sat on the unoccupied bed under the window. The others watched me as I studied the room. Boxes sat under the man's bed across from me. Plastic figures and thin books with bright red and blue and green people rested on the table. In the closet, several T-shirts hung on wires.

The round-faced man sat on the other bed, grinned, and reached over to the table to pick up a small plastic figure with green eyes. He held it up to show me. The woman spoke to me while tapping the back of her wrist, then she waved to the round-faced man, who shook my hand again, put the plastic figure in his pocket, and jogged away. I started to follow him, but the woman put up her hand. Wanted me to stay there.

They all went away, scattering into the hall, leaving me there with the door open. I didn't want them to leave. I stood in the middle of the room. My room. Free to move. Free to stay. I shuddered, afraid to take a step. The open door felt like jaws. I didn't know how to be free.

BELOW

THE FIRST TIME I was put below ground, it was dark outside. I was pulled from my bed at my mother's house. She'd just given me a new blanket, a blue one with long wavy lines. I petted it before sleeping.

I'd smelled the man before I felt him shake me awake. He smelled bitter, like split iron. He whipped off my blanket and carried me out of the room with one hand. He had red hair and a beard that flashed in the hallway light. My mother pulled on his arm. Hit him on the shoulder. Every room was full of smoke, full of spent words. He shoved her against the wall. She kept hitting him. I cried and kicked, trying to get loose. I'd seen the man visit my mother a few times before, but I didn't know until much later that he was my father.

He hauled me out of the house, knocking my toes against the front door. My mother screamed at him. He spat words back at her. *Fuggin. Ahmtagginim.* She lunged for me, but his free hand shot out and punched her in the nose. She fell backward. I reached for her. She was all I knew. He dragged me across the yard that was just lumps of mud and roots, opened the backseat of his truck, and threw me inside. My head hit the door on the other side.

My father started the truck and backed out. Through the window I screamed at my mother, who whipped her fists down on my father's window. Whenever I scream, it rises hot from my stomach and scratches my throat and brushes past my teeth on its way out. I hit my father's seat. He swung the truck out and almost hit my mother.

He steered along a gravel road, leaving her behind. The world opened up into an enormous gullet—the truck's lights glared out into nothing. We could've been driving in the sky.

I punched my father in the back of the head. He swung his arm back and elbowed me in the face, and I fell back against the backseat. My nose bled. I cried harder. Screamed into his ear. I pulled the knobs on each door, but they wouldn't open. I lurched into the front passenger seat and tried to open that door. He seized me by my hair and shoved my face into the dashboard. Twice. I didn't feel pain. My head was knocked empty. I ended up lying on the seat beside him. I stared up at the dome light thinking it was a large crystal. The yellow light from his radio made him look like a lizard.

Sometime later he opened his door, grabbed my hands, and dragged me out into the darkness. Cold air whipped against me. My head filled with heavy pain; the gravel hurt my feet. To him I was a sack of dirt.

I slumped in his arms, my head hanging back. I saw his house upside down— it was bigger than my mother's. Another truck with big tires stood outside a building made of grooved metal. Two men stood by the sliding door speaking to each other. I reached out to the men, cried for them. They made faces and said things to my father, then smiled and watched my father drag me toward the house. I couldn't see much else, but I could sense the empty prairie around us.

My father didn't look at me. I tried to yank my hands free. From the top of the metal building, a strong white light shoved its way through the darkness.

My nose bled onto my pajama shirt. As I cried, my nose spurted more and more. I coughed and kept trying to yank my hands away from my father. He hauled me around up the back steps, twisting my wrists to keep me still, and opened the back door.

The house smelled like a crowd of my father. A bitterness I can still taste. He pulled me through the kitchen, where a man sat at the table smoking. The tiles on the floor curled upward at the edges near the wall. The window had a red piece of cloth with a blue X in the center of it and white stars inside the X. I saw part of the living room, which had a couch and a deer's head on the wall.

My father opened a door leading down into darkness. I screamed and pushed against him. He turned on the light, wrapped his arm around my chest, and carried me down the steps. His heavy fingers dug deeper into my side with each step. I bit his hand. He slammed me into the wall. The walls were gray and had no paint, and the floor was all concrete. I smelled wet skin. He hauled me down a short hallway by my neck and opened a door to a small room. He shoved me inside and closed the door.

The room had no windows. White splotches pocked the unfinished gray walls. A single light bulb burned white. The floor was cracked and broken up. A stained mattress sat in one corner. Its edges were frayed. I cried and beat the door until I grew dizzy and fell back into a sitting position.

I huddled on the mattress and hugged my knees to my chest. There was no switch inside the room to turn the light off. It pressed down on me, pushing against my eyelids. I pulled my shirt off and draped it over my head. The light softened but remained. I smelled and tasted metal.

My bladder lurched. I got up and banged on the door. A cement chip dug into my foot. I clamped my legs together. My mother had thrown hard words at me when I'd pissed in her kitchen. Her smoke had spurted out at me, and she'd grabbed my arm and yanked me to the bathroom and pointed at the toilet. She held an imaginary penis and aimed it into the bowl. I watched her. She shook her head and walked out. She never hit me.

In the small room, I kept my legs together and banged on the hard white door. Then I banged on each wall. Nothing gave. No one answered. My bladder lurched again, and I pulled down my pajama pants and pissed on the wall. The puddle on the concrete soon spread under the door.

I was thirsty. I yelled and made a cup with both hands, one of the few things I knew I could communicate. My mother always understood what I wanted when I did that, and she'd give me water or milk or juice. I hoped my gesture would float through the door or through the ceiling. I called out. I had no idea how I sounded.

No one answered. I wiped my nose on my pajama top and huddled back in the corner. I pulled at the waistband of my underwear. They itched; I'd worn them for many days. My mother didn't buy many things for me. Didn't bathe me much. I was always covered in stains. I lay on the mattress stretching my legs apart to soothe the itch. I covered my face again with my pajama shirt, and the white light shone through the bloodstains.

I woke up later with no idea if it was day or night. The sameness of the light made me unsure. Something in my head—some crucial mechanism like a compass—was knocked loose.

The room stank. The stink was mine. Your own stink is easier to breathe. When I went to the wall to piss again, I saw the previous puddle had browned and settled, like soup.

As I pissed, I saw a spiderweb between the wall and the floor. A black spider scuttled up and down, hanging the delicate strings with precision.

I sat on the mattress and pulled at the frays at the edges, watching the spider expand its web. I gathered the blue threads from the mattress and tried making a web of my own, pulling it between two fingers and laying it out on the concrete. The way the spider could climb material from its own body amazed me. The last time I'd seen a spider, I tried to push silk from my ass and ended up making a mess in my mother's backyard.

When I tried touching the spider, it scurried away from me. Its speed frightened me, and I left it alone.

A man with long hair brought a bucket and a bag of chips one day. I slept, ate, drank, shat, pissed, hid from the light, watched the spider. It always looked asleep. It didn't move much, and when it did, it walked slowly. I got excited whenever it moved.

I sometimes touched its web to rouse it, but it never worked. It drew its legs tighter against its body, like it was angry with me. Its tiny eyes poked at me, warned me.

One time a line of ants trickled along the wall and a few wandered into the web. The spider snapped awake, grabbed them in its jaws, and wrapped them in webbing until they were snug. It held them, squeezed them, killed them with its embrace. They hung like decorations, like the deer's head on my father's wall.

I saw the long-haired man the most. He brought me my food and emptied the bucket. He brought me napkins and later rolls of paper towel for me to wipe with. He had drawings on his arms: green snakes and red lions and black skulls. I wondered if they had grown out of him like freckles and if pictures would grow out of my arms too.

Once he brought me a book full of words and pictures of monsters with enormous yellow eyes. Their teeth bristled up at me. I touched their teeth with one finger to see if they would prick me. The monsters traded arms and legs and noses and eyeballs with each other, so some had one short arm and one long arm and others had eyes too big for their heads that kept falling out. Yet they always smiled. Words trailed across the page like dead ants.

I took a chip of concrete and started scratching shapes into the wall. I studied the monsters and tried to draw them. White dust fell from the wall; sometimes whole chunks broke off. I drew a small monster, then I drew the same one but much larger. I got one of its eyes just right and held up the book beside it and felt proud. The concrete chip snapped. I picked up another one and scratched more monsters into the wall, giving them teeth I could feel, claws I could touch.

The long-haired man came in. He smiled. Shook his finger at me. He took the chip away and swept up the others and left me alone again. I threw the book at the wall. The pages bent.

I took it back and sat with it on my mattress. I stared at the words. I did what my mother had done once—dragged my finger under the letters—hoping something would become clear. I stared at them hard, hoping to make them dance, hoping to will them into meaning and to pry open a part of my brain that remained shut tight. To me the words were just more pictures with sharp edges. I grew tired and propped the book over my face to block out the light. But the light curled under every surface like water.

I MADE UP a game where I would stare at the light for as long as I could until I blinked. The heat of the light sank into my eyes, and I blinked many times. I kept staring. With time, my eyes hurt a little less. When I looked away or closed them, I saw spots. My eyeballs stretched to let in all the light and everything in the room looked cloudy.

A layer of crumbs and sweat and dirt formed on my clothes. No one washed them. I rotated between two pairs of underwear—I changed them when they began itching or became too stained. I had two pairs of pants and three shirts. No socks. They washed me maybe once a week, always with the hose outside. Sometimes it was easier just to be naked. My asshole festered and I rubbed it. One time I propped the mattress against the wall at an angle and crawled underneath it. When a tall man with thick arms and a round hard stomach came in and found me like that, he pushed it down and it dropped on top of me.

My clothes soon started shrinking. My shirt sleeves crept up my arms. My underwear clenched around my waist. I stopped wearing underwear. I didn't know how long my hair had grown until the bigger man yanked on it. They washed me once in the snow, then didn't bring me outside again until the snow was almost gone.

When I closed my fists, my nails dug into my palms. I felt like one of the monsters from the book. I stopped bending the pages; I flattened them all out. To protect the book, I kept it in the corner, wedged between the mattress and the wall. It was all I had.

The long-haired man came in one time to give me new clothes. His face twisted, and he covered his mouth and nose. He dropped a white plastic bag beside my sandwich.

The man watched me. I waited for him to leave. He didn't. When I finished eating, I opened the bag and found shirts and pants. I pulled on a green shirt with a wolf on the front. It hung off me. I felt warmed by it. They were new. They had tags. I tried on all the clothes. He studied my body.

A short time later—maybe a few days—the bigger man came in with a pair of scissors. When I saw the silver blades, I tried to run out the door and almost made it, but he grabbed me by my hair and yanked me back into the room. A few hairs broke off my head. He kept his hold and started cutting. When I saw the hairs floating to the ground, I screamed and tried swiping at him with my long nails. He shoved me to the floor and pinned me down with his knee on my back. He tossed my hair all over the floor. Light brown pieces of myself. I felt like I was becoming less, like I was shrinking.

Afterward, the man seized me by my neck and pulled me up the stairs and out the back door to the gravel pile. The light from the metal building flooded the darkened grounds. He turned the hose on me and blasted me with cold water, then picked up a bottle of green liquid, poured some into my hand, and rubbed his hands together. I didn't move. He gripped my hands and rubbed them together. *Jeezus*, he said. White bubbles formed between my hands. I soaped my body, my face, and my head. My hair was patchy.

Over by the metal building, two men smoked cigarettes and smiled at me. I hollered at them, pleaded to them with my eyes. I wanted them to take me away in one of their trucks. They said something to the bigger man. The bigger man spat words at them. I think he was ashamed to be washing me.

It happened maybe once every few weeks, being washed. Always outside, always under the black sky.

At one point, I developed rashes on the inside of my thighs. My thighs turned pink, then red, then purple. They opened up.

When I squatted to shit, I made sure not to let my thighs or ass touch the edge of the bucket.

The rashes stank. I kept my legs apart when I walked so my thighs wouldn't touch each other. When I lay down, my legs formed a wide V. Liquid oozed from my thighs onto the mattress. The mattress was now a part of me. It was my island.

I cried quietly—I no longer expected anyone to answer me. In a cloudy way, I sensed that pain—and not just the pain in my legs but pain in general—might be permanent, that all the gross festering wounds that life had to offer would form the foundation of my life from then on, and that was why I was there in that underground room. My heart had swollen with fear and outrage when my father had taken me, but when the rashes came and no one did anything to help me, my outrage dissolved. I accepted that I deserved it, through my ignorance, my ugliness. I let the rashes take in the air. Sometimes I splashed them with water and breathed on them until they healed.

They never washed my clothes. They just brought me new ones that were too big or too small. I piled them at the end of the mattress as high as I could and pushed my hands into their softness so I could feel rich. Whenever they took me outside, I watched my father or the bigger man or whoever was around and tried to find out more about them. I watched for gestures, habits, expressions, tics, the small things that make up a human. The bigger man rolled his tongue around his mouth whenever he hosed me or fought me—it bulged out his cheeks. The long-haired man scratched his neck and leaned on the doorway when he watched me eat. I sometimes imitated the men. I wasn't in school. That was all I could learn.

MY FIRST REAL big laugh was in that room. The kind of laugh where you fall out of your chair and lie on the floor holding your stomach.

I'd stepped on the spider.

The long-haired man had brought me a sandwich with a new red drink. Somehow it was both sweet and bitter. I swallowed it in one gulp. I ate one half of the sandwich, then picked apart the other half, pushing the sticky flaky meat around. I held the bare side of the bread against my face, and the soft bread formed a dent the shape of my cheek. I was hungry for texture. Soon I started running from one side of the room to the other, crashing into the walls, thinking I could break through them. I jumped onto the mattress and bounced on my knees. I shouted. Later, Felix would tell me my speaking voice was an unbaptized child. I don't know what that means.

My hands shook. The room shrank. The walls rushed in on me. I stopped bouncing and lay on my back and stared at my hands. Every bone and muscle vibrated like something new and grim and electric had come alive in me and taken over my body and was getting used to new surroundings. I stared at the spider in its web. Its shiny top side fully faced me. I saw all its legs at once. Its eyes tiny bristling black drops. It stared back at me. It wanted me to feel smaller, small enough that it could clutch me and embrace me in its webbing and sink its teeth into my guts and feast on me. I ran over and stomped on it. I stomped it into the floor and ripped down its web. I yelled at it, hoping that I looked like the bigger man did when he yelled at me. I kicked the web into the wall and stomped on the spider again—it stuck to my foot, and I dragged my foot over the edge of the broken concrete, and its small crushed body snagged on the edge and tumbled off. I laughed. I lifted my hands and jumped around and danced around the small corpse. My brain floated freely in my head like a shark. I dropped to my knees and laughed, covering the small body with my laughter, aiming my laughter at it like I wanted it to fill the spider's empty body. I pulled strands of webbing from my toes. They tickled, and I kept laughing. I pulled the webbing through the air, and it floated beautifully. Thin and delicate. I put the web next to the crushed spider.

I was alone. I stopped laughing.

The ceiling pushed down on me. Something hot and bristly swelled up from my stomach. I yelled and ran at the door and battered it with both fists. The poor spider. My grief was too big to fit in that room. I screamed at the door, punched it. My knuckles bled but I felt no pain. I couldn't punch hard enough. I pushed away from the door and overturned my mattress. I flopped it around the room. When it landed on top of the spider, I screamed and pushed the mattress off and carried the spider and its web back to the corner. I arranged the web as close to the previous state as I could, but it remained a messy pile.

I lay on my stomach, crying, the little corpse a hand's length from my face. I wanted my cries to stir it back to life and then I would cover its body and keep it safe. I still felt angry. My body wanted to move without me. I lay there vibrating. My bloody hands trembled. The light pressed down on us, glittering in its empty black eyes, highlighting my crime.

I GOT USED to the room. Got used to the weight of the house above me. Blank spaces have rhythms. The most boring rooms have a beat that you settle into over time. My cell had a beat, slow and heavy like a whale's heart. I lived within that beat, moved to its music.

Sometimes I put my hand on the wall to feel for vibrations from other rooms. Once, I lay against the door and felt someone knocking. I knocked back and put my hand on the door. Whoever it was knocked again, *knock knock knock*. I did the same, *knock knock knock*. I made a sound with my mouth. The knocking stopped. I knocked again. Someone punched the door. I stopped knocking and waited. I made another sound with my mouth. No answer.

The long-haired man brought me apples and small pieces of candy. Sometimes he talked to me, opening his mouth wide, lips peeling back over his blackened teeth. *Wuhddashaym*. His eyes glistened. He patted my back, squeezed my shoulder. I kept my eyes away from his and studied the drawings on his arms. He wanted me to like him. He brought me paper and pens. He took a pen and scribbled a little. Drew a smiling face to show me what to do. He gave me the pen and said a few words and walked out of the room.

I drew a smiling face like the one he drew, a circle with two dots and a curve at the bottom. I drew it again. I drew more faces with different mouths. I added ears and hair. One had squiggly line for a mouth, and I laughed. I added necks, arms, bodies to the circles. I lay one of my shirts on the mattress and drew its T-shape onto one of the figures and filled it in black.

After I'd used most of the paper, I set it all aside and sat straight. The stiff gray walls pinched in on me. Many of the monsters I'd carved into them were incomplete. The lines of their necks and ears and teeth stopped or went nowhere. I put my pen to an unfinished tooth line on the wall and brought the tooth to a sharp point. I drew another line to solidify a monster's eye. I picked up the book and used it as a guide to fill in the remaining lines and finish all the other monsters. For some of them, I scribbled hair on their heads.

When I'd finished, all the monsters had mixed outlines of black and blue and white. They looked uneven—it was hard to tell what some of them were. I started filling in all the white parts with the black pen. I drew more monsters. Filled an entire wall with them. The ink ran out and I started using the blue. I wanted to fill all four walls and make the room mine.

I pressed the pen hard into the wall, etching in scales on their arms and backs, filling them with fresh details. I added pictures of words whose edges snagged on my eyes. I didn't know what they meant but I wanted to add them all the same. One of them looked like this:

LOOk

I drew it as big as my hand and filled another wall with blue monsters. Words hung around and beneath and over them. I sat on the mattress. The two walls formed the corner where I slept. I was proud. I nestled down on the mattress, looking at the monsters upside down. They watched over me with their beautiful teeth and claws.

The long-haired man brought me a sandwich and a banana. He smiled at the walls. Nodded his head and showed me his thumb. I showed him mine. His smile widened. I think he laughed. He patted my head and walked out. I ate the food, then covered my face with the book of monsters and had the best sleep I'd had in a long time.

28 JUNE 1973

Dad's losing his job. St. Patrick's is closing the kids have to leave, I wonder if they'll go live in the woods and become trolls going into people's houses stealing food fighting coyotes. Mom worries about money saying no one will hire dad because he is Deaf. She says to me you see, you see, you need to learn. Mom says grandma won't give him grandpa's shoe shop because he doesn't have the skill Mom threw the bills at him called him loser dad said with his hands shut up shut up shut up. He put up the tent in the backyard and stayed with me. I asked if we're going to be poor he said be quiet he came out to get away from mom who's being a bitch he never called her that before. I asked if he knew any ghost stories he told me about how he and his friends went to Saint Louis saw a bright light coming at them through the bushes, he said his friends thought a train cut off a man's head and the man is still there swinging his light looking for it. Dad thought it was a little boy chasing fireflies on the tracks. I asked if the boy was hit by the train he said the boy's not real told me to grow up there's no such thing as ghosts. I asked what the light was he said it's passing cars I asked if Deaf people are ghosts probably he said. I asked if grandpa was a ghost he said leave me alone it doesn't matter. I said that grandpa believed in ghosts. He said Felix I'm not happy here. I told him speaking therapy at school makes me feel weird the person keeps touching my throat and I want to bite him want to go to the Deaf school instead but dad turned away so he wouldn't see my signs and went to sleep.

29 JUNE 1973

Can't stop seeing dad as a loser, mom's word sticking to him, grandpa used to ask what kind of man I wanted to be when I got older not like dad like a sad dog lets people kick him, no fight. Loser said I can't go camping this summer. I want to go with Wendy like me Wendy has hearing aids but she doesn't sign only blahblahs. Wendy's mom won't let her. We made a castle out of sticks and watched scary movies. We made up our own signs for ~~Crist~~ Christopher Lee and Peter Cushing and we laughed. I taught her signs for bad words asshole fuck bastard she asked for them, after we watched Godzilla Wendy showed me how to use a spray can to make fire held the match in front of the can and pressed down FWOOSH like a comic book burning her mom's curtains. Her mom the frizzy asshole came to our house told mom what happened like it was my fault and mom said I got to stay in my room for a week, no movies, no playing. I acted like Father Hoff in the mirror and gave grandpa a better funeral in sign to send him up to Heaven right. May God see him at last and his journey into the golden light be blessed.

WHERE I'M SUPPOSED TO BE

IN THE MAIN room of the prison's biggest building, the TV is always on, and sometimes the other inmates argue about what they want to watch. They change the picture, and I see other worlds. Mountains that spit liquid fire. Giant creatures with sharp teeth that swim underwater and eat men whole. Flowers with unreal colors that open as soon as the sunlight hits them. Everything seems miraculous. The world is infinite, always making new things. It's impossible to see all of its possibilities. I try to think how big it is, and how many places there are and how many people and creatures and plants, and my brain goes soft.

A few nights ago, I sat at a table drawing, as I have just about every night for the last several years, and I looked up and saw my father on the TV. I gasped. His picture was all gray and white, but his eyes stared right at me. I threw my pencil at the screen and yelled and signed, Dick fuck you dick, at his picture and swept my drawings off the table and ran out of the room. Two guards chased me and forced me against the wall. I cried as they led me back to my cell.

The next day, a lawyer visited me with an interpreter. They showed me the same picture of my father. I stiffened. Made a noise to let them know I didn't want to see him. The lawyer asked me if I knew him. I said yes.

He asked, How do you know him?

He's my father, I said.

How do you know?

He kept me in a basement room for a long time.

We've been chasing him for years. Where did he keep you?

In his house.

Which house?

There was a tall fence around it. A deer head on the wall.

The lawyer told me he needs to do some research, but he wants to talk to me again. I said I don't want to see his picture again and they should talk to my mother instead.

The sign for "sex" is two V hands knocking together. Seems right—my parents must've crashed together to make me. Just sacks of flesh knocking into one another, no gentle act of love. The few times I saw them together, I never saw love. They hardly looked at each other or at me. They avoided my eyes, feared my smile. Anger tingled in the air. When they neared each other, I winced, as though they'd start a fire by touching.

One time at my mother's, I spent a whole day in front of the mirror. It was the first time I remember seeing myself. Dirt covered my face. My hair rolled down to my shoulders. My eyes looked bewildered—I couldn't believe they were mine. I stared at them, the tiny red lines curling through the whites, the grayish-blue circles, the little black dots in the middle where everything fell into my head. I pinched my cheeks, smiled, and frowned. I ran my thumb along my teeth and stuck out my tongue. I let my tongue dry and held it between two fingers. I saw how I moved—my elbows and knees left welts on the air. I hated the way I moved. So clumsy and stiff. I imitated my mother and her friends. Their gestures and expressions. They had more rhythm, more control.

I said things to the mirror. I made sounds. My breath fogged up the glass. I spurted sounds as though the mirror could harden them into objects I could understand. I breathed on the mirror and drew lines and circles and zigzags. My mother had people over—no one was watching me. Each drawing cleared the fog from the glass and revealed her sitting across the room, a bottle in her hand. She smiled at the people. Our faces were shaped the same. Her eyes were darker than mine. My father's, I saw later, were lighter. He and I have the same eyes.

I couldn't do much at my mother's—her yard was mud and roots—but fields surrounded her house. Green and yellow. I rubbed flower petals between my fingers and petted the green fur with my hands. I loved how it could be sharp and soft at the same time. I stayed out there until dark most days, pulling flowers, chasing bugs, watching birds.

One day I came back from the field across the road and saw the man I'd later learn was my father there on the front steps, spitting words at my mother. He held something in a small bag. My mother said nothing, didn't look at him. He put the bag in her hands. She looked at it like she didn't want it, then held it close like she was hugging it. She didn't want it but at the same time she did.

Later that day she walked with me down the road into town. Not sure the name of the town. She led me to a small square building. Blue and yellow letters looped up and down the front window. As soon as we walked in the door, my mother hugged me and smiled at everyone sitting at the counter. I hid behind her leg as she bought a pack of cigarettes. I breathed in deeply—the smells of candy and cooking meat were so different from the stale air at her house. She kept patting my head and talking to everyone there. They didn't seem to say much. I waved and made a noise that I hoped sounded happy. They stared at me, puzzled. I shrank back to my mother's side.

The wall beside the counter was covered in small brightly colored packages, and I thought about reaching for one but was too nervous to leave my mother's side.

Once we left the building, my mother broke away from me and walked fast. I had to run to keep up with her.

Back at home, I took out my black and blue and red pens. Her table was covered in piles of thin books with shiny pages showing pictures of people and bottles and clothing and food, and I drew shapes on them while she smoked and watched people playing guitar and shooting each other on TV. My fingers became smudged with black and blue as I traced the people. I drew faces on them. Sometimes I gave women mustaches. Once I drew shapes on the wall. My mother threw a cup at me and put me in my room.

My room had a small bed. Clothes in a dresser. A painting on the wall. The painting showed the prairie, but it wasn't the prairie I knew. I recognized the shape of the fur and the flowers on the ground, but the fur was bright red and the flowers were purple and looked more like grasping hands. The sky was black, and the clouds bristled with white and gray barbs always on the verge of forming clear shapes. The moon was pure white and enormous. It cast a glow onto the purple and red prairie. I stared at that moon each night wondering if I'd ever see that version of the prairie.

While my mother was always busy smoking and watching TV, I explored the rooms, the cupboards, the closets. I'd act out things I saw on TV—gestures and facial expressions. As long as I didn't break anything, she didn't care what I did.

Once she tried teaching me to read. She wrote what I think was the alphabet across the top of a flyer. She put her finger under each letter and watched me like she thought I'd understand. She tapped on the first letter and held something invisible in her hand and took a bite out of it and pointed to the letter. I understood she was trying to tell me something. I just didn't know what.

When people came over to smoke and drink, they pushed me away and stepped between my mother and me, closing me off. They filled the rooms with smoke, their words sticking to my clothes.

One night, I left the house. I didn't run away—just walked down the gravel road. I wore shoes too big for me. One of the visitors might've brought them. I looked back. The house looked sad, like someone who hadn't slept.

I walked, kicking at the gravel. My feet shifted in my shoes. The sky was a fuzzy gray-blue. After looking at that painting each night, it seemed possible that I could rub my face against the sky, that I could walk beyond the gravel and dirt and fur and houses and step off into that blueness. I walked until dark.

I walked past dark. I never felt tired. I felt free. The cold air held me. The sky kept rolling away from me. I kept trying to touch it or at least reach its edge. I kept thinking I'd reach it soon.

In the morning, I saw kids running up to a long yellow vehicle. They had bags on their backs. They smiled. Their clothes were colorful and clean. I waved at them. Made a sound.

They got into the yellow vehicle, and it drove away down the road. I held up two fingers in front of one eye, watching the vehicle grow smaller as it drove away, and squeezed my fingers shut along with it until I could no longer pinch it between two fingers. It seemed like it drove off into the sky. I wished so much I could've been on it, because it seemed like it was going somewhere I was supposed to be.

THIS WORKBOOK BELONGS TO:

Felix Jimson

13 OCT. 1974

Yesterday Jeremy the fucker kicked me in the face. I was trying to get up onto the slide and he sat at the top of the ladder like a greedy troll. He said things to me, in my hearing aid he sounded like a fish flbblbblbbl. I laughed and said he sounded like ass and tried to pull him off the ladder. I'm the boss his lips said and he kicked me. My nose was bleeding. My hand had lots of blood and I chased after the shitty jerk with it saying didn't hurt, didn't hurt. I smiled with blood in my teeth like Christopher Lee and he started crying.

17 OCT. 1974

~~Me and dad~~ Dad and I moved to a smaller house. He works as cleaner at the church. I put a Frankenstein poster on my wall. He let me watch the ~~exorst~~ Exorcist at the theatre but for some parts he covered my eyes with his hand but he missed when she stabbed herself in the crotch with the cross. The first words Max Sydow said were spelled out at the bottom of the screen but none of the rest were spelled out which was bullshit. I asked Wendy if she could go but she couldn't cause of the frizzy asshole so I asked dad what the priest says again and again. The priest I guess was the good guy who didn't hit anyone and said the power of Christ compels you, which means what? Dad didn't know.

Wendy has a curfew. I walk down the alleys at night sometimes or by the river. I walk alone and never wear my hearing aid. The air is full at night and like Sydow in The Magician I feel in the air all the magic all the things people dream or won't say and I feel close to seeing them.

THE BLONDE BOY

I SPENT A while just closing and opening the door to my room, enjoying the click of the doorknob in my hand. I smiled at the people who passed in the hall each time I opened it. I'd open it a little and peek through the crack then whip it all the way open. People spoke to me, frowned at me, smiled at me.

The eyebrow woman stepped in from the hall and pointed at the door and pushed it all the way open. She kept her hand on the door and spoke to me. Her black eyebrows had been carefully drawn, with precise edges. She waved at me and cocked them, deepening their angles so that she looked like a beautiful devil. A question. I nodded. She waved me after her.

Everyone in the building had lined up along one wall, waiting to be let into a large room with long tables. I smelled something juicy and browned. The eyebrow woman stood beside me, while a few other women and a handful of men wearing white stood near the doors.

Up ahead, a boy with shiny blond hair and a yellow shirt approached the line clutching a book. One of the uniformed men, who had a drawing of a lion on his arm, put both his hands together and bowed toward the boy. The boy waved toward the people in line—his eyes skated across mine. He opened his arms and spoke to everyone with his mouth. The man with the lion dropped a hand on the boy's shoulders, ducking his head to aim words at his face. The boy didn't look at him. Didn't blink. He clutched his book to his chest and kept his eyes forward as the man walked him toward the back of the line.

Everyone filed in through the two doors and scattered to sit at tables with people they knew. Other people emerged from a swinging door to bring in silver trays full of food. White meat. Potatoes. Salad. Yellow cake. The eyebrow woman sat across from me. I didn't see my roommate, the round-faced man, so I sat alone near the people in uniform who ate in the corner near the door. I ate quickly, then waited for everyone else. The eyebrow woman smiled and offered me her cake. I took it.

The blond boy set his food on a table near the window. He bowed his head and touched his forehead and shoulders. The lion man walked over to him and reached for the boy's book. The boy slapped his hand down and moved the book under his leg.

The man scooped potatoes off the boy's tray and shoveled them into his mouth. The boy formed shapes with his hands like he was yelling through his hands at the man, hurling his feelings at him. Everyone else's hands moved in random flicks or shrugs or quivers, but this boy's hands moved specifically. They danced. Crisp. Ordered. Every finger in sync. His movements meant something.

A few young people sitting near him tossed the same gestures at the man and the other people in uniform. The lion man held up his middle finger and returned to his table.

The boy ate only a few bites and then got up. As he left the room, his eyes rattled like plugs trying to hold something in.

After everyone had finished eating, the eyebrow woman took me all the way to the other side of the building, to a room where a man with no hair was cutting another man's hair. The walls had pictures of people's hair done up like oiled rugs or bird nests. One wall was all mirrors, and I cringed when I saw myself in such clear color. My hair was tattered and shiny, my face a sickly white. My tight red shirt looked like a joke, and my ribs formed grooves that rose through the cloth. My arm looked like it'd been wrapped all my life. Nothing about me matched. I looked like a child had put me together.

I sat down, and a few minutes later the man with no hair wrapped a cloth around me and picked up a bottle of water and a black plastic thing with thin teeth. He squirted water onto my head and dragged the teeth through my greasy tangles. Some of my hairs snapped off my head like when my father's men jerked me by my hair. I breathed fast. My feet sweated. I looked at the woman. She held up her hands to reassure me. I gripped the arms of the chair.

The man took his time working his way around my head with the toothy thing until my hair was all straight lines. It hung over my eyes down to my belly. Something silver glinted in the mirror. The man held up a sharp snapping instrument. A little silver jaw. I bucked out of the chair; the cloth fell off me, and I backed against the wall. The woman held up her hands. *Oh-hay*. She touched my arm.

I edged further away from the chair. The woman sat in the chair herself and spoke to the man with no hair. He held a few strands of her unnaturally yellow hair and cut off the ends. The woman stood and dialed her open hands toward the chair. *Soh-hay*, she said.

I sat back down.

The man put the cloth back over me, then gently held my damp straightened hair between two fingers. I stared at him in the mirror. He smiled and snipped off several inches. I winced, though it didn't hurt. He did the same thing; I winced again. He kept going. Soon, I stopped wincing, and brown shards of hair crosshatched the floor.

When he saw my torn ear, he paused, then took extra care cutting the hair around it.

When he was finished, he put a shiny glue into his hands and pushed it through my hair, so that my hair softly framed my face. It stopped just above my jaw now while still covering the stitched ear. The woman smiled. I nodded at the man with no hair.

He swept all the hair on the floor into a green pan and dumped it into the trash. I stared at the trash can, feeling like part of me had been thrown away.

As we stepped into the hall, the lion man rushed past me. Down the hall, another uniformed man was hauling the blond boy out of a bedroom. The lion man seized the boy's arms. The boy hung between the men and shook his head. Everyone in the hallway stared.

The boy's lips kept repeating the same movements: *Whyoodoodis whyoodoodis.* The two men started leading him away, but the boy whipped his head back and forth, gritting his teeth and straining to pull free. *Nononono.*

The lion man gripped the boy's arms while the other grabbed his legs, and they lifted him and carried him away down the hall. Fear gushed from the boy's eyes, and he screamed. For a moment I felt the same kind of panic as when my father had taken me in the night. I stepped toward him, but the eyebrow woman nudged me on the shoulder, directing me toward my room. Then she followed the small blond storm twisting and thrashing down the hall.

When I got back to my room, I found the man with the round face and glasses sitting on his bed reading a thin book with pictures full of color. I stopped in the doorway. The box from under the bed was open and was full of similar books.

He stood and shook my hand again, then pointed at my arms. I walked over to my bed under the window. He showed me the cover of his book. Someone dressed in red and blue with large white eyes crouched atop a building. Words popped out in thick blocks.

He opened the book, and the pages flopped over his hands. He spoke and pointed at white ovals full of tiny black words and more drawings of the man in red and blue talking to people and punching them. He put the book down beside him and said something. I nodded. His face twitched and he spoke again. I nodded. His face twitched again. He shook his head and said, *Oh-hay,* and touched my shoulder. I cringed a little, and he pulled his hand away. He smelled like fresh laundry.

He lifted his shirt to show a clear plastic tube poking out of his belly. He grinned and prodded it with a finger, then went back to his bed and picked up a metal can with the top cut out. He spit into it, said something, and put the can down. Then he picked up a pen and came back over to inspect the white wrapping on my arm. He drew a face on it and added a circle with words inside it.

When he started reading his book again, I lay back on my bed. Settled into the comfort. Through the window, I could see the underside of the roof and part of the sky. Across from me, my roommate kept reading and spitting.

There was another meal in the evening, but my roommate didn't go. He waved for me to go ahead of him, then turned and went elsewhere.

The blond boy wasn't in the dining room either. I ate with the eyebrow woman again. The young people watched me. A boy with a black mustache and a few girls smiled at me. I turned away and smiled to myself.

That night I didn't sleep. The blond boy's hands had poked a hole in my brain and sprung a leak of some bristling electrical substance that spiked through my limbs and left me charged up. I sat in my bed peering out the window and glancing back at my sleeping roommate now and then. He'd propped himself up with three pillows so that he sat almost upright on the bed. I'd never slept in the same room as someone else. Everything about my roommate was soft and gentle. As his chest rose and fell, I found myself mimicking his breathing pattern and soon I became calmer.

The prairie blackened then disappeared into the night. There were no houses in the distance, no streetlights, no passing vehicles. The black freighted air flexed and pressed against the window. Late in the night, lit by an open door in the building, two men in white came around a corner and walked through the field toward a square of white rocks. One held a flashlight and a shovel while the other pushed something in a wheelbarrow covered by a brown blanket.

They stepped beyond the reach of the light stretching from the building, and the flashlight began sweeping across the field, briefly awakening its dull brown color. The men propped the light against a gray stone and took turns digging a hole. I couldn't see their faces.

The darkness crowded around the edges of the light, wait-ing to claw in and grab the men. When the hole reached the depth of their knees, they lifted the load from the wheelbarrow, keeping it covered by the blanket. My breath had clouded the window, and I wiped the fog away. Between the two of them, the load was light, easy to carry. A white arm dropped out from under the blanket just before they set it down in the hole. I made a noise and looked at my roommate. He remained asleep.

The men began filling the hole with dirt. When they finished, one of them straightened and turned toward the building, looking directly at me.

My father grinned, his teeth shining through his beard.

I ducked away from the window and coiled into a ball on my bed. I wanted to cry, but I couldn't. I gripped my knees. My chest hardened. Trying to breathe was like trying to suck water from a stone. A shadow from the hallway slid across the bottom of the door. I squeezed myself tighter, wishing for the darkness to hide me.

The light cracked on, breaking the room open. My room-mate put on his glasses and strode over to me. He spoke to me. Rubbed my shoulder. Hugged me. I felt his chest against my back, his soft warm belly sinking and rising. I grabbed his arm and matched my breathing with his. He kept holding me like he wanted to absorb whatever I was afraid of.

After a while, I sat up straight. He took off his glasses and wiped his eyes on his elbow. His cheeks puffed out—he'd been crying too. He grabbed his pop can from the table and spat a fat glassy gob into it.

I looked out the window. Outside, the men and the wheel-barrow were gone. The room smelled like my roommate's breath.

I stayed up until blue and pink light started blooming along the prairie's distant edge, and I fell asleep wondering how long it'd take to reach that edge, for it still felt possible to march out and step off it.

Felix Jimson

15 JUNE 1975

Mrs. Olafsson said I have to stop writing bad thoughts in my workbook so I do it at home now no matter.

Old prick Father Hoff talked to me in his office wanting me to read his lips but his white nose hairs wooshwoosh when he breathes so I told him to write. He knocked on the table and told me to look at him, asked if I love God and what I would do to feel his light. His lips were squishy like old worms, I couldn't look so he had to write.

His writing was full of loops like olden days. I'm Deaf, I said, I'm a ghost and already feel light. He said dad told him I want to be a priest one day, said God is careful when choosing those he wants to speak through he does not speak through the ~~affic~~ afflicted so I should stop talking about becoming a priest my ambitions are worthless and I should think of doing something else because embracing Deafness is welcoming the devil with open arms he said that with his pen. You've never met God I said so how do you know? Your attitude is outright blasfummus he wrote Deafness is a punishment an evil brought by lack of faith. Christ healed the Deaf so you must pray to be healed underlined the word Ephphatha. I sat there thinking about grandpa wanting to choke Hoff with his beads like rabbit shit on a string I whispered fuck you, said it out loud FUCK YOU he hit my hands my knuckles bled and my hands were still shaking when I got home. I pulled out the new bible I ordered read the invocation toward the conjuration of destruction. At night I turned the old bible upside down put on candles and wrote a wish about Father Hoff having his eyes pecked out by magpies I signed the invocation on the air but it ends with hail Satan and I couldn't complete it with grandpa's picture staring at me from the wall. Dad came home from work looked at me kneeling in the living room and walked down the hall to bed.

18 JUNE 1975

Jeremy Roy and others held me down and pulled my tongue out. Their lips said fix it fix it Jeremy with a knife about to saw a line down the middle Ms. Bonney saw and walked out then as Jeremy cut the tip of my tongue in two Mrs. Olafsson stopped them I went home stopped to cry by the garbage cans went to the cemetery to see grandpa with the cross on his stone my mouth still bleeding they're turning me into a devil.

19 JUNE 1975

Bump in my tongue keep feeling it. Mom hasn't sent me a letter in a long time.

I asked dad if I could visit her during the summer he said she doesn't want to see me. Our table's covered with court papers—

He asked me how I'd feel about him seeing Colleen who worked at St. Patrick's too she's gross picks feathers off the ground and puts them in her purse she's uglier than mom and smokes a lot I said no. He said they've been seeing each other I said she's a hearing woman he said he's going to bring her here for supper I said I don't want her here transgression is at work if people blahblahblah. He told me I'm a wart on his ass and he couldn't wait for me to grow up and leave. I threw my glass at the wall and dad said which of your magic rituals is that and he slapped the back of my head and put me in my room. I took mom's shirt out of the closet and held it, she wanted me to be good but she's not here.

Be not silent to me. If thou be silent to me I become like them that fall into the pit.

HOW THE SUN DIVIDES THE DAYS

BEING IN THAT brick building hardened the days into clear blocks. It took me a while to get used to the way the sun divided the days and even longer to understand the rules. All the doors must be kept open during the day. Everyone must take their medication every morning. Kids must study each weekday in the common room. Group talk takes place before lunch. Everyone eats at the same time. No one leaves the floor without permission. No one goes outside without a nurse. Family visits must be supervised. Anyone who causes trouble is taken up to the third floor.

The building had no fence, no loops of wire to keep us in. In the field a short walk away, the wide awkward square of white rocks formed what looked like a dinosaur's mouth, and inside it gray stones poked up out of the ground like rotten teeth. I watched the square waiting for something to happen, but nothing did in the daylight.

Each day, I stuck to the walls and made myself small as I watched everyone. How they lit their cigarettes. How they ate their food. How they walked and rolled dice and held books. I spent whole days watching and imitating everyone who walked past.

In group talk, everyone sat in a circle and looked at the floor and smoked while one person, usually someone in uniform, spoke. A brittle tension settled on the room—no one wanted to speak. At study time, I was shown into the common room with the teenagers and young adults, and I watched them read and talk. Their books had no pictures.

The boy with black hair and a weedy mustache kept approaching me. Unlike most of the other people who had pale or splotchy or pinkish white skin, his skin was smooth light brown. He spoke and wrote on my broken arm and showed me pictures from thin shiny books. In the pages, men with long hair pulled back from their faces wore suits with clashing colors that hurt my eyes. Thick gold necklaces were trapped in their chest hair, and women in yellow and green dresses smiled up from the pages and held cigarettes or glasses filled with red drink. He pointed at the people in the images, and I nodded and made a noise. Some of the other teenagers joined us and looked through the pages. A few of the girls wrote notes and passed them to me. One of them, a girl with pink streaks in her black hair, drew pictures of flowers and birds. She gave me a piece of paper, and I drew a monster. She and the others smiled and wrote on my broken arm.

I kept seeing the men in white burying the body at night. Even if I never looked out the window again, I could feel them out there: the small body under the blanket, my father staring up at the window. One night, I stuffed my head beneath my pillow, and terrible memories crawled their way up. Dogs biting at my arms. Blood popping out of the bigger man's chest. My father and his men pulling me toward the hole in the ground. I screamed and kicked at the air above my bed and punched the wall. My roommate came over to my bed and hugged me again. I tried to push him off, but he held on.

Eyebrow woman came into the room. She sat on the bed, and both she and my roommate spoke to me and waited with me until I relaxed. Then the woman left, and my roommate patted my shoulder and walked back to his bed.

One day I saw the man who'd been restrained in the bed beside me when I first arrived. He was in the hallway, drawing something in a book with a pencil, when he looked up and saw me too. He focused on my scarred, unbroken arm. He reached out, shook my hand, and started drawing on my broken arm.

It was a face with sharp cheekbones and thin hair that I soon realized was his own face. When he finished, he smiled up at me and started drawing in his book again.

The blond boy didn't re-emerge for weeks. Then one day, he walked into the dining room during the morning meal, after everyone else had sat down. He looked tired. Thinner. His eyes flat. He still carried his book and sat alone.

The boy with black hair and mustache had started sitting with me at mealtimes. I sat at the end of a table near the staff, and he sat across from me and spoke to and smiled at me.

I kept turning toward the blond boy. Black mustache showed me a piece of paper with writing on it. He held it over top of my plate and pointed at my scars. I nodded and pushed the paper aside and kept eating my eggs.

Eyebrow woman went over and spoke to the blond boy. Touched his arm. The blond boy did nothing. Black mustache shook his head. He said things as he looked at me, pointed at the blond boy, and spun a circle on the air near his temple.

Lion man pointed at black mustache's tray. His food sat hardening in front of him. He waved lion man away, and when he left he flashed his middle finger at his back and took a bite of eggs, then spat them back out and slid his tray away. I touched his tray, and he nodded. I pulled it over.

The blond boy didn't eat. He wrote in his book and held the cover at an angle so no one could see what he was writing. He did the same thing at study time that day. Everyone else read or wrote on loose pages or played board games. I was the only one doing nothing.

Someone had taken my usual seat along the wall, so I sat at the big table with everyone else. A nurse with bright green fingernails brought me a book from the shelf in the corner. There were two boys on the cover.

I turned away. She propped it open for me and traced lines across the page with her long thumbnail. She set the book down and tapped the page. I shrugged and pushed the book away. She pulled it back and tapped the page again. I closed the book. When she opened it again, I threw the book across the room. The other kids all looked at me. The nurse said something and brought the book back.

The girl with pink streaks in her black hair spoke to the nurse, and the nurse threw words back at her. I threw the book again and made a noise; it was like asking me to eat a plate of rocks. The nurse shook her head at me and the girl. Two uniformed men watched me from the door. The blond boy put down his pen, gripped me with his eyes, and formed a blade with his right hand and chopped it into his left palm. Stop. A smack of clarity. His eyes flickered like black fire. No one had looked at me that directly before. I was shocked. Thrilled. He spoke to the others with his mouth, then added more with his hands. Everyone sagged. He pointed at me, then picked up his pen and resumed writing.

Every part of my body dialed toward him. Waiting for more. His lips moved like he was speaking to himself. I repeated his motion and made a flat blade of my hand and slapped it into my palm. I did it closer to him so he'd notice. Other people at the table started doing it too. Black mustache smiled as he chopped; pink streaks thrust her chopping hands at the nurse and into another girl's.

The blond boy said something with his mouth. The others smiled, though not with their eyes, like they weren't sure what to say, and the blond boy grabbed his book and walked out of the room.

When we lined up in the hall for the evening meal, the blond boy walked close to the front like he wanted to speak to everyone again. He peered back at the uniformed men, who tilted their heads, warning him. The boy walked toward the back of the line.

As he passed me, I shuffled backward to give him room in front of me. He stopped. Smiled at me. He stepped into the space I'd made in the line and said, *Thenkoo*.

We ambled into the dining room. I sat beside him at the end of the table by the window. Rain made scratch marks on the glass. The prairie was a soaked rug—in the gray light, it seemed impossible that anything could grow out there. We sat stiffly. I slowly chopped my hand into my palm again. He said something with his mouth. I did it again. He turned to me with his eyebrows sunk down over his direct eyes. Then, with his upturned index fingers and thumbs, he formed beaks that opened and closed.

I repeated his motion, chopping my hand into my stiff, white-wrapped palm.

Stop, he said with his hands.

Stop, I said with my hands.

Oomuckinmeh, he said with his mouth. He thrust his thumb outward from under his chin and shoved his open hand at me and turned an imaginary valve on his nose. His lips read *Nawtoorklown*. He did it all so smoothly that his movements seemed to be one motion.

I tried making the same gestures but I couldn't keep up. The wrapping on my arm hindered me. I waved for him to do them again.

He snapped his index and middle fingers against his thumb and pointed away from the table.

I did an awkward dance with my hands. Hoped my raised eyebrows and widened eyes asked enough of a question that he'd understand.

He stood from the table and walked to the door. Lion man stepped in front of him. The boy tried to step past him, but lion man stopped him and said something to him. The boy stood there shaking. He returned to his seat beside me and said nothing.

The trays of food came. He ate one bite and put down his fork. I finished my food and took a bite of his. He slapped my hand. Patted his chest. *Mine!* Touched his nose with one hand-shape and flicked another handshape at me. *Bissawff.*

I made the same motion, and his face swelled red. His hands curled into fists.

When the doors opened, he scurried out of the dining room. I followed him.

He slipped into the bathroom. I tried pushing the door open, but he held it shut. I shoved on it, and it swung open and knocked him back against the wall. He screamed *Fuhawff* at me, stepped back out into the hall, and ran away. I was much taller and could keep up easily.

I tried gesturing to him as I ran alongside him. He kept swatting me with his book. We ran all the way to the other side of the building, where he ducked into his room and closed the door. I tried the knob, but it didn't move. I knocked. No answer. I sat on the bench across the hall and waited.

A painting hung on the wall beside his door. A man's face. His wide white smile stretched well beyond his cheeks. His eyes were uneven. His long hair curled down and formed some of the trees in the background. It was both ugly and beautiful.

The hallway darkened. The nurses started putting everyone in their rooms. Green fingernails approached me. I hoped she would open the boy's door, but instead she pointed down the hall and tapped her watch. When I didn't move, she pointed me down the hall again. I fixed the painting of the smiling man in my head so I'd know where to go the next day.

Felix Jimson

2 APRIL 1977

I found a book about Manson. His mother left him and he was poor so he stole things and begged in the streets, I was halfway done when dad took it away. He said I was too young but I took it back and he said fine it's your brain.

Manson saw himself as Christ but he was evil, selfish. Christ wouldn't kill. True love is selfless, blessed are the peacemakers.

What's the difference between a follower and a disciple? Would John or Simon kill for Jesus?

3 APRIL 1977

Dad took another job making deliveries for the bakery, saying we need the money. The loser just doesn't want to be home. Fine with me.

Grandma brings food and I read and watch movies and sit with my ideas to change the world. My tongue against my teeth feels weird but good. Dad says there's no mark there but I feel it. Grandma says dad should marry again, I hope he doesn't. I said we should move. The other Deaf people here are nice but boring. They don't like me or dad. Grandma makes him and me go to church, and we all helped at the bake sale yesterday, I showed a little kid my tongue and he laughed and squirmed, I told him to get me some juice and he brought it, then his mom called him away, glaring at me.

When the bake sale was over, I walked past Father Hoff's office. The door was open and I saw today's sermon on his desk with all loopy writing talking about being good citizens. I said to the ceiling HORSESHIT and took his red pen and crossed it all out and wrote, If we are all made in God's image why must we be corrected? People have twisted the word of God to serve themselves, which is Satan's work. The people we see as afflicted are full of divine beauty. I felt grandpa's hand on my hand as I wrote, pictured myself signing this to a stadium full of people with grandpa in the wings, people cheering, hands fluttering beautiful. Father Hoff came in and grabbed my hands. I ran out of his office and found grandma and dad but the old fucker told dad what I did and dad said go along then back to the office where Father Hoff made me say four Hail Marys as loud as I could. In my head I went hail mary full of beans because grandpa used to say I was full of beans, and I laughed. Hoff took off his belt and hit my hands so hard he broke two knuckles. Grandma yelled at him, her face all red, pointing at him, she never uses her mouth voice but she did yesterday. She brought me ice and at the hospital I said to dad what's wrong with you, why would you let him do that to me. He said why can't you be normal, why can't you be good.

7 APRIL 1977

Hard to write with my knuckles wrapped. Keep thinking about the other bible "I am mine own redeemer" and "Satan represents opposition to all religions which serve to frustrate and condemn man for his natural instincts." Does that include signing? I'd ask grandma but she'd never say—
   I walked past Wendy's house last night saw her changing into her pants and waited before I waved at her window. I said with my mouth I wanted fire cause she had firecrackers

under her bed. Her chest is getting bigger. We ran into the alley and put the firecrackers into a garbage can, before she lit them I asked if she liked me and she said nothing I asked if she thinks I'm nice she said sure and lit them and as we moved away she tipped the garbage can over with her foot and the firecrackers spilled out. Someone next door had thrown out towels with oil on them and they caught fire and the fire jumped onto the garage. We ran to Wendy's house, stood behind the bush breathing hard my prick all the way hard I said you should be my girlfriend and tried to kiss her. She held me back and went home didn't say anything.

I SEE YOU

ABLACK DOG was charging toward me when my roommate woke me. I rubbed my eyes and nodded at him. I pulled on a red sweatshirt that sagged off my limbs, and together we went down the hall and stood in line. A nurse gave me a glass of water and a small round pill in a paper cup. I didn't know what it was for.

My roommate sat on a chair and winced while a nurse pushed a needle into his shoulder. The nurse spoke to me. My roommate raised his upturned thumb. I swallowed the pill and the water.

As everyone ambled down the hall toward the dining room, I walked toward the blond boy's room. Lion man stepped in front of me; the lines of the drawing on his arm were runny and green. I tried to move past him. He patted me on the shoulder and encouraged me toward the line. I watched over his shoulder for the boy, then fixed my eyes on the front of the line where he'd gone before.

Black mustache and pink streaks walked past me. The girl waved and spoke to me. The boy kept pulling his snarled hair to one side. His black eyes glowed when they settled on me.

I sat at the blond boy's place near the window. He came in after everyone else, headed toward me, then walked past and sat at another table.

Black mustache sat across from me. I hardly looked at him the whole meal. I kept turning and watching the blond boy's hands. Whatever we ate that day, I didn't taste it.

After the meal, the nurses guided him out. I followed them. He nodded toward the bathroom, and they let him go inside and stood outside the door. When I approached, they let me pass.

The bathroom had stalls with no doors. The bright blue tiles had been scuffed white in the middle of the floor. He'd propped his book against the mirror by the faucet and stood over the sink washing his face. He saw me in the mirror and whipped around. *Wahoowan.* He stared. *Fuhawff!* He said. His hands thrashed and whirled at me; his fingers slapped his forehead. His palms opened and turned upward and seemed to weigh invisible balls and he drew the balls closer to his chest. I imitated him, pleading with my eyes.

His body slammed to a halt. He stood straight and held me in place with his direct eyes, searching my body. He pointed at me, then with his index finger touched his ear, then his chin. He did it again. *Oodef?*

The leak in my brain burst. Lightning arced through my limbs—my entire body vibrated and hooked onto his hands. I yelled and jumped and nodded hard and pointed at him with both hands.

The boy slashed his hands through the air. I did the same. He clapped his hands down on my shoulders. Held me still. The nurses threw open the door. The boy waved them off. So did I.

The boy dried his face on his shoulder. You're Deaf, he signed.

You're Deaf, I signed.

A nodding fist: Yes.

Yes.

He wagged two fingers between the two of us. We're Deaf.

We're Deaf. Yes.

I nodded my fist hard, using my whole arm and bouncing it through the air. He squeezed my arm and snapped two fingers against his thumb: No.

No.

He pointed to his politely nodding fist, which he kept fixed in place and bent at the wrist. Yes.

I did the same. Yes.

You're Deaf.

You're Deaf.

Not me. You.

You.

He turned my pointing finger toward my chest: I. Me. He pointed toward his chest: I'm Deaf.

I'm Deaf.

Yes.

Yes.

The nurses approached. The boy said with his mouth, *Sohhay*, and waved me toward the door. I stepped past the nurses. I blinked. Everything in the hallway now glowed and rattled with secret life. Chairs. Paintings. The floor. The doors. The people. I wanted to wake up every object and every person with the same lightning the boy had given me.

My roommate passed us and waved at me. I'm Deaf, I signed.

He grinned and showed me both thumbs.

The boy clamped his hand over mine. He spun his index finger in front of his chin and pulled me after him. He kept pulling me back to him as I signed, I'm Deaf, to everyone we passed.

He led me to the common room, switched on the light, and shut the door. I started for the hallway—I wanted to sign to more people, but he pulled me back and sat down at a circular table. He motioned for me to sit across from him.

He cinched the fingers on his right hand together and touched his temple, then spun his index fingers around each other. You know Sign Language?

I raised my eyebrows to match his. I stretched my left hand and moved my stiff fingers as best I could: Know Sign Language?

He arched his index finger at me.

I shook my head.

He did it again: I'm asking you. You. Know. Sign. Language. You?

Sign Language you?

He waved both hands. He made two fingers into eyes that scanned his palm. You read?

He pulled a magazine from a nearby shelf onto the table. The cover had a yellow border and a picture of a gorilla holding a camera. He underlined the words on the cover with his finger. Read, he signed.

I shrugged.

He hit one index finger with the other: You can't read?

I shrugged again.

He put the magazine back on the shelf. That's okay, he said. He joined his index and middle fingers on both hands and tapped them against each other to make an X shape. I did the same motion.

No, he signed. He touched his chest and tapped his fingers again, then joined his index finger with his thumb and drew a circle around his head.

I started to draw a circle around my head but he stopped me. His hands formed five distinct shapes. His index finger joined his thumb while his other three fingers fanned out, then his four fingers drew back against his palm like hissing teeth, then his thumb and index finger made an L, then his pinkie stood alone from his closed fist, and then his index finger formed a hook.

He waved for me to join him.

F.

F.

E.

E.

L.

L.

I.

I.

X.

X.

He drew another circle around his head. Felix. My name.
My name.

Not your name. My name.

Your name.

Yes. What's your name?

My name.

He waited. He didn't blink or look away. Something in his
gaze encouraged me to please him. I didn't know what to say.
I didn't know what a name was. I repeated the sign, forming
Xs with my two hands, hoping something would occur to me.
Name, name, name.

Felix flicked his flattened hand outward from his temple.
You don't know?

Don't know.

He smiled a little. That's okay, he signed. With his left hand,
he cradled his right: I'll help you.

He squeezed my arm, warmly covering my scars. I shuddered, swallowed my tears, relieved.

ROYAL SASKATCHEWAN PSYCHIATRIC HOSPITAL—WAKAW, SK

PATIENT PROGRESS REPORT

Patient Name:	DOB:
Felix Jimson	30 Oct 1963
Admitting Psychiatrist:	Admittance Date:
Dr. Harrison Pearl	2 March 1980
Reporting Psychiatrist:	Report Date:
Dr. Lyle Okimasis	6 May 1980

ACTIVE MEDICATION(S)

Serentil—100 mg oral tablet (recommend in-
crease to 150 mg injection)

PROBLEMS AND PROGRESS

—Initial diagnosis: paranoid-type
schizophrenia—

Since his admittance, Felix has oscillated
between participating in patient activities
and complete withdrawal. Much of this has to
do with his hearing impairment. When he does
participate, it is done visually, with pen
and paper, though he loses patience quickly.
Not an excuse for disobeying rules, which he
clearly understands. He is an energetic and
pious young man who often reads the Bible
and writes in his journal, yet his thought
processes (shown through preaching) incorpo-
rate a range of ideas, including Satanism. The
end of the world is a constant theme. He has
not shown overly violent behavior, but due to
frequent disruptions during group talk, he
has been moved temporarily to the third floor

where, under Dr. Pearl's care, he is receiving insulin therapy. (See Dr. Pearl's notes dated 4 May.) Not my recommendation; will revisit in conference.

I have submitted a requisition for an interpreter to attend two days a week but have received no reply. Staff have attempted to write him notes or play games with him or help with his schoolwork, but he shows little interest in school. "I know all I need to know," he says.

One nurse expressed a concern that Felix has not been taking his medication. I asked him about this – he admitted it. He will receive his medication via injection after his insulin therapy is complete.

RECOMMENDATION(S)

Follow up in two weeks to check on medication's efficacy; continue observation with goal of clarified diagnosis; continue asking for interpretation for therapy sessions. Felix possesses a unique energy and charisma for someone his age. If he can direct his energies toward doing good work, he can make a clear difference in this world.

NOTES

How are you, Felix?

Sleep well?

Sorry about the restraints. You'll be fully released from them in a few days.

Dr Pearl's a fucking nazi

I don't agree with restraint. It won't be much longer.

when can I go home

I'd like to read some of your journal. That okay? Why not?
Can you tell me why you burned down your school's library? You're always reading + writing—you seem to value books.

the way the world is now serves only some people while so many beautiful people die without their voices ever being heard. if the world really wants to welcome everyone it must be torn down and rebuilt with everyone in mind.

Like the flood? Like Noah's ark? You admit you burned it down? Violence solves nothing, only hurts people.

I'm not violent, people don't understand

Understand what?

do you realize how much better the world would be if people just listened to us?

May I please read your journal? I don't want you to go to prison. The sooner you work with us the better off you'll be.

WHAT LOVE IS

IN GIVING ME language, Felix gave me love. My blood glowed. The world shimmered with incredible potential—even dust pulsed with life.

My questions overwhelmed him. I pointed to every single object and person in the institution. Several times, Felix stared at me and asked how I didn't know about something. A few times he delayed naming things because he thought I should know them.

What is this?

A door. You know that.

No, this.

What?

I slid my hand over the door's surface. Is there a name for this?

He smiled. A door!

This is not this. I patted the hard cold wall.

That's wood, that's brick, or do you mean the color?

What is color?

He bit his lip. My questions were so basic.

His hands danced their names for me. Colors. Shapes. The alphabet. The bright light in the sky was an outstretched hand throwing imaginary light back on his face. The fur on the ground was his fanned-out fingers brushing his chin. The toothed machines the people fed cloth into was an invisible needle pulled across his flattened left hand. I wrapped myself in language. I practiced them all before I slept—sometimes my roommate helped. I grew drunk on Felix's hands. I'd ask him to sign things three or four times even when I understood the first time.

Every person had a unique name shape. Felix scraped his M-hand against his stomach to name my roommate: Marvin. Black mustache was a G-hand drawn above his lip: George. Pink strands was a B-hand drawn back through his hair: Bernice. For the doctor in the white coat, he pulled his index and middle fingers outward from below his nose, then extended his flattened hand all the way out in front of him: Dr. Pearl. He tapped his open palm with an O-hand for the doctor in striped suits: Dr. Okimasis. Eyebrow woman was both hands tracing lines above his eyes: Ms. Beddim.

Can you give me some time alone? Felix signed. You can find something to do. Away from me.

What is do? What is something?

Do is doing. Moving, doing something.

What is something?

Everything is something.

What is everything? I don't know everything.

He gritted his teeth together and led me out of his room.

The whats led to whys. Why is the fur on the ground green? Why does the sun disappear each night? Why are letters shaped the way they are? How many words are there? Where are we right now? How big is the world?

Why are people's skin different colors? Or their faces shaped different? Bernice and Dr. O and others.

Bernice is Asian. George and the doctor are Native, First Nations. Different races.

What is race?

Kind of people. You and me are white.

I scanned my arm. Felix had pointed out white to me the day before using a piece of paper.

I'm not white, I signed. My skin's pink and has dots and ugly spots.

You're white. Most of us here are white.

He stuck out his tongue and pointed at the tip. A rough line slashed down the center, forming a small groove in the meat.

You see a line here?

Yeah.

His eyes gleamed. Another kid took a knife and did that to me years ago, he signed. But I forgive him. It's part of my final form.

Okay, I said. But I didn't understand what he'd said, and I still didn't understand about race. Why are people different races? I signed.

That's how God made the world. Not everyone looks alike.

What is God?

God made the world. Made you and me.

And the people in white clothes? I signed. They're a race?

No. They're just assholes.

They're here why?

To make sure we follow rules.

What are rules?

What you can and can't do.

I can't do things?

You can't hurt people, skip medication, go outside.

They make the rules?

Felix shook his head. Rules hurt people, he signed. They use rules to control us.

Control.

After I practiced my words and lay down to sleep, my mind still brewed with questions. I couldn't know enough.

I mimicked him for weeks. He told me what people had written on my broken arm. "Best wishes." "Stay out of trouble." "Stay sexy." I asked who wrote that, but Felix couldn't read the name.

Happy. Angry. Sad. Feelings were difficult. Not just because I couldn't see them. Not just because I had to learn how to aim my facial expressions after years of living without a mirror. But because as soon as I pinpointed my emotions and cradled them in my hands, I felt them so much that they spilled all over, and Felix had to help me clamp them down. Happy was one hand sweeping up from the chest as though the heart is a fountain of light. Angry was both clawed hands ripping outward from the chest. Sad was drawing a curtain down over the face.

If Felix was writing in his book, I had to wait until he was done. If I tried to ask a question, he'd grit his teeth and hold up his hand. He did that several times a day. He dictated the pace I learned at. Once I tried pulling on his sleeve, and he jerked his arm away. I learned to wait.

I met him every morning at medication time. I swallowed mine while he sat in a chair and Ms. Beddim injected something into his arm.

What is that? I signed.

Medicine.

What does it do?

Supposed to keep me calm.

Why is yours different?

Because we're different.

What am I taking?

Felix pointed at me. Ms. Beddim said something with her mouth.

She can't say.

Why not?

It's supposed to be private.

What's private?

Only you know.

Felix said something with his mouth. Ms. Beddim did too. Felix spelled it out for me: M-i-d-a-z-o-l-a-m.

What's that?

Felix shrugged. His shoulder was splotchy with brown and purple bruises. He pulled down his sleeve.

Ms. Beddim said something more. Felix frowned. He didn't like watching people's lips.

What'd she say?

Morning-eat, Felix signed. Breakfast.

We went down the hall toward the dining room, and once we sat down he wrote in his book for a few minutes. I waited until he closed it.

What'd she say? I signed. She had said more than *breakfast*.

They might have to change your medicine, he signed, because they thought you were—Felix slapped his forehead with his fingers, then circled his index finger beside his head.

What's that?

Delayed, or psychotic. Why are you here?

I stiffened. I don't know, I signed.

Did you break down? Hurt someone? Kill someone?

No.

Did someone hurt you?

I made fists. Said nothing.

They told me your name is John Smith. Is that a fake name? Are you hiding?

I cringed. Shook my head. The questions needled at me. Not having a name made my body feel runny.

I don't know what my name is. People take me places.

Where were you before you came here?

I don't know.

How'd you break your arm? What happened to your ear?

The enormity of all that had happened to me boiled up then turned to steam before it reached my fingertips. All I could get out was, I was in a car.

Felix crashed his fists together and raised his eyebrows. In an accident?

I was in a car that came here.

Who brought you?

Men.

What men?

Men in white. The car had a—

I scratched bars on the air then gripped them like I was stuck behind them.

A cage?

Yes.

His outstretched fingers crossed over each other. Were you in jail?

Yes, I signed.

What'd you do?

Nothing.

People go to jail because they did crimes.

What are crimes?

Stealing, lying, breaking things, hurting people.

I'm not bad. My bed was white. They wrapped my arm, sewed my ear. I couldn't move. Then they drove me here.

That's a hospital.

What's hospital?

They help people who are sick or hurt.

A uniformed man gave us our trays. Eggs. Potatoes. Milk. Orange slices. Felix pushed his tray away. George and Bernice sat beside us with their trays. Bernice slid a note over to Felix. Felix shook his head and spoke to them.

They want to know about you, he signed.

Why are they here? I signed.

Bernice's parents brought her here—she tried to kill herself. I don't know about George.

Kill? Herself? Why?

Who cares? Want to go somewhere else? I don't like them.

Felix kept pointing at them. Bernice swept her hand across the table, trying to knock Felix's finger down.

You can kill yourself? I signed.

I stared at Bernice. Snapped my *No* hand at her. She blinked.

George watched me like he wanted to sign. Bernice tapped Felix and spoke, but her lips moved too fast for me to understand. Felix replied. Bernice said something else and put her hands together.

Felix turned sideways so that he fully faced me. How'd you break your arm? he signed.

I fingered the tiny ridges in the white wrapping. I was frightened of what might happen if I shared but also grateful that someone was asking. Bernice and George watched me, their eyes bright. I raked my hooked fingers through the air, trying to dredge up the proper words. I couldn't carry the images out of my head and hold them in front of everyone. I slammed both hands on the table. Everyone in the dining room looked at me.

Ms. Beddim approached, but Felix waved her off. She said something to him and walked away.

I circled my fist over my chest. I'm sorry, I signed.

It's okay, Felix signed.

Bernice's hands fluttered on the air, waiting to know what I'd said. Felix picked up his fork and, as he ate, he told them what I'd said. They studied me the whole time, then George spoke to Felix.

Nuthertim, Felix said.

I scanned the room. Some people ate with their fingers. Some flicked eggs around their tables. Others picked through their food looking for something. Felix pulled my broken arm closer to him, pointing at some of the writing, and spoke to Bernice and George, who smiled and nodded.

Why are we all here? I signed.

Felix put down his fork and sat up straight. Everyone is here because they're more truthful and more beautiful than the world can handle, he signed. Everyone here has shone a light on a dark corner of humanity, and people hate us for it. The world doesn't listen to us. The world doesn't trust us. People out there, they hate us for how we look and what we do and what we need and what we say, so they hide us away in this place and make us feel shame. The world doesn't like truth.

What is truth?

What is real. Everyone here has more courage than most others, including you. The world is based on lies, rules that are only for a few people. People like us find love and beauty only outside the rules. I'm here because I followed the real path of Jesus and questioned the path of my church and my elders.

Who's Jesus?

Felix spelled the name then added a name sign: middle fingers pushed into each open palm. He was a beautiful man who suffered horrible treatment, he signed. My father put me in here.

What is father? What is suffer?

In pain for a long time.

I suffered, I signed. I'm like Jesus.

Felix smiled. In a way, we all are.

He spoke to Bernice. She smiled and took my good hand in both of hers and nodded at Felix. He pulled my hand away from her.

What's in your book? I signed.

My gospel.

What's gospel?

A beautiful way to live life.

What is beautiful? What is love?

Felix smiled. I'll teach you, he signed.

IN GROUP, THE two of us sat side by side and signed to one another while the others spoke. The nurse wore a green uniform and had long brown hair and wore a button with words on it. Felix told me they spelled *Mrs. Koepp.*

Marvin can't swallow, he signed. He has to get food through that tube in his stomach. That's why he never comes to breakfast.

Why are we here? I signed.

We're supposed to talk, but how can we understand anyone? It's tiring, reading everyone's lips.

Mrs. Koepp gave Felix a note. She smiled at me as she stood waiting for his response. Felix shook his head. She said something else, and Felix took out his pen and quickly wrote on the back of her note. She read his words then spoke to him. Felix turned his head so he couldn't see her lips. She walked back to her chair.

I don't like speaking their language, he signed. You know what sound is?

No.

Sound is what comes from your mouth, your voice. Most people speak in ghosts—you can't see their words, only the shape of their lips. Our language we can see. The language of beauty and love.

Beauty and love, I signed, hugging my hands to my chest.

Felix turned his chair toward me. His eyes were almost black. They can't see us, though, he signed. Not really. We need to stick together. When things go wrong, disabled people are the first people everyone blames and the last people they save.

Why would things go wrong?

The world's not built right. Everyone has to bend their lives to suit it. You can't build a world that leaves people behind. When the world ends, people will forget about us.

The world will end?

My grandpa used to say that we'll be left behind while everyone else walks toward death and hellfire, and we'll remain here and be able to rebuild the world the way we want, because we know how to survive. It'll take the end of the world, he said, for people like us to have the lives we want.

He leaned forward as he signed. His hands danced with beautiful fury. I didn't understand most of what he said but his excitement pulsed off him like heat.

I loved that he kept saying *We*. As though I would always be with him.

Why would the world end? I signed.

Ignorance, Felix signed. The ultimate sin. People don't take care of each other.

Felix's signing churned the air, animating the dusty pink room. Many of the group members turned to watch him, as if his hands were brewing a thunderstorm.

Mrs. Koepp waved at him and pointed to George, who'd been speaking. Felix circled his *sorry* hand around his chest.

If the world was properly built, he signed, we could understand everyone here.

Mrs. Koepp gave Felix another note. Felix said, *Waddoowannehttado*. Mrs. Koepp pointed us toward the door.

He picked up his book and stood. Mrs. Koepp stared at me. Felix tapped my shoulder, and I followed him out.

You see? he signed. What do you do if the way you're built is against the rules?

We sat on a bench a short way down the green hall. The man

who'd been restrained in the bed next to me was there, sitting by himself and drawing near the dining-room door.

Who's that? I signed.

Anders. Felix scribbled his A-hand down his palm. He sees things that aren't there, and he draws them. He's extraordinary.

How does he do that?

That's how his brain works. Sometimes he sees things that aren't really there, but they're real to him. Only he can see them.

He sees people?

Sometimes people. Sometimes lights. Whatever it is comes from him: his fears, his joys. We don't get to see or talk to our feelings the way he does. People don't understand.

I craned my neck to try and see his drawing. All I could see were whorls of green and purple.

Everyone has a different reality, Felix signed, and the best world accepts them all.

I see people at night, I signed. They follow me. They want to hurt me.

That's right, Felix signed. People like us, like Anders, like Bernice and George, we're more aware, more conscious, more open to truth. We see things the rest of the world doesn't see, but the world doesn't see us. That makes us holy. We want to make the world better, but the world doesn't want that, so we have to wait for it to end. God watches what we do. He knows everything and guides us through the world.

Felix patted my hand. His eyes settled on me, embraced me. As he leaned toward me, the black circle in his eyes widened and the hallway faded away. We could've been in space, and I wouldn't have noticed.

You are special, he signed. You are holy.

How am I special? What's holy?

I believe God kept you pure and brought you here for me, to help me in my work. Will you be my first apostle? He smiled, his eyebrows cocked.

Yes, I signed. What's an apostle?

A good follower who does good work and stays loyal.

Good work. What's loyal?

Felix's eyes glittered. Loving no matter what, he signed. Do you feel love? That warm tickle in your chest?

Yes.

Do you feel that for me?

Yes.

He held up his hand, his index and pinkie and thumb outstretched. This is how you say *I love you*. I'd like you to say this to me everyday.

I smiled. I love you, I signed.

Felix grinned. You'll be the perfect apostle, he signed.

HE STARTED COMING to my room first thing every morning. I smiled every time; I always had questions. Marvin would wave at him and show his comics and toys. If I spent too much time playing games with Marvin, Ms. Beddim, George or Bernice, or any of the other patients, Felix's eyes would crackle and his shoulders would cave and he'd shrink to the size of a child. He always had to be around me and have all my attention.

Once, on a bright blue day, Ms. Beddim invited me outside. She waved me toward the door, her eyebrows raised to new heights, while a uniformed man held sticks and small white balls. When I pulled on my coat—a thin brown coat that always felt damp but wasn't—and walked past Felix, he thrust both his thumbs out from under his chin.

What? I signed.

He did it again. Thrust both thumbs out slowly.

What's that mean?

D-e-n-i-a-l.

Are you coming outside?

They won't let me. I told you.

Why not?

He signed something too quick for me to understand.
Something boiled behind his eyes. His lip twitched. I glanced
out the barred window.

I want to go outside, I signed. It's bright.

Stay here with me, he signed.

I want to go outside.

I don't have anyone.

I want to try. Why can't you come?

They won't let me!

Felix's hands trembled. His shoulders shrunk inward.

You okay? I signed.

He stared away from me. Fine, he signed. Go.

I went out. My first time outside since I'd arrived. I enjoyed
the cool air like it was a bath. I made the sign for grass as I
petted it. George and Bernice and a few others came too. We
had to knock a white ball into narrow wire U-shapes stuck in
the grass at the back of the building, out of view of the stones
out front. The sunlight highlighted George's smile. He stayed
close to me, bumping against me, tapping me on the leg with
his stick a few times. Bernice wagged her finger at him and
took my hand and pulled me beside her. George jumped up
and down, happy to be outside. I kept hitting the ball too hard.
George did the same and knocked his ball out toward the
fields. Bernice swatted her ball into the building's brick wall—
and it bounced back so hard and she had to dodge it. She and
George laughed. I laughed too. I peered up at the windows and
saw Felix watching us. His face sagged with sadness.

When we walked back inside, Bernice held my hand as we
climbed the stairs to the second floor, her thumb brushing the
fingers of my broken arm. As she tucked my hair back behind
my torn ear, something blushed between my legs. My pants
grew snugger, as if my body had sprouted a new limb. I slowed
down and fell behind her and George and Ms. Beddim. Then
I ran to the bathroom and stood in the stall farthest from the
door. I faced the wall and undid my pants. The thing between
my legs had hardened. It stood straight out, long and thin. I
flicked my finger against it and gasped—a hot thrill echoed

through it. I moved my hips, wagging it back and forth. I tried squeezing it smaller. It grew harder. I aimed it at the toilet, thinking I might have to piss. Nothing came out. I waited until it slowly started to sag.

When I got back to Felix's room, he was sitting on his bed reading a book with red words on the cover that looked like blood. I waved at him. He didn't look at me.

What is this called? I signed, pointing at my crotch.

Felix grimaced. Why?

It was standing up. I flicked my index finger outward to illustrate.

Get out, Felix signed. That's disgusting.

It's called disgusting?

He snapped his *No* hand at me and shut his book. Get out! Why?

Felix pushed me out of his room and closed the door. I walked down the hall and the thing hardened again. I slapped it—it scraped against the inside of my pants. Mrs. Koepp came down the hall toward me. I pointed at my crotch. One of the men smoking in the hall grinned and put his hand to his mouth. I kept slapping at it to go away. Mrs. Koepp rushed over to me and took me to my room.

Felix didn't speak to me for the next few days. One day before group, I found him sitting on a bench writing in his book. When I approached, he held up a finger before I could say anything. He finished writing then looked up at me.

The world doesn't revolve around you, he signed. You need to understand how I see things.

Okay.

You know what a promise is? You say something, and you make it true.

I waited. Said nothing.

Promise you'll never leave me.

I won't leave you.

Everyone in my life has left me. My family, my friends.

I won't leave you.

You hurt me.

No I didn't.

You left me the other day, when you went out to play.

I went outside. I came back.

It hurt me. I asked you not to leave, and you left anyway. You don't feel bad for hurting me?

I stood there feeling small. I understood the words, but I didn't understand what he was saying. I didn't hurt you, I signed.

Felix's eyes gripped me like blue claws. You're such an animal, he signed. Ignorant, empty. You said you were my apostle.

I wanted to try the game.

I don't like being alone. The staff want you to play their games. The other kids, too. They want to pull you in, to control you and take you away from me.

Tears leaked from his eyes. His cheeks strained like he was trying to suck the tears back in. They want you to be like them, he signed. They want to take your purity and ruin it and mold you in their image. That's how the world is. Only I can teach you. I'm all you have, and you're all I have. If you leave me, we both have nothing.

Felix wiped his eyes. I sat beside him. I didn't understand most of what he'd said, but I knew he was hurt.

I'm sorry, I signed.

You won't leave me?

I won't leave you.

Felix nodded and smiled a little. He peered up and down the hall.

It's called a dick, he signed. He made the letter D and touched his nose with it. That. It's called a dick.

Dick. Why does it stand up?

It gets hard when we like someone. Do you like someone?

WE TRIED GOING to group once more before Mrs. Koepp again asked us to leave. Dr. O then started private sessions for just the three of us. We sat in a tight brown room with a narrow window and stuffed bookshelves. The room felt like a hand about to close around us.

Dr. O leaned backward in his wooden chair and wrote his questions while Felix translated. He again wore a suit with different color stripes.

Green, blue, white, I signed, pointing to his suit. Right?

Right. Plaid, Felix signed.

Plaid. I like it.

My grandpa said it looks like bad TV reception.

With his curved fingers, Felix drew scraggly lines on the air and stuck out his tongue. I laughed.

Dr. O smiled, the wrinkles in his cheeks bunching up and underlining the glow in his eyes. He held a piece of paper out for Felix. Felix held up a finger.

Watch out for him, Felix signed to me. He seems nice, but he works with Dr. Pearl. They're not on our side. The doctors want to keep us here so they can study us and get famous.

Dr. O wrote and showed Felix his note.

What'd he say? I signed. I shook out my arm; my wrist often cramped from signing so much with one hand.

Asking about your arm. How it feels.

Hard to sign. When does it come off?

Felix spoke, and Dr. O wrote back.

Another month, Felix signed.

How long is that?

Thirty days.

I don't know thirty.

Dr. O showed Felix another note. Felix nodded. Dr. O pointed to me.

Felix signed, He said you don't need to have me in here if you don't want to.

Okay.

You don't want me here?

Yes.

You want me to go?

No, don't go. I want you here. I faced Dr. O and signed, I want him. Yes.

It was hard for them to know how to help you because you couldn't communicate. Now they'll try to figure out how to treat you properly.

Help me how?

Another note. Felix smiled.

He's asking about your roommate, he signed.

What?

Felix scraped his M-hand up his stomach. Marvin, he signed. How you're doing with him.

Fine. He helps me a lot.

Another note. Felix shook his head.

He's asking if you know your real name.

No. I don't have one.

You will soon.

Felix smiled. So did I.

You should sleep in my room, he signed.

Can I?

Felix spoke. Dr. O wrote a note.

He says he'll look into it, Felix signed.

Dr. O put down his notes and pen. He slowly signed, I'm learning Sign.

I smiled. Good! I signed.

I don't know much, Dr. O signed, but I'm learning.

Dr. O pointed at Felix and tapped the thumb of his fanned-out hand against his temple. Father.

No, I signed.

What? Felix signed.

Not my father, I signed.

We're talking about my father, Felix said, not yours.

Dr. O started to sign but then wrote another note instead.

My priest is coming to visit, Felix signed. My father won't.

My father's grinning face swelled through my head. I pulled on Felix's sleeve.

Father's a bad man, I signed. He's the night man.

Enough, Felix signed. I'm trying to talk.

I have his eyes, I signed. I don't want his eyes.

Dr. O wrote another note and pointed at me. Felix said something, his mouth a tight circle. The walls squeezed closer. My breathing thinned.

He hurt me. He— My hands stammered. I jabbed my finger at my chest. Me! Hurt me!

Felix faced me directly. Your father hurt you? he signed.

He tried to put me in a hole.

Your father tried to kill you?

My body clenched. I snapped my fist up and down. Yes! He tried to put me in a hole!

I thought of the dogs at my father's house. The men kicking their bodies aside. Their slumping weight. Their open mouths. The blank looks in their eyes. I yelled.

I don't want to be dead, I signed.

All of us will die one day, Felix signed.

My breath skidded up my throat. Why?

That's how life works. Don't worry, you're not going to die for a long time. And I'll make sure you go to Heaven.

I sobbed. I don't want to die, I signed. I don't want my father in my head. I don't want him! I flung my words at Felix and pointed at my invisible father, who did not feel invisible at that moment. The whole room seemed infected with his presence, his face. That man's ugliness swam in my blood the way the ghosts swam through the air above the prairie. I shouted and slapped the books and papers off Dr. O's desk.

Calm down, Felix signed, or they'll send you upstairs and put you in a coma.

My thoughts crowded within my fingers. My hands stumbled on the air. He's in my head, I signed. I see him at night, in the dark. He's waiting for me. He'll find me and put me in a hole. He wants me dead.

Why? Felix signed.

Men had guns. Things bit me.

Dr. O wrote a note. Felix shook his head and stood up, took my arm, and led me out of the office.

We sat on chairs outside the group therapy room, and he brought me a glass of water and waited with me until I calmed down. Marvin and Bernice passed by and spoke to him. He nodded at them and waved them away.

Your father seems like an asshole, he signed.

Asshole?

Mean. Bad man.

I flicked my fingers out in frustration. I don't have the right words, I signed.

You'll learn in time.

We sat just breathing for a moment.

They send you upstairs for the worst reasons, Felix signed. If you get a little emotional, or if you break a rule without meaning to. I think they've diagnosed me wrong, too.

Okay.

The doctor said they're bringing in an interpreter for us both, so he can talk to you on your own.

Without you?

Privacy.

I don't want privacy.

Felix sagged. I'm tired, he signed. Okay if I have a sleep?

It's not night.

People can sleep if they're tired. Teaching you has been hard work. So many questions!

He smiled, got up, and started walking away. I followed.

No, you stay here, he signed. I'll see you later.

What do I do?

Draw me something, or practice your signs.

I thought you don't want to be alone.

I'm never alone when I sleep.

He carried on toward his room. I followed him, until he turned around and stopped again.

Sit down and stay here, he signed. I'll come find you when I wake up.

He walked away. I stood there, focusing on stopping my feet from moving toward him. I slumped when he stepped out of sight. My hands hung at my sides, like I'd been unplugged.

For a few moments I forgot how to name everything. The water fountain. The doors. The windows. The paintings. The people. Everything had lost its certainty. Chairs could be weapons. Doors could be instruments to cut food. Everything could move at any moment and serve any function.

People passed by, and some of them smiled or tapped my shoulder. Anders waved at me and knocked on Dr. O's door. People filled the hallway. Peopleness filled it. Their smoking, talking, trading, laughing, drinking at the fountain. It warmed me, and I settled down.

George walked past and waved for me to come with him. When I did, he put his arm around my shoulder and pulled me down the hall. He peered into the rooms as we passed, watching for other people.

He led me to a small windowless room at the far corner of the building. A room full of strange objects. A large brown box with rusted white and black teeth. A tall wooden device with strings feeding into it. A U-shaped device linked by a cord to a panel with buttons. He shut the door. I couldn't see anything.

A tiny flame blinked from the corner. Bernice's face bloomed orange out of the shadows. She grinned.

George sat down on the floor beside her and pulled out a plastic bag full of twigs. He opened it, held his hand near the flame, and put two twigs into his palm. They had tiny shriveled bulbs on the ends. He patted the floor beside him. I sat.

What's that? I signed.

Bernice said something. I shook my head. She held the flame inches from her face and brushed her hair back. Her eyes glittered as her lips said, *Muh-shrooms.*

George offered me the bag and held up his finger. *Wun*, he said.

What is it? I signed.

George smiled. Patted the air. *Soh-hay.* The light changed how he looked. His lips glistened. Shadows ringed his eyes, made him look more mannish. I wanted to cup his soft face.

Bernice said something to George, who shook his head. *Naw.*

He took a third twig from the bag then passed it back to Bernice. He gave me one and held his two close to his mouth. I couldn't see it clearly. It smelled like shoes. It might've been a weed.

Bernice lifted two twigs to her lips. She and George tilted their heads back and opened their mouths. I did the same. They put the twigs into their mouths and started chewing. I did too.

The twig squeaked between my teeth. Tasted like dirt. I coughed. George put his hand on my mouth. *No, no, no*, he said. *Soh-hay*. He swallowed. Traced his finger from his throat to his stomach. I swallowed too.

He and Bernice nodded. She patted my leg while George tucked the bag into his pants pocket. The two of them ambled around the room, picking up and fiddling with various objects. Bernice stroked every string feeding into the tall wooden frame; it looked like the skeleton for a boxy car. George picked up an old nurse's hat and perched it on his head, then pulled a dusty white coat from under a desk. The coat had straps and narrow sleeves. He held it up and spoke to Bernice; she grimaced and shook her head, and George tossed it away.

After a while—a few minutes? An hour?—Bernice came to sit next to me. She spoke to and smiled at me. My crotch began to blush—I crossed my arms over my lap. She pointed to the flame, then pointed to her chest and drew lines under her eyes and smiled. I stared. She did it again, then reached over and drew two stick figures on the dusty floor, one big with a huge bald circular head, one small with long hair. She pointed her fist at the bald figure and wiped the figure away. She said something and kissed her finger and touched my cheek with it. George did the same to her, then to my other cheek. My skin tingled. I smiled.

Bernice's fingers wrapped gently around the wrist of my good arm, and she lifted it and held the flame closer to examine the latticework of scars. George's eyes snapped wide. He laughed and pointed at my crotch—my dick stood straight up and strained against my pants. Bernice turned to him and dropped the flame. The room went dark.

I crossed my legs and went still. Bernice and George scrambled around the floor, bumping into my knees. I felt the air around us thicken and bristle. A small noise scraped up my throat.

I shut my eyes as they searched for the flame. On the inside of my eyelids, I saw colors that swayed whenever Bernice or George brushed against me.

I glanced toward where I thought the door was. My father's grinning face blossomed out through the darkness like a prickly gray flower and slid on the air toward me. As it approached, it quickly swelled to the size of a truck, filling the room like an ugly balloon, his outraged eyes leering and pressing down on me. His mouth whipped open and stretched into a dog's snout—his sharp teeth chomped at me.

I ducked and screamed. Someone patted my shoulder and helped me up. Someone else grabbed onto me, and we all stumbled toward the door.

Light split the room as the door opened, and my father's face washed away. We filed out into the hall. The light jolted me. Too many people moved at the same time. The hallway was a long gullet; its walls seemed to breathe in and out. I saw the vague outlines of everyone's words—the air swirled and curved like smoke as they spoke. I squinted hard, trying to force them into clearer shapes.

George looked at my crotch. My penis had shrunk, but he smirked and held out his two flattened hands like measuring the size of something large.

We walked slowly through the halls. People's hands moved like lizard tails, their mouths like empty eye sockets. Eventually, everyone lined up along the wall outside the dining room. I turned away from the line—my stomach had shrunk to a marble—but Ms. Beddim pointed me forward. I stood behind George and Bernice and stared at the floor, trying to will the walls into staying still. But the walls closed in inch by inch. To the hallway, we were food, slowly being digested. Everything was wrong. I made a noise. Bernice squeezed my shoulder and waved at me. *Soh-hay, soh-hay.* Strange shapes outlined her and George and each person in front of me, like someone had drawn lines around them on the air, each of them full of shifting colors, hovering and seizing to a rhythm that fit the person's manners. Bernice's outline gently floated on the air, its purple and orange and gold dapples surrounding her head like a halo. George's green and silver outline arched smoothly around his body. Others were black, green, pink, orange, wavy, spiky, jittery. When people touched, their outlines and colors merged and blended, and I realized I was seeing the beautiful rattling glow that lived inside each person. I smiled and screeched. Everyone turned to me, then glanced away.

Someone tapped me from behind. I turned to find Felix smiling at me. His outline was jagged, bubbling with red and black. I reached out above his head to touch it, and it jerked away. Half of his blond hair spiked up at an odd angle. I dabbed it down, but it sprang back up, and I snickered. I mashed it down and it sprang up again, and I laughed. Everyone stared at me again, but my laughing seemed to will the walls away. I bounced my hand on his head and petted his blond hair, guffawing, and he grabbed my wrist.

Enough, he signed.

I gripped his hand back. Rubbed it with my thumb. The hot blush between my legs pulsed. I kissed him. Felix jumped back from me. Bernice put both her hands to her face. Other people frowned or said things I didn't understand.

What are you doing? Felix signed.

I pulled his hand toward my crotch. He yanked it away, and his face reddened. Two men in white watched us, including Mr. Creel, the lion man. Felix stood still for a moment. Shaking. Then he walked quickly down the hall.

I tried to stay as still as possible for the rest of the day. Instead of eating, I pushed my dinner around my plate and watched how people's outlines pulsed and blended with each other. After dinner, I settled on a bench and watched the hallway throb and the people saunter past. I saw fibers in the air. It had muscle. It held things—it fixed me in place. I felt an odd peace. The world was trying to bend itself to match the way I saw it. My crotch ached.

Toward bedtime, the hallway had hardened into its usual self. I went to the washroom, walking slowly in case the walls reawakened.

As I pissed in the urinal, I felt someone's footsteps behind me. I finished and turned. Felix stood there, his hands closed together.

I waited. Then signed, Hi.

He stared away from me, breathing quickly, opening and closing his fists like he was preparing to fight. I was afraid, he signed.

Afraid?

Felix shook his head. I've been selfish, he signed. I need to show more devotion.

He stepped over to me. A thin margin between his body against mine. He waited like he was getting used to being so close. Okay? he signed. I nodded. He kissed me. A small touch on the lips. Then a deeper one, his mouth opening up to mine. He stood on his tiptoes to reach me. He glanced back at the door, then pulled me past the stalls toward the shower room adjoining the bathroom.

We can't do this out in the open, he signed. People won't understand. We have to do this in private.

Private.

He touched my crotch. The hot blush bloomed fresh. I nodded to him. Felix unzipped my pants and pulled out my dick. I swallowed.

Equal love, he signed.

He sank down to his knees and wrapped his mouth around my dick. I gasped. He held my hand—I settled a little. The heat in my crotch rose to the heat in his mouth. His mouth slid up and down. He started sucking and pulling, his grooved tongue licking at the end. I kept watching for people coming in. The heat in my crotch swelled and started to fight its way out. I put my free hand on his head and thrusted into his mouth. He kept sucking. He squeezed my hand. The heat churned. I grunted. The feeling was too good—I tried to push away, but Felix kept going. With a rolling bulge, the heat heaved up through my dick and burst out into his mouth. I slapped the wall and made a noise.

Felix stood up straight. Put your pants on, he signed.

I zipped them up. He smiled at me.

You know what love is? he signed.

Do anything for the other person.

He kissed my hand. Don't let anyone tell you you're unloved, he signed. You are loved.

20 DEC. 1977

Last night hallelujah I had a dream Jesus knew sign language. He smiled at me held my hand and signed like spinning gold on the air and kissed my hands. His hands had bloody holes in them so some of his signs were hard to understand. His face had been torn apart then sewn back together, his eyes different colors, his hair poking out in weird clumps. I kissed his hands with the holes and tasted his blood and he blessed my hands. He had grandpa's smile. He left a glow on my hands the way mom left ~~moistí~~ moisturizer on my hands.

A naughty person, a wicked man, walks with a froward mouth, winking his eyes, teaching with his fingers?

No.

1 JANUARY 1978

Wendy went to Jeremy's house was kissing the fucker all night. ~~I waited down the street then ski mask on went after~~ what the hell's wrong with me

THE CAGE

MY TOOTH BEGAN to hurt at about the time I started to fit into the cloth man's bigger shirts. The cloth man was my own creation. All the clothes my father's men had given me were too big or too small, so I'd stuffed them all into a T-shirt and stood it up on my mattress. I added a drawing of a man's face and tucked it into the neck hole. Over time I drew hair onto the face and colored in its eyes. I slept beside it each night. Punched it. Hugged it. Tackled it.

I had a habit of gnawing on the inside of my cheek. That day, I was biting down, and my teeth slipped and clacked together, and my back tooth made a red crunch in my head. I spit blood onto the floor and felt around my mouth. My long fingernail jabbed my cheek. I pried loose part of my broken tooth. The other part was still lodged in my gums. The blood came fast.

I spit more of it out and tried putting the broken piece back, but it wouldn't stay. I began pressing against the shard with my thumb. My gums throbbed. I coughed—the loose piece tumbled down my throat. The blood was sticky and warm on my fingers. The shard clung to my gums, stubborn as the trunk of an ancient tree.

It came off later when I was eating my sandwich. I bit down on it; it folded and loosened from my gums, and I pulled my sandwich out of my mouth. The shard hung from the bread.

Later still, my father came into the room. He closed the door behind him. I sat up against the wall, my body rigid.

He held a brown glass bottle in his hand. His breath cut through the other smells in the room. He sweated and made a face like he was trying to smile but couldn't lift his lips. As he drank from the bottle, he looked at the cloth man on the mattress beside me. The blood stain on the floor. The reeking bucket. He walked over. I moved into the corner, under my monsters. He sat down on the floor, touched the cloth man's paper face, and then touched the monsters on the walls. He drank some more. I watched the door. I wanted the red drink.

He sat beside me, leaned back against the wall, and opened his mouth. Water spilled from his eyes. He gripped the bottle with two fingers, then seized it with his whole hand. He shook his head and covered his dripping eyes. His face was red. The drips slid from his eyes down into his beard.

His breath covered my face. I started to move further away. He pulled me into his chest and covered me with both arms. His embrace was warm. Salty. I fit there. His chest shuddered up and down like he had trouble breathing. The drops from his eyes fell onto my head. I put my arms around him. He covered me tighter. He put his hand on my head. I cried.

Then he straightened up and wiped his face. Shook his head. The door behind his eyes had slammed shut. He shoved me aside and took up his bottle and walked out.

I wiped my eyes and nose on my shirt. I waited, hoping he'd come back. My mouth dried. My stomach prickled.

The long-haired man came in with a tall glass full of the red drink. Only the drink—no sandwich or fruit. It tasted fully bitter with no sweetness at all. I drank it down. The cold liquid soothed my still-bloody gums.

I shook the glass at the long-haired man. He watched me like he was waiting for something to happen. He took the glass and went to leave. I followed him and tried to barge past him out the door, but he shoved me back. I clawed at his hand with my long nails. He shoved me harder, and I fell. He snapped the door shut.

I ran at the door, yelling at him, my nails folding back into my palms.

The drink dropped like a cold light into my stomach. Its emptiness shined. I shouted, hollered, bellowed. My blood screeched. My father's brief embrace had awoken an appetite I didn't know I had. I hungered, starved, in every way.

I breathed quickly. My body trembled—it wanted to move faster. I paced and spun and skipped around the room. My skin grew wet. My stomach clenched then relaxed. The room lurched. It couldn't stay still. I sat down, waiting for the room to stop moving. My legs vibrated. My skin grew wet and left streaks on the floor.

The door opened. I jumped up. The bigger man grabbed me by my shirt and hauled me out and up the stairs past the living room. A pink pair of underwear hung from the deer's head.

We went out the door into the night. He shoved me even though I walked with him and didn't fight. Instead of taking me to the gravel pile where they usually hosed me, he pushed me past the metal building. My father and the long-haired man and several others stood around a chain-link enclosure. Lights shone from their trucks into the cage, where a dog sat. Tall. Shiny black fur. Pointed face. I stopped walking. The bigger man seized me by my neck. I kicked and fought against him. I sank to the ground, hoping to make myself too heavy. He dragged me by my shirt—until my shirt ripped. He jerked me to my feet by my hair. I clawed at his arm. I felt stronger, better able to hurt him. He showed me his teeth and slapped me, then shoved me into the cage. The dog tensed, lifting its lips over its teeth. I spun and pulled on the cage door. My father locked it. I tried to snag his eyes with mine, but he talked to the other men or looked at the ground. I turned toward the dog—it looked at me sideways, its teeth still showing. The bigger man stood beside my father. In the hard lights coming from the trucks, the bigger man looked thinner. Fallen leaves lined the ground along the cage walls.

The dog snapped at me. Its nose and mouth trembled. I shook the cage door. The men passed around small pieces of colored paper. I reached for my father, but the bigger man knocked my hand away. My heart shuddered. I yelled at my father. Yelled at all the men. Some of them were drinking from glass bottles and tossed foamy brown liquid at me. I ran from one corner of the cage to the other, my feet quickened by deep panic. The men spat words at both of us. I couldn't see straight. The dog faced me directly and snapped its teeth again; it seemed to squat, like it was about to jump. I moved to a corner of the cage. A man poked me in the back with a stick. I grabbed the stick from him and threw it away. The men grinned. My stomach clenched as the red drink churned inside me. My muscles twitched; steam rose from my sweaty skin. I tried to flex my hands and keep them still, but I was not in control of myself. I was terrified. And angry. By giving me the red drink, my father had planted anger inside me.

The men pointed at the dog and at me. Their breath made clouds that crowded above us. The dog took a slow step toward me, snapped at me again—its breath made a hard clear cloud. The men pounded on the cage. The dog leapt at me. I raised my arms, but it knocked me down and bit into one arm. It planted its feet on my chest and hauled back on the flesh. I shoved it away; it fell back then launched itself at me again, biting down on my ankle and squeezing its teeth into my skin. It yanked and tried to drag me backward. I swung at the dog and missed—my fist sliced through the clouds its breath left on the air. Its black eyes flashed in the truck lights. It twisted its head side to side and pulled the skin off my ankle. I screamed. The men shouted and shook their fists at the dog.

The dog bit into my arm again. Bit until its teeth scraped bone. I held my hands out to the men, but they would never help me. I kept screaming—first in pain, then in outrage. My terror and anger rolled all the way up into a hot clenching ball in my stomach. The dog's breath rose into my eyes—my blood stained its teeth. I roared and raised my fist.

That ball of anger pulsed; my body filled with quivering redness. I couldn't stay still. I had to spend my energy. I moved in skids, dashes. The men's faces became a singular snarl, all of them melting together into one horrid angry mass. My heart-beat filled my body with its concussive beat.

I swung my fists, slashed my nails, kicked my feet until the red pulsing inside me quieted, then I hunched and wiped my bloody hands on my shirt.

The cage door opened. My father stepped in, grabbed the dog by its neck, and tucked his gun between its ears. The gun gave a small flash—the ground jarred beneath my feet. The dog fell onto its side. I blinked. It made me sick how quickly it went still.

I fell to my knees and crawled over to the dog. I stared at its empty eyes, touched its black fur. With its warmth, it still seemed alive. The terror drained from my body. It felt wrong that the dog would no longer jump or snap its white teeth or form clouds on the air with its voice. I put my hands on its flank and felt its muscles coiled up, like it was waiting to charge.

The men passed more colored paper around, then most walked away, back to their trucks or to the house or to the metal building. But my father remained standing over me. He said nothing. I don't know what his face was saying. It was like he wanted to smile, but he didn't.

The bigger man stepped into the cage and pulled on my shoulder. I shook my head and covered the dog with my body and held onto it. He yanked on my shredded arm, tearing me away from the dog, and pulled me out of the cage and toward the house.

I watched the dog the whole time. It got smaller and smaller until it became part of the ground.

Back in my room, the long-haired man cleaned my ankle and arm and tied cloth around them. My blood blushed through in little spots. Afterward, I lay on the mattress facing the wall. My body kept vibrating. I brought my knees up to my chest and hugged them and sobbed.

Later, he came back with water and a sandwich. I didn't move from the mattress. The man lay beside me. He put his hand on my ribs. His body was close to mine. I felt him move.

Felt his other hand move against my back. I shut my eyes. I saw the dog. The man's hand patted against my back with a regular rhythm until the other hand squeezed my shirt. I felt something warm and wet on my back and thought it was blood. I turned, and he was gripping his dick. I scrambled off the mattress, yelling. He got up, took a shirt from the cloth man, and wiped himself off. I kept yelling and yelling until he went away.

A short time after, my father came in. Two other men held the long-haired man behind him. His nose was bleeding. My father held a knife. He pulled down the long-haired man's pants, grabbed his dick, and held the knife above it. The long-haired man shook his head. My father lifted the knife, then lowered the knife. He stared at me—he was asking me a question. When he lifted the knife away from the man, I nodded. When he lowered it, I shook my head.

He said something to the other two men, who took the long-haired man away. My father nodded at me, then closed the door. That was our first conversation.

Felix Jimson

1 MAY 1979

I asked grandma last week if there are any Deaf saints. She said St. Francis a frenchman is the saint of the Deaf. Is he Deaf I asked she said no, I said why? I don't know she said. I asked if the church thought it ~~sacretigo~~ sacrilegious to make a Deaf person a saint she said she hoped not or she'd give the pope a talking to. I asked if there are any Deaf saints. She said she hasn't heard of any and I said I'd make history and be the first Deaf saint spreading love with my fingers.

9 MAY 1979

Grandma's dead. Was sick for a while, never told dad or maybe she did and he never told me. Lots of other Deaf people came from all over and signed things about grandma they loved her. Dad said nothing at her funeral cause he was thinking about her house and the shop and people had stiff faces when they shook hands with him like they didn't want to. I waited until everyone left then did a prayer for her in sign—may your love keep giving me strength—before they put her in the ground.

When I got back to school I found out Wendy's moved to alberta never told me just left how dare she how fucking dare the fucking bitch ass fucking bitch bitch BITCH

THE WEIGHT OF WORDS

YESTERDAY THEY PULLED me from my cell and walked me past the guard station into a small room where a man waited for me. Said he was a lawyer. Came with an interpreter and another lawyer. They showed me a picture of my father and asked me if I knew him. The police have caught him, they said. He tried to sneak into another country by hiding in a truck full of toys.

When they showed me the picture, I winced. He looks the same—his hair's just longer and grayer. He's on his way here to Prince Albert. The lawyer says he'll go to court and will be kept here at the prison.

There's no paperwork to show I'm his son, but there's a test I can take. They need blood or spit. They usually don't do this unless they find blood at a crime scene, but because I've seen so many things, they need me to tell them. In court.

When he arrives, they'll test him too, and if the tests show that we're family, they'll move me to a cell on the other side of the prison. Away from him.

The men here yell all the time. They yell so hard they almost throw out their backs or shove their eyeballs out of their heads. It's strange that the air doesn't bend when they yell or that the temperature doesn't rise or that their words have no edges. With that much effort you'd think there'd be physical evidence of their words. You'd think that people's words would soothe sores or splash bruises on their skin or crush their bones into pieces. I've seen people crumple under the weight of words. I've also seen words brighten people's eyes and hook the corners of their mouths into the widest grins.

I make license plates. I work as much as I can. I feel safest at my bench working with the metal. The rest of the time, I stay close to the walls. When I pass people in the hallway, I keep my back to the walls and walk sideways. They laugh. But this way, no one can sneak up on me. I'd rather be cornered; I can see everything then. When I was first put in prison, people snuck up on me all the time, like it was a game. They slapped my head, kicked me in the back. One guy tried to stick a piece of metal into my neck. I turned just in time to trip him, and he fell face-first into a metal bar, breaking his nose.

My cellmate sleepwalks at night. He walks into the door and into the wall; his leg bumps against my bed. He makes a motion with his hand like he's pouring something, maybe acting out a past memory. I'd rather remember when I'm sleep than when I'm awake.

He ends up sleeping on the floor in the corner beside his pile of books. He reads all day. He keeps blaming me for the bruises on his face. Points his finger at me and says words through his teeth. I think his name's Alistair.

A few nights ago, Alistair sat at the edge of my bed. Didn't look at me. His thin mouth softly framed words. He seemed to want to be near me and at the same time away from me. I waited. If I don't understand what's happening, things usually move along if I wait long enough. He lay beside me, his back against my chest, and pulled my arm around him. I stayed still, then hugged him close. He rested his head on my pillow. We lay together like that, the warmth between us soft and comfortable. My crotch blushed a little, but I kept my hips well back from him. Didn't feel right.

A short time later he sat up and went back to his bed. He nodded at me and lay back and faced the ceiling.

18 JANUARY 1980

Dad took me to the winter carnival by the river. Colleen walked away from us holding hands with some other man. Some of the kids from school were playing hockey Jeremy shot a puck that hit me in the leg stuck out his tongue gave me the finger the others waving me away with their sticks. I read their lips, freak, fucking weirdo, go away Deaf boy.

Dad was sitting by himself, watching people, hoping. People took a long path around him and it's sad how lonely he is but it's his own fault, but it's also not. I don't know how to talk to him. We're both ghosts going faint. That's what the world wants, to treat us like ghosts until we become ghosts.

21 JANUARY 1980

The police came today to ask me questions, sat in the living room and wrote their questions while dad watched. While they asked, he kept asking me in sign are you telling the truth, are you telling the truth, like he wanted me gone. After they left dad couldn't look at me the rest of the night.

There's so much that can be better and we have the power to do it but people choose not to

Love has been twisted so much that we can't recognize it anymore.

THERAPY

AT BREAKFAST I beamed at Felix. I wanted him to love me again and had to fight to keep the blush between my legs quiet.

Maybe again after? I signed.

Not today. Felix made forks with both hands and had one following the other.

What's that?

F-u-n-e-r-a-l. Bury a dead person outside.

I turned over an invisible body with my hands. Who's dead?

Man named Clark. Older man. He was here for years. Ms. Beddim told me he died upstairs the other day.

Felix touched his forehead, then both shoulders. Dr. Pearl probably killed him, he signed. He made a knife of his thumb and pulled it backward across his palm, then tapped his head and spelled out the sign: He had a l-o-b-o-t-o-m-y a long time ago. Dr. Pearl removed part of his brain. I saw the scar.

His brain? Where his thoughts are?

Yes.

That's sad, I signed. I felt much more than sadness—the image of someone cutting thoughts and pictures out of my head was horrifying—but *sadness* was the most available word.

I said a prayer for him, Felix signed. Do you want to watch the funeral, so he's not alone?

They bury him?

In the cemetery outside.

No. Don't want to.

I'm going to watch.

They buried a boy, I signed. At night.

When?

A few nights ago. My father buried him.

Felix shook his head. It's just a dream, he signed.

He's coming for me. I don't like people being buried. In the dark, all alone.

Who was buried? What'd you see?

A boy. He was covered with a blanket.

They don't bury people at night. Just a dream.

Tears swelled through my eyes. I don't want to die, I signed.

Felix leaned close. Don't worry, he signed. You and I won't be buried here. We're meant for better things.

Our trays arrived. Pancakes with apple slices. I nudged mine aside. I have questions, I signed.

I'm hungry. Felix spread butter on his pancakes.

I don't like people being buried, I repeated. All alone in the dark. It's big sad.

Yes.

When can we love again?

Felix didn't answer. Bowed his head and kept eating.

Why can't we talk about it?

I told you. Rules. Stop asking.

No one understands us.

They understand enough.

Felix peered around the dining room and made himself small.

Later, he watched the funeral from the corner window in the common room. I sat across the room studying pictures in magazines. He sent several signs out to the small crowd walking to the cemetery: Peace. Beauty. Heaven. Sleep.

I thought if I watched the burial, I'd see my father standing beside the hole.

NEW PEOPLE CAME. A woman named Irene whose arms and legs moved without her permission. A girl named Hortense who used long metal sticks to help herself walk. George and Bernice made friends with Hortense, and the three of them kept asking me to spend time with them. Play games. Go for walks outside. Go to the storage room. They tried passing notes. Tried drawing what they wanted from me: stick men with thin smiles and twigs for hands. They invited Felix too, but he was too busy reading and writing so they just gave me the notes.

They just want us for entertainment, Felix signed. We're not their clowns.

I wanted more love from Felix, but the closest we got was hugging and lying beside each other one afternoon. During meals or study time, I'd touch his leg under the table and he'd shove my hand away. The ache in my crotch persisted until it became pain. Hortense once smiled at me and swung her head asking me to follow her, and I started to, but Felix pulled me back.

Each night the sun arced over the prairie and left red and pink smears on the sky. Why don't they build houses here? I signed. Have more people? There's nothing out there. Empty. It's boring.

Felix signed, No, it's not. Everything's here. Every possibility.

I feel the breath of ghosts whenever I'm out there. I'm never safe.

That's just wind. The land, the air is full of possibility.

Like love?

On a hot day when our shirts clung to our shoulders, Bernice approached me sitting alone in the hallway. Felix was writing again and had told me to do something else until dinner. She led me down the hall toward the storage room. She waited for some uniformed men to walk past, then opened the door and nudged me in ahead of her.

George stood there, holding a lighter. Bernice tucked a chair under the doorknob, and George let the orange light go out.

I stiffened. All the objects felt closer in the dark windowless room; I thought I might trip or jab myself.

George bunched his body up against mine—soft on the surface and hard underneath. His chin touched my forehead as he wrapped his hands around me; his dick dug into my hip. Bernice pressed up beside me and took my hand and put it underneath her shirt. She smelled like soap and pink sugar. George smelled like sweat and fire. Bernice kissed me. I felt her and George kiss each other, then George kissed me, his mustache brushing my lip. I tasted toothpaste. Bernice pulled my hand down and tucked it in her pants. George undid mine, and I shut my eyes. The darkness wrapped around us. Hid us. Protected us. We began stroking, kissing, petting, settling into a rhythm, leaning into each other. I felt soft hair, warm skin, slippery folds.

The heat in my crotch surged up, and white lights popped through the darkness. I made a noise through my teeth. Bernice covered my mouth. We all stopped. For a moment we breathed as one, each of us with a hand on each other's shoulders.

The small flame opened, and I saw George's sweaty face and Bernice's breasts just as she pulled her shirt on.

I smiled back. Thank you, I signed.

They both smiled at me. Bernice pointed at the door and said something. George lifted the chair away and pulled the door open a small bit. His eyes searched the hall, his face stiffening in the light. He said something and waved us after him.

Bernice straightened her shirt and hair, and the two of us followed George out into the hall.

Bernice's eyes widened; she pointed at my pants. A small white smear spread out from my crotch. As I tried to wipe it away, two men in white walked past us. One of them, Mr. Creel, laughed and spoke to George, whose mouth pinched. He looked at the floor. Bernice spoke to the men. Mr. Creel stopped walking and pointed, spitting hard words at her. She ushered George and me away.

At dinner, all the uniformed people watched me, George, and Bernice. Felix did too.

In his room after dinner, he signed, You have sex today?

What's sex?

You have love? With George?

And Bernice.

Felix scoffed.

We just used our hands.

Did you kiss?

Yes.

Felix held his head in his hands. What did I tell you? he signed. It's dangerous. People can't know. It's supposed to be just you and me.

You never want to.

Stop being a child.

I'm not a child, I signed, making fists.

Felix's face slackened. He held up his hands to calm me down. We have to hide, he signed. There's a time and place. You can find other things to do. Draw, paint, build something, play a game.

I don't understand. Why don't people love all the time? In the halls and bedrooms and the common room? It feels good.

I know.

Why do we have to hide?

Men can't like men.

Why? I don't understand! You said we had to find love outside rules.

Felix nodded. Then shook his head.

The next day, Mr. Creel said something to me. He grinned as he looked me up and down, his narrow eyes like holes punched through the wall. He made a gesture like stroking something. George ran over and punched Mr. Creel in the face. The two of them started fighting, George standing his ground and using his long reach to keep Creel away. Mrs. Koepp called for other nurses, and they grabbed George and injected him with something, but he kept fighting. It took four nurses to hold him still so they could take him away.

Felix sat still, staring at George and the nurses until they disappeared.

Later we saw Bernice standing in the hallway near the nurses' station talking into a shiny black handle. I made a Y out of my hand and put one finger to my ear and the other to my mouth.

Phone. Right?

Felix nodded. The man who invented it wanted Deaf people to speak orally and stop using Sign Language, he signed. All so they could use his invention.

She misses George, I signed.

When I first got here, she thought I was twelve.

We sat on the bench across from Bernice. Just above our heads, dusty air seeped from a vent. Felix dragged his finger up and down over the diamond-shaped holes in the white metal vent cover. Bernice waved at him and shook her head. Felix stuck out his tongue and dragged all five fingers against the vent. Bernice held the phone between her head and shoulder and signed, Stop. Felix smiled. Mrs. Koepp stood up from the nurses' station and said something to Bernice, who pointed at Felix then tried talking again. Felix's hand skidded over the vent covering. He stomped on the floor, beating out a rhythm to which he dragged his fingers. Bernice clamped her hand over one ear and pressed the phone hard against the other.

Felix said something with his mouth, and she dropped the phone and strode over to us.

Whuzzerproblum, she said.

Felix put up his hands. *Jessajoke*, he said.

She pointed at me and spoke again, then walked back to the phone.

What'd she say? I signed.

She says I'm a creep and I should stay away from you.

During study time, Felix tapped Bernice and said, *Ahmsawwrybout hutherday*. Bernice waved him away.

Ms. Beddim had given me paper and pencils, and I'd spent the period drawing giant monsters stomping across the red and black prairie. I showed them to Felix. He nodded without looking at them and said something to Bernice I didn't understand.

She pointed at me and spoke.

What is it? I signed.

Nothing, Felix signed.

Bernice shook her head and kept pointing at me.

Why'd she and George pick me? I signed.

She thinks I'm using you like a puppet, Felix signed. She and George are trying to protect you.

Felix spoke to her again. *Nawoorfugginbidniss.*

Yehdunluvim, Bernice said. *Ooluvnuwwin. Oorasykobath. Ehmnod. Ahluvevwun.*

Fuggoff.

Bernice pointed out the door and said more. Felix tensed. He looked away from her; her words were gnawing at him, digging into him.

I tapped Felix on the arm. What is she saying?

Oodonnowuhluviz, Bernice said.

Felix jumped to his feet and opened his arms and spoke to everyone in the room, shoving his voice at them, his teeth flashing, his eyes stretched wide. He began signing at the same time. I understood only a few things. Beauty. Holy. Light. Afraid. World. His body shook. He looked about to cry. Then he leaned across the table and kissed me on the mouth. I sat stiffly. Ms. Beddim averted her eyes from Felix, then looked back with her eyebrows halfway up her forehead, like she didn't believe what she'd just seen.

Felix sat breathing deep. His body rattling.

At dinner that night, I waited for Felix. I caught Ms. Beddim's eyes across the dining room.

Where's Felix? I circled my F-hand above my head.

She pointed to the ceiling. I pictured him under a heavy blanket. Tubes stuck in his arms. His body cooking in the heat.

Bernice sat across from me, her eyes lowered. She touched my hand and said nothing.

I had difficulty eating. I didn't know whether to start with the meat or the salad. Didn't know when I should drink my juice.

When we left the dining room, Ms. Beddim waved me toward the main room where a group of people sat talking, smoking, reading, and watching TV. Bernice and Hortense lay on the couch watching the TV. In the corner, Anders drew with red and black markers. Irene sat under the TV, facing the room.

Too many people. I walked back to my room.

THE NEXT DAY Felix was still absent, so I went to Dr. O's office alone. He and a woman with a long face welcomed me in.

Sit down, the woman signed, her fingers fluttering like twigs.

I sat down and gripped the chair arms. Dr. O wore a green plaid suit. The woman stared at me. My ear. My arms. Her shoulders rolled. The sight of me disturbed her.

My name's S-i-o-b-h-a-n, she signed. She gave a name sign, her S-hand tracing a long arc above her head. How are you?

What is this? I signed.

The woman spoke with her mouth to Dr O. Their eyes fixed on me, then his words came to me through the woman: She's here to help. She'll interpret so the two of us can talk, and so you can have the help you need. Understand?

I mimicked her sign. What is interpret?

Help you understand me.

Her? Or you?

Dr. O pointed at himself.

She's speaking for you? I signed.

Helping me speak with you. I'm sorry it took so long—money has been limited.

The woman's signs were tighter and more reserved than Felix's open, expressive signs. Her face was stiff, and she held her hands closer to her body, like she was trying to keep her signs secret. It was hard to understand her.

What is money?

Helps you buy things.

Buy?

Dr. O reached into his coat, pulled out a small leather square, and opened it up. He pulled out pieces of colored paper. Something coiled in my gut.

You trade this for things you need, he said. Food, clothes, things you want.

Trade that? Is that a rule?

Yes, it's a rule.

I don't like that, I signed. Put it away.

Dr. O nodded and tucked the money back into the leather square.

I pointed at the woman's hands and signed, This is weird. Your hands are different.

Dr. O smiled. You have the right to privacy, he said. You know what privacy is?

I mimicked the way the woman tapped her lips with the thumb of her closed fist.

Only you know what happens to you, Dr. O said. No one else does, unless you choose to tell people.

You don't know what words I know. I understand Felix.

It's important for you to learn without Felix.

When's Felix coming back?

He's in treatment.

I winced. Something brushed against the back of my neck. The air around Dr. O and the woman seemed to shift. I smelled sweat and piss. A gruesome presence was slowly leaking into the room, turning the air to thick putrid muscle. I tightened my body, drew my hands back into my lap.

Don't hurt him. With the blanket and the needles.

He needs special attention. Dr. Pearl's taking good care of him. The woman's fingers were so thin I thought they might snap when they moved quickly.

My eyes widened. Dr. Pearl cut into someone's brain! I signed.

Dr. O grimaced. Let's talk about you.

What about me?

I have good news. You're having your cast taken off soon.

I looked at my arm. So many people had signed it that there was no white space left. I'd been looking forward to having the cast removed and signing with ease, but now I didn't want to lose it and become more exposed.

Something thunked down on the floor behind my seat. I glanced over my shoulder and wrinkled my nose—the smell of the basement room crowded around me.

Dr. O opened a folder with a few sheets of paper. The woman waited for him to speak. Her stillness bothered me.

We don't know much about you, he said. Your name, where you're from, your family, your history. It's like you dropped out of the sky. Everyone here has a lot of questions, and until now we've been unable to ask them.

I want to see Felix, I signed.

You'll see him soon.

What does that mean?

Let's start with your arm. How'd you break it?

I felt like something would soon jump out from a corner of the room and bite me. I drew my hands close to my chest and hunched forward, sweating. The basement smell clung to my nostrils.

It smells in here, I signed.

Are you okay?

I smell the downstairs room. I want Felix.

Can you tell me how you broke it? Do you remember?

Felix!

Do you have any questions? You probably have a million of them.

I can ask questions?

The woman's hands slowed. Yes, whatever you want.

I relaxed a little. You won't lie to me? I signed.

Dr. O frowned. So did the woman.

No, he said.

Felix says you want to control us. You lie, Dr. Pearl lies, the nurses lie, because you want us to stay here.

For a moment Dr. O looked like I'd slapped him. He blinked the expression away. The woman's hands slowed.

I want you to get better, he said. To get better, sometimes people need to stay here, but they don't stay forever. You have an excellent chance of getting better and leaving this place, but that starts with us having a conversation. Understand?

I flexed my fingers together, unsure which question to ask. They whipped through my head like leaves gusting past. The books and papers in the room seemed full of answers. So did Dr. O.

Why is love between men bad?

The woman sat straight like the question bit her.

That's a big question, Dr. O said. I don't think it's bad.

The woman pouted at him. I breathed deep. Signing seemed to waft away the smell and whatever else filled the air.

Why is Felix not here? Why does Mr. Creel do this whenever I walk past? I made the stroking motion.

I'll talk to Mr. Creel. That's unprofessional.

Why are people here? Why can't we change the rules?

I can't discuss other people, Dr. O said, but generally, people are here because they're having a hard time on the outside. They have difficulties, so they come here to get better.

Outside where? In the fields?

Outside the building. The real world.

This place isn't real?

Of course it's real. It's just a phrase, real world. People live in houses and apartments. They go to work, go to school, spend time with their families.

I didn't understand a few of the woman's signs so I fixed on a sign I did understand.

Felix told me about school, I signed. He said they hit his hands.

It might be difficult for him because he's Deaf, but school's where young people belong. We're not sure how old you are, but you look like a teenager. Maybe fifteen or sixteen.

What's fifteen?

A number.

Can I go to school?

That's the goal.

Goal?

That's what we want for you.

I didn't understand. The newness of the woman's signs was too much. The smell of piss and shit and blood hooked into my nose, and the thing hovering behind me started to squeeze my head. I moved in my seat. My signs became quicker and broader.

Why do I have pictures in my head? I signed. All the time I see pictures of things that happened to me, and I don't want to.

Those are called memories.

I don't want memories. Can you see all the pictures when you cut into a brain?

Dr. O smiled. Certain pictures appear in certain parts of the brain, but you can't see them if you remove the brain. Not like a movie or a photograph. No one can see those pictures but you.

That's sad, I signed.

You have a lot of pictures in your head? Dr. O said.

Yes.

What kind of pictures?

People. Men. Shouting at me. Hurting me. Animals.

I grunted. I still lacked the words I needed. Felix can help me, I signed. I need more words.

Let's go slowly, Dr. O said. Can you tell me how you broke your arm?

A man pushed me down the stairs.

What man?

My father's man.

His friend?

I don't know.

Where was this?

I shut my eyes. Breathed through my mouth. My father's house, I signed.

Where's his house?

I don't know. I want to leave.

Soon. This is important. Did you live there?

Live there?

Did you have a room?

Yes.

What was the room like?

Below ground. Something to sleep on.

The woman signed "sleep," then added a flat shape in front of her. A mattress?

Yes. And a bucket.

Why a bucket?

Piss and shit. I unfolded pieces of paper from my pocket, each one full of monsters I'd drawn during study time. I drew monsters on the wall, I signed. When I wasn't fighting.

Who were you fighting?

Things. Animals.

What animals?

The air around my head tightened. I made jaws with both my clawed hands. They made me drink a red drink before I fought, I signed.

They made you fight alligators?

They had hair all over. Legs and tails. Like this high.

I measured a height above the floor. Dr. O's eyes hardened. They made you fight dogs?

The sign for "dogs" was a soft snap of the fingers and a slap against the thigh. Too meek. Couldn't have been right. I made the jaws again.

Is that how you got those scars on your arm?

I fought them in a cage.

Your father made you do this?

Other men watched. They yelled at me and passed that paper, that money, around. I mimicked the men's expressions. Bulged out my eyes. Flashed my teeth. Jabbed my finger down at an invisible me on the floor.

Where was your mother? Dr. O said.

I don't know. My father took me from her.

How do you know it was your father?

It's a feeling. I look like him a little.

How long were you in the room in the basement?

I don't know.

Weeks? Months?

I thought for a moment. My head couldn't reach the ceiling when I went in, I signed. It could when I came out.

Dr. O put his hand in front of his mouth. The woman knuckled the tears from her eyes. The air in the office loosened. I smelled papers and fabric.

I'm sorry, I signed.

Dr. O waved his hands. No, no, no, he said. Thank you so much for sharing. I'm proud of you. I can't imagine how long you've been wanting to say those things.

I smiled.

We have a lot of work to do, he said. Everything we thought about you was wrong. But we'll make a plan, and I'm confident you'll be able to leave this place and have a brilliant future.

Future, I signed. A fanned-out hand arcing forward from the body into the air.

Dr. O reached out and shook my hand. He spoke to the woman. The woman's hands didn't move.

I have a question, I signed.

Yes, of course.

I saw a woman outside. The day I came here. She was crying and trying to get in the door, but Dr. Pearl was keeping her out. Why was she crying?

I imagine there was someone she wanted to visit, maybe a family member, but she couldn't.

Why do you bury kids?

Dr. O's face slackened.

I see kids being buried at night, I signed. I don't like it.

We have a cemetery here—you've probably seen it. Sometimes people die, and they have no family to claim their bodies, so we bury them here. But we never do that at night. How often do you see this?

Every night.

It sounds like a dream. We can give you something to help with that.

My fingers hung before me. I had to dig into my stomach a little for my next question. Why do you and the people in white want to stop our beauty? I signed. Everyone here is beautiful, but they all get hurt. Felix gets hurt, and George, and Bernice. People get scared.

Dr. O leaned back in his chair. He started to say something then stopped. It took him a few moments to answer.

We're trying to help, he said. We're doing our best.

Felix Jimson

28 FEBRUARY 1980

Dad says I can't be here anymore. He says I'm lucky I'm not in jail, he doesn't trust me cause I'm sick and I'm headed down a bad path and he doesn't know how to help me. I said what do you care he says I need to go somewhere else where people can help me, I asked what he meant he waved me away and made himself a drink. Do you ever think about being a fucking parent I said you don't teach me like a real dad and he turned away and didn't answer.

1 MARCH 1980

Dad told me to pack my things, said that mom was right she didn't leave him, she left me. I told him he's weak and I hate that his blood's inside me. He told me the devil lives inside me I stuck out my tongue and said good the devil had the strength to do the hard thing and I threw his lousy ceramic Charlie Chaplin at him SMASH. He tried to grab me and I ran out into the street past all the houses all the way to the river, touched the water and prayed for help. Police came to get me, cuffing my hands behind my back and watching me like I was an animal that could bite them. They put me in the back just like CM for all who live a godly life will be persecuted.

7 MARCH 1980

Nobody thinks I'm sane and I don't know how to show it.
If I sign people look at me like I'm a clown if I speak no one
listens I don't know who will help me or who will punish me
I never know the right thing to do. I try to reach out but the
nurses and doctors and patients don't understand. The air
here stinks. They won't tell me when I'm getting out.

   How can they expect me to do what they want when they
don't communicate right? What would a Deaf Christ do if
he was locked in an asylum? What would the devil do?

RESISTANCE

FELIX HAD TRIED teaching me about time. He'd formed clocks with his hands, counted out the seconds, scratched out calendars on the air. Like a kidney made of iron, my body wouldn't accept it. Wouldn't accept that all the things that happened to me could be broken into seconds and minutes and weeks and years, that the blob of time I spent in that room in my father's house could be hardened into numbers and slotted into shelves that had been waiting for them all along. When I was first arrested, they argued for days over whether I should be tried as an adult, and now, every once in a while, my lawyer tells me I have a few more years before I can apply for parole. I don't know what that means. Telling time is trying to use a glass to control a river. Time is a way of controlling. Time means nothing if nothing changes.

In that basement room, I'd grown until my head started bumping the ceiling, while my father grew heavier. His hair shortened. The bigger man grew even thinner. He wore the same clothes, and his body disappeared within them. His belly shrank, his skin grayed. The long-haired man never came back.

But my hair had grown. On my head and under my arms. Nobody cut my hair anymore. The men enjoyed it when a dog yanked me around the cage by my hair. I hurt my neck many times. My nails grew long and the only way to keep them short was clawing at the dogs and at the ground and at the walls. I lost one nail when a dog ripped it out.

Sometimes the men had tossed things into the cage. Rocks. Pieces of wood or metal. Shards of glass. I fought in rain, snow, mud. I never knew when I'd be finished. Sometimes the hard earth would be littered with soupy blood and desperate claw marks, and I'd still have to fight. My father kept opening the cage. He was testing me, seeing how much I could take. Maybe he was proud. My arms hardened as scars piled on top of scars. My fists sharpened. My mind flattened. The angry smiles of the men and the sorrow and outrage in my heart never faded. Time meant nothing.

When the fights were finally over and the bigger man hauled me back down to the basement, I continued to see the dogs' teeth chomping at me. If I closed my eyes, I saw their stilled claws and slackened tongues. They fought me in my dreams. Tore at my clothes. Snapped at my face. I punched at them in my sleep. Broke two knuckles like that. I tried to stay awake all the time, staring at the light that never went out.

If I didn't dream about the dogs, I dreamed about the monsters. They'd step out of the walls and out of the pages of the book and surround me and hold me in their clawed hands. They stared at me with their enormous green eyes. They let me touch their teeth and stroke their heads. Their bodies were as flat as the walls and pages they stepped out of—their arms and legs curled when they moved. They smiled and never said anything. They never had to. I hugged them, and they hugged me back.

One time the bigger man came to get me. He brought me the red drink; I'd been thirsting for it. When I finished, he grabbed my arm. He'd been losing weight and his fingers were bony. He tried pulling me, but he couldn't shift me. I saw a chance and kicked him hard in the ribs. He stumbled back. I was thrilled. He was still bigger than me, but there are different ways to be bigger than people. I punched him in the eye and shoved him out the door into the hall.

I ran past him and up the stairs. A man stood in the kitch-
en, a cigarette between his lips. He wore over his back the red
cloth with the blue X. He spread his arms, and the cloth looked
like wings. On the counter was a container of red drink and a
white bottle. The man stepped toward me. I slapped him, and
the cigarette flew out of his mouth. He reached for me. I ran to
the back door and opened it and ran outside.

The crowd was waiting by the cage. The biggest dog I'd ever
seen walked around inside. White and brown with bored eyes.
Some of the men saw me. My father saw me. The men chased
me as I ran around to the front of the house. Many cars and
trucks were parked there. I weaved between them. The gate
was open for someone driving in. I ran for the opening. My
legs stretched. My lungs bloomed—freedom was suddenly
close. The car veered in front of me. I tried running around
it, but someone hit me from behind and slammed me into the
front of the car. I whipped my elbows backward. Many men
tackled me and piled on top of me, shoving my face into the
gravel. I thrashed and bucked against them. Their breath clung
to my face. Through the mess of legs and arms, I saw the open
gate. The road led out into that immense prairie churning with
insects and possibility. I kept fighting.

Multiple hands seized each of my limbs and lifted me up. A
few men punched me. They'd watched me fight for a long time,
and they wanted to hit me, just to touch me. They carried me
to the back of the house. One of them jerked my hair side to
side.

My father and the bigger man stood by the cage. The dog
lay in a corner, a tired mass of fur. The bigger man slumped.
He held his hand to his ribs. My father spoke to him, pointing at me. He shoved the bigger man's head back. My father
was smaller than many of the men but in a different way he
was bigger. The bigger man winced. He straightened, rolled up
his fists, and came toward me. My father held him back. He
touched the cage door and motioned to the men.

My nose bled. My cheek was swollen. I smelled the dog
and the men. The men smelled worse. They gripped me hard

because they feared me. They knew I could beat them one on one. My father opened the cage door. The men threw me inside and gathered around. Some of them spoke to the bigger man and slapped his back. The bigger man grimaced and spoke through his teeth.

The dog slowly stood. Its bulk swayed. It easily weighed more than me. It didn't show its teeth, but for some reason I felt more afraid of this dog than any of the others. I tried to see past the men toward the gate. The lights from their trucks blocked my sight. I slapped the cage, yelled at the men. I shoved my arms through the wire and tried to grab them. They smiled and jumped back. My mind was completely blank, full of nothing but red.

My father tossed a tool with a wooden handle into the cage. Its metal head had a flat side and a sharp side. I threw the tool out of the cage toward the trucks; it landed on the front window of one of the bigger ones. White cracks flowed out from a white circle like seeing the moon through tears.

One of the men started to climb over the cage to get me, but two other pulled him down. The dog watched me. I couldn't read its bored eyes. Someone gave the tool back to my father, who pointed it at me. He turned his chin from me to the dog and made his eyes bigger. He tossed the tool back into the cage. It landed by my feet. He nodded at me. That was our second conversation.

I picked up the tool and weighed it in my hand. The dog took a step toward me. Sniffed my hand, then walked away. I shook my head at my father. A few of the men had begun prodding the dog with sticks. My father tilted his head. I couldn't tell if he wanted me to survive or to stop embarrassing him. I ran over to the dog and raised the tool over my head.

The men shook the cage and shouted. The dog didn't want to fight. It wasn't a fighting dog. Probably none of them were. We were not enemies. This was not survival; it was cruelty.

When I finished, I dropped the bloody tool and sank to my knees and hugged the dog hard. I shivered. I'd almost tasted freedom. I wanted to cry, but the cry in me was too big to let out.

The bigger man and another man pulled me off the dog. My father took up the tool. The bigger man pulled my hair, and he and the other man took me back inside. I kept my eyes away from the cage.

The bigger man shoved me down the stairs. My arm folded beneath me and jarred against a sharp step. They threw me onto my mattress.

My forearm bulged. From the middle outward it had a new angle. I touched my hand, and hot pain spiked through my arm. Soon my skin turned blue. It was a long time before the bigger man came back in and saw my arm. He jerked it straight and taped a stick to it. Whenever I knock my arm against a wall or a table, a pulse of pain snaps out.

I see that dog every day, sitting right in front of me. I smell its warm fur, feel its gentle tongue on my hand. Sometimes I'm so sorry that I can't breathe. Sometimes I think I shouldn't be alive.

But I'm alive for a reason. Felix told me that. He said he had a plan for me.

And yet, in the end, he left.

STEPPING INTO THE MOON

ALISTAIR LEFT A few days ago. His time was up. He picked up his books and shook my hand and walked out. Someone else is in my cell now. Smaller man. Bald, eyes like pebbles. Cringes when I walk past him. He keeps staring at the scars on my arms. I'll miss Alistair.

Had a meeting with my lawyer yesterday. Needed my signature. I held the pen in my fist and scribbled. She always brings the same man to translate for me. Fingers like wieners. I hate the way they skid through the air. No music. No rhythm. Nothing like Felix's hands.

I dreamed about him the other night. It was like the night he left me behind. His blond head shining blue in the moonlight. Except he didn't leave me behind. He took my hand and pulled me with him, and we rose above the ground and ran on the air, higher and higher, our feet brushing the treetops. The moon was a bright opening in the sky, and we ran toward it. Neither of us looked down.

We stopped running. We were about to step into the moon the way you step into a room.

Felix signed, You ready?

The moon's white light washed over me, its glow like a soft weight on my chest. I didn't know what was on the other side of it. I signed, Yes.

You sure?

Yes.

He let go of my hand. We hovered in the air for a moment. Smiling at each other. His entire body glowed white. His eyes completely lit up. I reached for his hand to kiss it.

I fell. He stayed where he was. Still smiling.

I didn't scream. I wasn't surprised—only sad. He stepped into the moon and disappeared into that white light. I stared at the ground as I fell. Wind blew up at me. The prairie below got bigger and darker—the whole earth looked like an enormous hole.

I woke up before I landed, lying on my side facing the white brick wall, the taste of dirt in my mouth.

HE'S HERE. IN the prison. My father. When my lawyer told me, I punched through the table. I wanted to blow a hole through the wall and run. I thought I had more time.

His name is Kellan Gray. Knowing his name made me angrier—it was like naming a pile of shit. I picked up a chair to swing it through the glass in the meeting room, but my lawyer held up her hands and some of the guards pulled out their sticks until I put the chair down.

They're keeping him in the infirmary. He tried to escape and got into a fight; a guard broke his eye socket. They took blood from him while they stitched him up. I gave them my blood yesterday. When I asked my lawyer to move me to a different wing, she said they're working on it.

He's killed people. A lot of people. Sold drugs and guns. They found his marriage certificate, but they can't find Bethany, my mother. They think he might've killed her too. He hasn't said anything. He doesn't know I'm here. They said I'm a surprise witness. I asked what that means, but when the interpreter tried to explain, his thick meaty fingers wobbling through the air, I still didn't understand.

I don't know how my mother and father met. Don't know if they have brothers and sisters. Don't know if their parents are still alive. Don't know if she had ambitions, or if she ever escaped her house, or fought to get me back.

When I was at her house, she sometimes bathed me. Ran the water and put me in the tub. I couldn't enjoy it. She never paid attention to me the rest of the time, so when she pulled me toward the bathroom it always felt sudden. I thought she wanted to hurt me. Drown me. I fought her in the water until she was soaked and left me alone. The water was all over the bathroom floor and she walked out. I would wait until the water in the tub got cold before I left.

There was one time where I enjoyed it. I held my breath and let my arms float around. I let her scoop water into a cup and pour it on my head. I let her watch me with her sad eyes. I might've been sick.

They buried someone yesterday, in the graveyard behind the prison. A man whose head was crushed in a fight. I saw the burial from the window in the shop. Two men digging and lowering him in. All the graves have the same little rock.

I don't know what I'd do if I was released from this place. I can't see the future. My head is too full of what happened; I have to squint to see what's happening now. There are so many little things to know about how to live in the world, and it feels impossible to learn them all.

I will not be buried out there. I refuse to be put back below ground. I want to live in the air and stay in the light and touch the sky.

ROYAL SASKATCHEWAN PSYCHIATRIC HOSPITAL—WAKAW, SK

PATIENT PROGRESS REPORT

Patient Name:	DOB:
Felix Jimson	30 Oct 1963
Admitting Psychiatrist:	**Admittance Date:**
Dr. Harrison Pearl	2 March 1980
Reporting Psychiatrist:	**Report Date:**
Dr. Harrison Pearl	25 May 1980

ACTIVE MEDICATION(S)

Serentil—150 mg injection (suspended in favor of insulin therapy)

PROBLEMS AND PROGRESS

—Initial diagnosis: paranoid-type schizophrenia—

Patient continuously exhibits unruly behavior on Ward 2. He is unwilling to listen to instructions. His hearing loss has dulled his faculties and fostered an insular personality in which rules do not seem to apply to him. Delusions of persecution; has a pathological need for attention and disruption. After brief conference with nurses, his privileges were revoked, and he began insulin therapy on 7 May. Patient has responded well, demonstrating insulin's efficacy and bucking current trends. Tried and true. Had a seizure on 10 May but otherwise no serious side effects.

(Side note: Not many patients with hearing loss come through RSPH. Will save notes for future case study on hearing loss and schizophrenia.)

RECOMMENDATION(S)

Continue insulin therapy. Assess progress at
month's end. Insulin to serve as deterrent for
future misbehavior.

3 JUNE 1980

FUCK THEM ALL FUCK their rules motherfucking philis-
tine shit PIGS making fun of me why do they come after me
I wish no one pain I just want to love people unruly they say
someday they'll see my enormous power that can lift them to
the sky or reduce them to dust———my light is too bright it
warms the visionaries and torches the weak I am unruly because I have a sun inside my chest full of love + beauty they
keep punching it down trying to kill it they keep sedating
me tying me down I'm too strong to be sedated within the insulin sickness my soul leaves my body and I see everything
merely altered ~~conshusness~~ consciousness you can't put the
sun in a box I am unruly because I'm alive any silenced
person who wants a place in this world is seen as insane as
less as unhuman the world can be remade I've seen it and
it's beautiful I see the blood surging in the nurses' and doctors' heads I see their empty ideas how the truth skates across
their eyes instead of sinking in my words are mighty wind
flattening houses pulling trees out of the ground there is no
difference between earth + sky I hold the universe in my
hands and will share it with anyone who wants the TRUTH

4 JUNE 1980

I miss mom. Still no word from dad.
  I must pull the nails out of my own hands + rise.

CEREMONY

BECAUSE OF ME, Marvin didn't sleep much. I was either sitting up practicing my signs or watching out the window for more dead bodies or screaming and punching the wall while in the middle of a nightmare. One night I woke up with bloody knuckles. Blood had smeared over the wall above my bed. Across the room Marvin lay on his side facing the wall, his hands gripping his ears. I lay back down, searching for stars through the window. I hated that I'd disturbed such a gentle person.

George returned before Felix did. He lurched into the dining room during dinner. Black and purple bruises shone on his arms and neck. From where I sat, I thought he'd had drawings put onto his arms like the long-haired man with the snakes and skulls. His eyes moved quicker. I tried to sit beside him during meals, but he kept moving away. Bernice sat with him. I sat near the nurses. Ms. Beddim had learned a few signs—no, yes, food, medicine, read—but we couldn't talk much beyond that. In the dining room, everyone's words surrounded me, scratched at me. I sat there, watching, bristling.

I walked past George in the hallway after dinner. He was alone. The white light overhead slid along his black hair. He smiled like his lips were weights he had to lift off the ground. That hot blush in my groin returned. I followed him. It was lights out soon. Most people were in their rooms or at the nurses' station receiving their evening medicine. George slowed—he knew I was behind him. I took his hand. He squeezed it a moment, then let go. I pointed back down the hallway toward the storage room. He shook his head and kept walking. I grabbed his hand. He said something.

What? I signed.

I lifted his hand to my mouth. He yanked it away. His eyes flared. Hardened. He shoved me a little and jogged down the hall. I stood watching him.

Bernice tapped my shoulder, and I took her hand and started for the storage room. She stopped. Pulled me back. *Weecand,* she said. *Thuhno. Thozemudderfuggers.*

A DAY OR two later, I saw Felix at his usual spot receiving his morning injection. The sunlight flashed through his blond hair pasted flat against his head. His face a gray decayed flower. Eyes like rocks, absorbing nothing.

I gulped down my meds, then ran over and hugged him. It was like hugging a pillow.

You okay? I signed. I waved my hand before his face. What happened?

Tears seeped from his eyes. He reached out for my hand and squeezed it hard. Red streaks sliced down his forearms. A bruise curled around his neck.

At breakfast we sat apart from the other kids, who kept looking up from their food at him. He ate little, said little. Just yes or no. He never blinked.

I waited. He pushed his tray away.

Did they hurt you? I signed.

He didn't answer until study time. We sat in the corner table—he had three or four books open at once. The other kids again sat apart from us.

They tried to drown me, he signed. That asshole Dr. Pearl held me underwater in a huge tub. They beat me, too. Hit my face, my arms. Strapped me to a bed. Felix stabbed invisible nails into his palms. Like a crucifixion. I think they did the same to George.

Everyone's been watching me, I signed. Like they don't like me.

Felix made a note in one of the books, then put down his pen. My priest came to see me again, he signed.

The man in black clothes?

He said my father has a new job. Why would I care? He wasn't even supposed to visit me, but Dr. Pearl let him because he's a priest. He tried touching my hand, but I didn't let him. I asked if my mother knew where I was, and why my father hasn't come. The priest wouldn't say.

I thought you didn't want him to come.

Felix peered around. They divide us, he signed. That's their goal: treat us like dogs and make us despair until we do things their way or die. Can you imagine what we'd accomplish if we were allowed to just be? We'd make a light brighter than God himself could make.

He wiped his eyes. I saw everything clearly while I was up there, he signed. My life, my path, the way of the world. Everything I've seen and learned rolled up into one beautiful vision. One night, while I was strapped down, I was thinking about why everyone who was supposed to love me left me. My mother, my grandparents, my friends. Then I looked up, and I saw God. God visited me. He came down from the moon and stepped into the room on a beam of moonlight and touched my hand. Felix held up his left hand. God is real, he signed. He confirmed the path I've been following is the right path. I need to keep going and grow stronger, and I need you with me. When the time's right, we'll leave this place together.

Dr. O said I have a good chance to leave.

Felix frowned. How did you talk to him without me?

A woman signed for him. I told him everything that happened to me.

Felix slumped. You gave him your story?

Yes.

Why would you tell him before you tell me?

You wouldn't let me tell you.

Felix's eyes hardened. I couldn't tell what he wanted—his eyes were like a shield for his thoughts.

I've been alone here, I signed. I can't talk to anyone. I'm having bad dreams. I didn't know what to do.

You didn't tell him about our love, did you?

I asked why men can't love men.

Felix glanced at the other kids and pulled his seat around so his back faced them. Why would you do that? he signed. Why tell him anything?

Felix said *Ferfoksayx* with his mouth, then reached for his pen and squeezed it in his fist. He scribbled on the paper, then dropped the pen, thrust his thumb out from his chin, and thanked me with both hands.

Ungrateful brat, he signed. I've spent the last few months answering all your questions. All I do is help you, but you don't listen.

My hands shook. I listen, I signed. I'm sorry.

I thought I'd failed you, but all you do is take. Without me, you'd be a fucking monkey, strapped to a bed wasting away. He held his head in his hands and clamped his eyes shut, trying not to cry or scream. I thought of a name for you while I was up there, he signed. But I can't give it to you now.

I'm sorry. Felix. I put my hand on his leg.

He shoved it away. Stop! What'd I tell you!

I backed away. I'll tell you my story, I signed. I'll show you.

I told Felix everything. My father. The basement. The empty house. The hospital. The other kids kept looking over at us. When I smelled piss and shit again, I signed quicker. The room began to shrink. I focused on Felix's face, clinging to it with my eyes. I thought my father's face would rush out from the corner if my eyes drifted.

Felix stared, never reacting, never interrupting except to help me find a word.

When I finished, he pulled a magazine off a shelf and showed me a picture of a dog.

Yes, I signed. One of them.

He snapped his fingers just like the woman did.

That's the sign?

Yes. Dogs.

I waved my hand in front of my nose. The smell lingered. Something breathed from the corner to my right.

I didn't tell Dr. O about the house, I signed. There was something there with me. I don't know what. I felt it through the floor. Didn't tell him about the lightning, either. There's something in here with us. I can smell the basement room right now.

Felix blinked, then smiled. Your father is an animal, he signed. How dare he treat you like that.

Felix cupped my face with both hands. He smiled. Eyes full of gold. His whole body rose and fell as he breathed deep. The others watched us. He ignored them.

You are a living parable, he signed.

A what?

Your Deafness has preserved your holiness, your purity. You had a terrible journey, but it didn't stain you, didn't break you, didn't make you a monster. You're a miracle. My miracle.

He sat back. His fists vibrated with excitement. His eyes slid across all the books he had open—he snapped them all shut. As his hands danced on the air, the room and the smell and the thing in the corner and the other people faded away, and I leaned toward him.

Like Lazarus, or the Golem, or the creature, he signed. I want to help you preserve your holiness and share your story with the world. You and I are holy spirits. The world doesn't see us, but we're here, and we can touch their hearts with light. The doctors, the nurses, even the other patients, they can't see what a gift you are. More proof of the rightness of my mission. That's why you were brought to me, so we can show the world what is possible.

He touched my hand. I'm sorry for what I said before, he signed. I didn't see you for the holy being you are.

He slapped his notebook down on the table and began writing fast. I stared, trying to feel his excitement. He'd dazzled me so much I didn't bother asking what he meant.

AT STUDY TIME I showed Felix my drawings of the monsters, with their jutting teeth and eyes that took up half their faces.

I saw these in my father's basement, I signed. Someone gave me a book, and I drew these on the walls.

Felix smiled. His fingers spelled out G-r-i-m-t-e-e-t-h. I know that book, he signed. *The Grimteeth.*

What are Grimteeth?

Monsters that trade their body parts among each other. All sorts of funny mixes—tall ones give their legs to short ones, and they swap noses and eyes so their faces look weird. A little boy tries to trade with them, but they can't. They ask to rip off his limbs, but he says no. It's like Frankenstein's monster but for kids.

I tried to spell the name he'd used. My fingers stumbled. What is that, what you just signed?

One of my favorite stories, Felix signed. A man gives life to a monster, and people treat the monster badly, including the man who made him, and the monster can't take anymore.

I pointed to my drawings. These are monsters, I signed, unsure if I was stating it or asking it. Are they real?

Monsters are real, Felix signed, but they don't look like that. Real monsters have human skin and hurt others. They're empty inside. They smile when others suffer. They don't know God, don't know love, don't have souls or faith. They destroy love and beauty and make you feel sick when you see them.

Empty inside. No heart? No guts?

I'd say that's right.

I plucked an invisible thread from my left fist. The sign for soul.

That's what lives inside, Felix signed. He tapped his chest with his fist.

Everyone here has souls? I signed.

Glowing, beautiful souls.

Marvin? Anders? Ms. Beddim? Dr. O? They all have one?

People without souls have no feelings. Your soul is where you feel your deepest feelings. It's what you feel when you're happy. When you first started signing, your soul lit up.

I smiled. Yes, I signed. It did.

Felix smiled. I could tell, he signed. Your eyes sparkled.

I want to read and write like you can.

You don't need to. You're pure. You're perfect the way you are.

You read a lot.

Knowing things is not always best.

There's so much to know.

More knowledge doesn't change what happens to us. We end up going the same way no matter what. Alpha and Omega, past, present, future—the Almighty sees all of it. He allowed me to see where my path leads, and I'm going to keep following it. Understand?

No.

Your path runs right beside mine, he signed. He that overcomes and maintains God's work until the end will receive power over the world. Felix watched me, his eyes gleaming and almost entirely black.

I'd like to talk to God, I signed. Shake his hand.

Everyone can talk to God. But God talks to only a few lucky people. No one shakes his hand.

Why not?

We have to remain humble.

I tried to picture all these things in my head: God, Heaven, faith, will, paths, power. I could not see them or hold them in my hand; they meant little to me. I picked up a pen and added a few hairs to one of my Grimteeth.

Your father will go to Hell, Felix signed.

I put down my pen. Hell was a finger thrusting downward then both hands mimicking flickering flames.

That's where bad people go, he signed. They go down below the earth, and they burn for all time, and all the worst things happen to them. My father will go there, too, and Father Hoff, and probably my mother. Definitely Dr. Pearl.

I imagined my basement room coated in fire, orange flames eating and churning and whipping along the walls. The hulking faces of dogs rushing up through the flames, snapping their hot jaws.

That's sad, I signed.

That image of the dogs lingered—I felt the heat of flames on my back. The air gusted out of me.

Hell is frightening, Felix signed. I wish all people could be good, but some people can't. He flexed his fingers. When Dr. Pearl goes to Hell, he signed, he's going to be in a room far underground. The rotted heads of all his loved ones will hang from spikes on the walls. He'll be strapped down to a bed, just like he did to us, and demons that look like us are going to inject him with insulin and heroin and gasoline and sheep's piss and Mello Yello, and they'll fuck in front of him and shit in his mouth and scream into his ears that everything he knew was wrong, and they'll cut into his head while he's still awake and rip away his hair and show him his brain and it'll be rotten and full of bugs, and he'll wake up and think it's a dream but he'll still be strapped down, and it'll start all over again, and every second will be full of fear and pain, and he'll never be able to scream loud enough, and he'll never know rest again.

Felix made a face that looked like a smile hiding a roar.

Hell is under the ground? I signed.

Mrs. Koepp showed Felix a note and tapped a small stack of papers lying in front of him. He'd scribbled a few spirals on them.

How can they make us do schoolwork here? He signed. School's useless, anyway. I know everything I need to know.

A FEW TIMES Hortense asked me to play board games in the evenings and during study period, but eventually she stopped. Everyone stopped paying attention to us, though I still felt a small blush whenever I walked past George or Bernice.

One day, Ms. Beddim took me downstairs to a white room where a man with a circular blade sawed through my cast, through everyone's words and drawings. Ms. Beddim held it up for me after, asking if I wanted to keep it. I shook my head. Flexed my arm. My muscles had thinned. The shape of the cast had been pressed into my skin; my scars seemed some- how deeper and redder.

At dinner that night, Felix grinned and signed, Go to the shower room after. I'll meet you there.

The shower room was just a small room off the bathroom with a drain and two shower heads. In the bathroom corner, a door opened into the water-therapy room, which had a metal tub and a table full of towels; a heavy silver box with glass eyes and a hose rose out of the floor. The door had no knob, and the hole where the knob should've been was always dark. I'd never seen anyone use the water-therapy room.

I sat on a bench near the shower room that allowed me to see into the bathroom. Anders came in and walked toward one of the stalls but stopped when he saw me. He looked over my shoulder, then jogged back out of the bathroom. A little while after that, George walked to one of the urinals. He started to undo his pants, then saw me and covered himself and went into the stall farthest away. I approached him. He finished and quickly washed his hands. I waved at him. His face was tight and grim in the mirror. He said something on his way out; I think it started with *Sawrry*.

Felix arrived holding his notebook to his chest. He wore black clothing and stood straight. Proud.

In here, he signed.

He pushed open the door to the water-therapy room and snapped on the light. All the silver in the room gleamed. He set his notebook on the ledge beside the tub and turned on the water.

What are we doing? I signed.

A special—

I didn't catch the last sign. Special what?

Special c-e-r-e-m-o-n-y, he signed. He repeated the sign, arcing his outstretched hands forward then turning his fists inward and circling both hands, both index fingers hooked.

I copied him. Ceremony.

Felix beamed, and I waited for its meaning to sink in. Felix shifted his upturned thumbs this way and that. Baptism, he signed. You need to be cleansed before we go any further.

I shower every day.

This is different.

When the tub was half-full, he shut off the water. Steam swirled up like the ghost Felix pulled from his fist whenever he talked about spirits and souls. He opened his book and began reading and signing over the water, his hands following whatever he had written there.

Physical matter is sacred matter, he signed. As water is physical matter, so is the divine covenant of my temple begun by blessing this water.

I leaned forward to ask what he was saying, but he held up a hand and closed his eyes. His face glowed. He signed slowly like he wanted his signs to sink into the water, his arms swaying in graceful arcs above the tub. I remember all his handshapes, the ideas he held in his palms and gripped in his fingers that I couldn't quite picture, but I didn't grasp what they meant until much later.

He signed, May those cleansed by the holy power of this water be blessed and welcomed into my temple, which follows the sacred Gospel of the New Prometheus, and may those who are cleansed always maintain their purity and faith from this day forth.

He balanced his book on his leg and held one sheet out straight, then slid his finger along the edge of the page, up and down, until blood seeped out in thick drops and trailed across his words. He held out his hand and let the blood fall into the tub; the red drops dissolved and became part of the water. Felix touched the water and drew a circle on his forehead. He turned to me.

Take off your clothes, he signed, and step into the water.

Why?

You must be naked to be reborn.

Reborn?

Trust me.

Felix shut the therapy-room door and propped a trash can in front of the door. It's okay, he signed.

Are you loving me?

In a different way.

I removed my clothes. He watched me with a soft welcoming smile.

Beautiful, he signed.

I stepped toward him. My dick pointed at him full and long. He put his hand on my shoulder and turned me toward the tub. I squeezed his hand and lifted my leg and stepped into it. The hot water gripped my legs. I knelt down. The water rose to meet me, rose to my shoulders. I felt a charge from the water, a buoying thrill.

Coming in? I signed.

I have questions, Felix signed.

The heat scoured my head clean. Made me dizzy. I planted my hands against the tub walls to stay steady.

Do you wish to leave all your mistakes behind?

Mistakes?

Bad things you've done.

The dog I killed with the hammer fell onto its side and crashed against the wall of my skull. I nodded to Felix.

Do you wish to do good in this world?

I reached up with my shining wet fist. Yes.

Do you love me and believe in me, as I love and believe in you?

I love you. In my soul.

Do you accept me as your teacher?

Yes.

Do you accept me as your— He pulled his S-hands outward, then filed his flattened hands straight down, outlining a
person: Save person. Saviour.

What's that?

Felix cocked his head, arched a brow. He had incredible control over his eyes. Do you accept me as your savior?

Yes, I signed.

I baptize you in the name of the New Gospel. May we find
our peace together.

He put his hand on my head and gently pushed me underwater. He held me in place for a moment, then cupped my
chin and pulled me back up. I rubbed my eyes.

Your name, he signed, will not be like other people's names.
Your name will not be written down. It will exist as proof of
the divinity of our people. It will require that people engage
with you on your terms. Here is your name.

He dragged his fist up from his stomach and opened his
hand wide, as though spreading the love that lived inside him.
I breathed deep and leaned back against the tub wall. The heat
had opened me up. I felt peaceful.

Understand? he signed.

I smiled. Snapped my N-fingers at him. No. The water flicked
off my fingertips. The head of my dick poked up through the
water.

This is your name. He signed my name again.

I blinked. My name.

Yes.

I signed my name, my hand brushing the surface of the
water. His blood clung to my skin, covering it, forming a protective layer.

The past is gone, he signed. There's only what we have
now and what lies ahead. As you share your story, you
become more holy. Jesus needed Lazarus to display his
power. You are the key to my temple. You and I are the first
true believers.

I signed my name again. And again. As I signed it, my body
flexed. My muscles felt fuller. My dick hardened even more.

I stood from the tub. Even with the slick tub bottom, I felt more solid on my feet, better able to stand up.

Thank you, Felix.

He took my hand and kissed it, then put his hand on the back of my wet head and pulled me toward him and kissed my forehead, his hands squeezing the water out of my hair. He touched his forehead to mine, and we stood like that for a moment, hands on each other's shoulders, him fully clothed, me naked, our breath gathering between us, the cool air settling on my shoulders.

GOSPEL OF THE NEW PROMETHEUS

Pastor Felix Jimson

30 JULY 1980

I was born a ghost
and ghosts cannot be killed
love endures

MONSTERS

HE KNOWS I'M here. He stared at me through the infirmary window, locked me in place with his eyes like he had to make sure it was me. He threw a chair and smashed the window and leapt through the frame and tried to stab me with a piece of glass. It set off a huge fight. Guards, prisoners, doctors. A guard pushed me out of the way, and two of my fingers jammed against a bar and snapped sideways and broke. I'm sorry if my signing is off.

They haven't finished the DNA testing yet, but they moved me to a new cell all the way across the prison. I'm alone in there. Can't work in the shop anymore. Can't go to the cafeteria or the gym. The cell is smaller, a closet. I look at magazines and draw pictures. It's like being in that basement room again.

My lawyer wants to make a deal. I have to go to court and say what I know. If they decide my story's true, then I have to tell more people. She says I could maybe have my time reduced. The problem is whether anyone will believe me; my father's lawyer will say I'm unreliable. They'll say I'm not his son. They'll attack me because I have no name. Because I'm Deaf. Because I can't talk. Because I'm a murderer. They'll make things up about me, say I'm a drifter, a bum, a monster. Someone looking for fame. They'll say my words mean nothing. People will hear my story and decide whether I'm lying and whether my father will spend the rest of his life in prison.

During that meeting my father's face swelled through my skull, filling it like cement. My hands wouldn't stop shaking. I had to ask the interpreter to repeat several times. At the end of the meeting, my lawyer said something, but the interpreter stopped and blinked. His body slumped.

What? I signed.

The interpreter made a fist and circled it over his chest, then pushed his hand toward me, then tapped his chin with his outstretched hand. He turned over an invisible body.

Your mother is dead.

My mother. She's dead.

Yes.

I signed more slowly, letting the words sink into my bones: Bethany. My mother. Dead.

We found the death certificate, my lawyer said. She took too many drugs.

Like the red drink?

Like what?

I shook my head. I felt lighter. Nothing held me to the ground anymore—for a moment I thought I might drift away. My lawyer said a few more things, but I didn't pay attention. I floated back to my cell, two guards walking beside me. My lawyer said she'd taken too many drugs but that's not what killed her.

I sat in my cell last night thinking I should do something or say something. I remembered Felix at the window during that man's funeral, so I said some of the same things he'd said, like peace, beauty, love, sleep. I signed them toward the back field and to the ceiling. She was out there somewhere in the prairie. So was Felix. I felt both of them there with me at the same time, and I fell to my knees and cried.

AS I ATE breakfast this morning I remembered walking past a small room near the nurse's station and seeing Ms. Beddim hooking a plastic bag full of brown sludge up to Marvin's stomach tube. Neither Marvin nor I had gotten much sleep, and when I'd sat up to get out of bed, he'd cringed at me and run out of the room, his eyes suddenly looking older.

I stopped eating. I'm tired. I've lost all my strength. I keep thinking I'm close to understanding how the world works. Why Felix and my father did what they did. Why my mother is dead. Why I'm in prison and Felix isn't. Why ghosts surround me and strain every second to dig into me. Why I'm always alone. But all of it slips through my fingers.

Felix said we are our own saviors. We must believe in our own power and create our own place in the world because no one else will. I hope to make a life for myself one day, live in a house where I'm free to leave and enter, to eat whatever food I want, to walk through the streets without feeling I'm about to be shut away again, to love someone who loves me back. I wish I could wrap my arms around the world; the world never seems to have enough love. Maybe it doesn't know how to welcome it, doesn't know how to hold and protect those who have the most love to give.

ROYAL SASKATCHEWAN PSYCHIATRIC HOSPITAL—WAKAW, SK

PATIENT PROGRESS REPORT

Patient Name:	DOB:
Felix Jimson	30 Oct 1963
Admitting Psychiatrist:	Admittance Date:
Dr. Harrison Pearl	2 March 1980
Reporting Psychiatrist:	Report Date:
Dr. Lyle Okimasis	4 August 1980

ACTIVE MEDICATION(S)

Serentil—150 mg injection

PROBLEMS AND PROGRESS

—Initial diagnosis: paranoid-type schizophrenia—

Switching to injection has by and large been beneficial for Felix—his mood has stabilized somewhat. The medication is only part of the story: while Felix remains defiant toward staff, he has found a companion who, like him, is Deaf and uses Sign Language. Felix appears to have found solace in teaching this companion, who did not know Sign Language previously.

There is concern that both Felix and his companion rely too much on each other for companionship; this companion appears to be younger than Felix and, because of his own vulnerable state, is quite impressionable. This companion has clearly been through some trauma; he follows Felix everywhere and mimics him in every way. (For more information, see the record for John Smith.) Also, given Felix's past behavior, I am wary that he spends so much time with this companion. I have encouraged Felix to continue reaching out to others, but with little success, and while he has admitted to certain transgressions (see Notes below), he has not expressed remorse for them; in fact, he feels they are justified.

Given the evidence, I am confident in the present diagnosis and recommend that he refrain from resuming his course of insulin therapy at this time.

RECOMMENDATION(S)

Continue to monitor medication's efficacy; requisition interpreter for therapy sessions (recommended separate from John Smith).

NOTES

How are you, Felix? How are things with your companion?

Does he know his name?

what is it?

I'm glad you've found a friend in here—have you interacted with anyone else?

I believe Father Hoff is visiting you again next week

why not?

don't feel like talking today?

we received notice that your school might press charges. how do you feel about that?

I agree but setting fires is not constructive

that's what we need to address, your anger

would you let me read your journal? please?

SINS OF THE FATHER

WE SAT IN the dining room pushing eggs around our plates, the two of us glowing together.

Will you do that for others? I signed. Put them in water?

Felix shook his head. No one believes the way you do, he signed.

He scanned the room. Sunlight flooded through the tall windows, brightening everyone's face, even if they sat slumped at the table. Outside, the sky was the same wondrous blue as Felix's eyes, and the ghosts on the prairie had for the moment relaxed and the fields bloomed sharp and green.

I hope their pain fades, he signed.

I want love.

They're watching us now. They'll take us both up there next time. No touching or kissing anymore until we get out.

When's that?

I hope soon.

Ms. Beddim approached holding a piece of paper. She showed it to Felix and pointed to me.

What? I signed.

Therapy today, he signed. Separate. They have an interpreter.

Ms. Beddim smiled at me. Pointed to my plate and gave a thumbs-up. I nodded.

She walked away. Her yellow curls were fading toward the tips.

She's been watching us for months, Felix signed, and she still doesn't know how to sign *good* or *bad*. She takes notes, too. She probably gives them to Dr. Pearl. He can't be bothered to leave his cozy office and see us himself. Then he'd have to see us as people instead of problems.

The previous night, I'd asked Felix why there are more white people in the institution than Asian or Black or First Nations. He said that in Japan and China, there are more Asian people, and in Africa there are more Black people. He said that white people have killed millions of others all over the world, including First Nations people here on the prairies, because they saw them as problems. The image of so many dead people forced the limits of my mind further and further outward until my head ached and creaked from the stretching, and I shuddered.

Bernice really wants out, Felix signed. Dr. Pearl took her upstairs before I got here. When she came down, she just sat in the hall and hardly said anything. Whenever Dr. Pearl looks at me, I see in his eyes he wants to cut my head open and play with my brain, or strap me down and zap me, or stick pins in my skin to see what I'd do.

I peered across the dining room. Bernice and Hortense were play-fighting with their thumbs. As Mr. Creel walked past them, they raised their middle fingers to his back.

I don't understand, I signed. Why do people hurt other people or kill other people?

Some people are greedy or petty or bored, Felix signed, and some people have no choice.

He pulled me closer. At your next session, he signed, don't give the doctor anything. Don't tell him anything about me, don't tell him about your baptism. That's our secret. Understand?

Okay.

What'd I say?

Don't say anything. About you.

I swallowed a forkful of cool eggs and broke off a corner of toast, then left it on my plate. I wasn't hungry anymore.

Felix held up a spoonful of jam and poured sugar onto it and shoved it in his mouth.

What did your father do to you? I signed.

Felix's eyes hardened. I told you, he put me in here, he signed.

Before you came here, what did he do? Did he hurt you?

Felix's eyes dulled. He fucked everything up, he signed. He's more a child than a man. He didn't look after me, didn't give a damn.

Felix sat up straight and snapped his hands sharply as he signed: He let my mother leave without a fight. He let people do what they wanted to me. Never defended me, never supported me. He makes things up in his head so he's never at fault. He's a fuck-up—weak, selfish, has no courage, believes in nothing.

I'm sorry.

I've written letters to my mother, but she hasn't come. I bet my father's keeping her letters from me, or maybe the doctors are doing it. Felix sagged. Both of them are horrible, he signed. I wish I didn't come from my parents. I wish I was put together from spare parts, that I didn't carry their blood, their skin, their eyes, their weaknesses.

He leaned close. If Dr. O asks you questions, just say, Everything's fine, I'm okay. Understand?

HOW ARE YOU? Dr. O signed.

He wore a green shirt with a collar. No suit. The same interpreter sat beside him. She'd cut her hair short; it made her smile look bigger.

Everything's fine, I signed. I'm okay. Understand?

He spoke, and the interpreter began signing. I locked onto her fingers, trying to remember their rhythm from last time.

You could use a shave, he said. Maybe a trim, too. I'll ask Ms. Beddim to arrange it.

My hair had gotten long, almost to my shoulders. Your hair's shorter, I signed to the woman.

We've been trying to find your family, Dr. O continued, but it's difficult without a name or address. Given everything that's happened to you, we don't want to return you to a harmful environment, but there are legal implications.

I swung my eyes around the small room. The bleak light outside made it look even tighter, like a fist aching to close.

May I ask why you're not speaking? he said.

I tucked one hand into the other. His words prodded at me like mosquitoes.

You sure everything's okay? Did Felix tell you not to say anything?

I met Dr. O's eyes, then looked at the floor. Everything's fine, I signed.

You're welcome to share as much or as little as you want, Dr. O said. This is your time. Nobody else gets to tell you what to say. In here, you get to share what you want, not what someone else wants. You have a much better chance of leaving here if we can work things out.

Dr. O leaned forward, trying to snag my attention with his eyes. Are you sleeping better? he said. I heard that you woke up screaming a few times.

I'm okay, I signed.

What about your relationship with Felix? Are you two seeing each other romantically?

I started to sign something but stopped and shook my head.

Dr. O slumped back. So did the woman. They seemed like two parts of the same animal.

Last time, you had many questions, he said. Whatever you want to ask.

I had to move away from the subject of Felix, so I signed the first question that arose. Why do people die?

Dr. O's thick eyebrows arched up. That's a big question, he said. Deaf is a part of life.

The interpreter signed his words, then frowned at him.

Excuse me, Dr. O said. Slip of the tongue. Death—death is part of life. It's natural.

Natural?

Happens all the time. Everyone dies.

But why?

We all have a certain amount of life in us, and eventually that life runs out. Sometimes it's taken from us.

The soul? The spirit?

That's right.

I don't want ghosts around me.

You see ghosts?

No.

Ghosts are okay. They can speak to us. They're nothing to fear.

Why do so many people have to die?

Dr. O took a moment. Are you afraid of dying?

I flexed my fingers together.

Do you have dreams about dying?

I thought for a moment. The question had nothing to do with Felix. I think so, I signed.

The interpreter snapped her fingers. The dogs? The men burying the body outside?

I saw them again last night, I signed. One of the men looked like my father.

It's the same men you saw before?

Yes.

How many times have you seen them?

I don't know.

Are you taking your medication?

Yes.

Have you told anyone else about this? Besides Felix?

I can't.

Dr. O nodded. I have some news for you, he said. The woman signed words I didn't understand. I caught *family, you, place.*

I tried to imitate the woman's signing. She was too quick. I waved my hands for her to stop.

What's agency?

Good people.

Please slow down.

The woman's hands slowed.

We're looking into taking you to a foster agency, where you'll be able to find a new family. We'd misdiagnosed you, so we're not sure the institution is the best place for you.

Okay, I signed. I still didn't understand.

The plan now, Dr. O said, is to make sure you're stable enough. Then the agency will help you find a new home. It'll take a while, but that's the plan, so you have to work hard. That means listening to me and the nurses and not causing trouble. Understand?

I worked to untangle the woman's signs. Work, I signed. No trouble.

Dr. O gave a thumb's up and started writing on a small pad of paper.

I'm going to give you a new medication, he said, something that'll help with the nightmares.

Did you say a new home? I signed. Can Felix come with me?

Dr. O shook his head. This is for you and you only. I can't discuss the plans for Felix or anyone else with you, and I can't discuss you when I meet with him. That's all private.

How will I talk to people without him?

That will be a challenge. The agency will do their best. You likely won't leave until after the new year—the agency moves slowly, and we need to get your nightmares under control, so there's a bit of time. I want you to spend that time thinking about yourself, asking yourself what you want out of life, what you might like to do, that kind of thing. Your life doesn't belong to anyone else but you. You're free to choose.

What I want to do? I signed. Like what? I don't know anything.

You can learn. You may have a long way to go, but you can learn. I suggest you don't tell anyone that you'll be leaving. Some people might get upset.

Like Felix?

You understand? Say nothing about what we talk about in here.

I say nothing.

Dr. O nodded and made a note in one of his file folders. May I ask what you and Felix talk about? he said.

No.

Why not?

Because.

Because why?

A cold sensation wriggled through my guts. I squirmed in my chair. I can't say, I signed.

Again, this is your time. Whatever you say in here will not leave this room. If someone is hurting you, or making you do something you don't want to do, that's our business. We're here to protect you.

I stared. Kept my hands still.

Has anyone done something to hurt you or make you feel uncomfortable?

No, I signed, my eyes fixed on the floor. I thought about telling him that I had a name now, but Felix gave it to me.

Are you sure? he said.

Yes, I signed. Everything's fine.

FELIX WAS WAITING for me outside Dr. O's office. Hands crossed in front of him. Face stiff.

Everything's fine, I signed.

She can see you. He pointed over my shoulder at the interpreter.

What's this? I pressed my two fists together on my chest and flicked my thumbs up and down.

Romance. Felix's eyes flared. What'd you say?

Nothing.

Felix shut his eyes and shook his head, then walked into

the office and closed the door. I took a drink from the water fountain and sat on a bench down the hallway. The bench had writing on it. Different colors, different letter shapes. I dragged my fingers across the wooden slats and flexed my left arm. It had grown stronger thanks to my signing.

Anders approached, wearing shorts and a T-shirt, his hairy legs thick and bowed. He carried a large black book under his arm. He walked a little past me, then stopped and looked back, as if he hadn't noticed me at first.

Hello, Anders, I signed.

He smiled, then looked over my shoulder, the way he had the day of my baptism. He sat beside me, opened his book, pulled out a black pencil and a red pencil, and started drawing. I started to stand. He pulled me back down and held up his hand. *Stay.* His eyes slid from my face to over my shoulder. I glanced behind me—there was nothing there but wall. He winced a few times as he drew.

I stayed still. Sweat slid down my face. I didn't touch it.

When Anders finished, he turned the page toward me. He'd drawn me exactly as I was, sitting on the bench, hair hanging over my eyes, my cheeks pinkish, a calm expression on my face, the hallway in the background receding into blankness.

Mr. Creel snuck a look at the drawing as he passed by. He smirked and patted Anders on the shoulder. Anders waved him away, then carefully tore the page out of his book and handed it to me. My face and arms were blocky, made of sharp angles, and my hair was a cluster of zigzags, but somehow it still looked like me.

Thank you, I signed.

Anders said something that ended with *airfull.* He walked away, and I studied the drawing again.

Over my shoulder was a black shadow with two rough red spaces that looked like eyes.

Down the hall, Dr. O's office door opened. Felix ambled out. I held up the drawing.

What did he say to you? he signed.

What's this? I signed. I pointed at the shadow on the page.

What did the doctor say? He was keeping something from me. Tell me what he said.

I folded the drawing and put it in my pocket. The cold sensation tightened around my guts. I don't know, I signed. The woman's hands were too fast.

Felix sat down. His knee brushed against mine.

He told me it's private, he signed. That means it's important. Tell me what he said.

Felix peered over his shoulder. The interpreter stood in Dr. O's doorway, staring at Felix. He took my arm and ushered me away to his room.

People filed past us toward the dining room and the smell of cooking meat. He shut the door. We sat on his bed—all his books had spilled out from underneath and spread on the floor.

I hate that interpreter, he signed. Hard to watch her. She has a face like a horse. She probably talks about us with her friends.

It's lunch time, I signed.

Are you trying to hide?

No.

Felix swatted my arm. I stiffened.

What did he say to you? he signed. Did he tell you not to say anything to me?

I stayed still, flexing my thumbnails against each other.

Felix's lips folded back into his mouth. You see what he's doing? he signed. That's how he pulls us apart. He thinks we're ignorant. But we're not ignorant, are we?

No.

We don't have secrets.

No secrets.

What did Dr. O say?

He says I can leave here in the new year. Someone will take me out of here and help me find a new family. I asked if you could come. He couldn't say.

Felix's eyes dulled, held me in place like weights.

He says he'll give me new medicine, I signed, because of nightmares.

Felix's door opened, and Mrs. Koepp stepped into the room. She pointed at the door and spoke to Felix, then put her hand to her mouth. *Food.* She pushed the door open all the way against the wall and walked away.

I didn't say anything about you, I signed. I promise.

I'm all you need, Felix signed. I don't want you hurt again by a new dad or mom. My dad worked at an orphanage—the kids came back all the time, and they were hearing kids. They'll put you in a hearing house, and the family will ignore you. They might have kids of their own too, kids who'll hate you and play tricks on you. Maybe they'll have a dog that scares you and bites you. It's not worth it.

Felix's fevered hands left marks on the air. I imitated him as much as I could. I understood only part of what he said, though his tone was clear. I repeated the sign for "family"—a small cozy circle made with both F-hands. Making the sign left a dent in my heart.

I'll try to stay, I signed.

We'll figure something out. If you behave badly, they'll hurt you.

Why would he ask me not to tell you? I signed. Is this what people do? Do they always hide things?

People don't like truth as much as we do. We're truthful people. The world is built on lies and secrets.

I peered around. Felix's room and the hallway outside, and even Felix himself, seemed to lose color and depth.

Why? I signed. Why are there so many words if nobody uses them right?

That's why they hide, because they have so many words.

You asked me to hide, too, I signed.

He ignored me. With so many ways to say the same thing, he signed, they can talk their way out of trouble. But signing—it's harder to lie when you speak with your body.

I shook my head. It's sad that people hide, I signed. I don't understand it. I hate hiding. I was— My hands spluttered. I clenched my fists, knocking them on my knees and on the edge of Felix's bed.

I hate hiding my love, I signed.
I know, Felix signed.
I want love all the time. When I can't have it, it hurts me.
We'll figure it out.
I took Felix's hand. He squeezed it. I kissed him, leaned into him. He pushed me away.

GOSPEL OF THE NEW PROMETHEUS

Pastor Felix Jimson

17 AUGUST 1980—and forever more

For posterity only, my gospel is as follows—

Nothing is truth but blood and bone.

I am my own savior. No one speaks for me but me.

God and humanity are one. I hold God in my hands and so am divine.

The world is my church—with my hands I deliver my message.

Just as Christ's hands revealed the truth of his suffering, so do my hands reveal the truth of my love.

Silence is holy. My people are holy and shall inherit the world.

My people are the oppressed, the forgotten; I shall lift them up whenever possible.

My people are legion, numbering in the millions. Our collective voices both crack and nourish the earth.

The tongue is the most treacherous muscle; I carry my gospel in my heart and my hands.

The physical is sacred; thus, sex is a form of worship.

Abandoning one's friend or blood is the same as abandoning God and is the worst betrayal.

All people are born beautiful but lose their beauty through the treachery of the tongue, with hatred being the worst treachery of all.

One's love, which is the same as one's beauty, must be preserved at all costs.

The world must be destroyed before it can be remade.

I am a holy ghost on earth, drifting until the End of Days, when my full holiness is achieved and I may pass my light unto others.

When humanity dies, my people shall live, for we know the meaning of survival and God shall bless us to populate the earth forevermore.

The oppressed have fallen through the cracks like seeds; they shall spring up and remake the world.

Those who oppress others are the worst evil; thus, only those who know the true impact of power can wield it.

Family is achieved not through blood but through common goals. There are no fathers, no mothers, no sons, no daughters.

Prophecy is madness until everyone believes.

The past has no meaning; only the present and the future.

FIRST SNOW

WHEN FAMILY VISITED at the institution, they always met in the main room with the TV. Ms. Beddim or Mr. Creel would stand outside the door, and I'd stop walking past and watch for a few minutes. Bernice's mom came. George's dad. Hortense's grandma. It was easy to tell who was family and who wasn't, not just by appearances but by how they came together. Some kind of energy surrounded them. They fit. They matched.

The man who visited Felix was tall with white hair and had a thick neck that pressed hard against his white collar. Felix always told me to stay away when he visited. I usually did, but the main room is too big not to pass by, and I was curious.

The man wrote notes and spoke with his mouth. Felix sat with his back to me. He didn't write or speak much; he kept his arms folded on the table. Next to the tall man, he seemed even smaller than usual, like his backbone had caved. The two of them did not match.

Hortense passed me in the hall, tapping me on the leg with one of her silver sticks. She did that sometimes to play around, but never when Felix was with me.

I waved. Hortense stopped.

Why do you go away from us? I signed. I pointed at Felix, then at myself, then at Hortense.

She glanced into the main room and saw what I was look-ing at. She waved her arms at me, then pointed at Felix. She flicked a hand in his direction, dismissing him. *Fuggim.* She said more, but I didn't understand.

She waited a moment, then walked on. Without looking over her shoulder, she waved for me to follow her. She turned around the corner.

I was about to follow when Felix spoke. He shouted, words snapping past his teeth, his hand slamming the table. He grabbed a piece of paper, scribbled hard, then thrust his middle finger in the man's face.

The man remained still, his face stiff. He seemed bored. He walked out a little while later, nodding at me as he passed. A nurse escorted him out the locked double doors.

Felix hunched over at the table. I sat across from him.

He says my father's coming soon, he signed. He wants me to tell the police, so they can take me away forever. Felix smiled, but his eyes didn't.

What are police?

Will Dr. Pearl tell them he pumped me full of insulin? he signed. Will Father Hoff tell them he broke my knuckles? Will my dad tell them he neglected me? Felix flicked his index and pinkie fingers at me. It's bullshit.

I don't want you to go away.

Please stop watching me in here, he signed.

I'm sorry.

It makes me angry, and I don't want you to see me angry. You're too beautiful for anger.

THE SUN WEAKENED, the hot weather faded into cool-ness, and the prairie changed from full bristling green to flat brown. Cold wind spurted through a crack beneath the window above my bed. I showed Mrs. Koepp, who taped over the crack. The tape fell soon off, and she gave me an extra blanket.

Why is it changing? I signed.

Happens every year, Felix signed. The Earth tilts away from the sun, so it gets colder. That's why we have four seasons.

I'd seen a picture of the Earth from a long way up in the sky, a bright blue ball giving off a soft white glow. I imagined it tilting, like a slowly falling building.

How far does it tilt? I signed.

It'll get colder and darker. You'll still see the sun.

Why can't it be sunny all the time?

Felix smiled. The Earth is too big for us to control. If we could lift it, we would.

Marvin had begun to hate me. I'd woken him up too many times. He wore earplugs but they didn't help, and he had started throwing his pillow at me. He stopped smiling at me in the hall, stopped looking at my drawings and sharing his comics when his parents brought him new ones. He probably asked to be moved, but the institution was bloated; most rooms on our floor had at least three or four people. Felix said the floors above and below us were crawling with people.

They think we're cattle, he signed, so they pack us in here and leave us to rot. If they wanted us to get better, they'd give us a better place to stay.

One day the staff dressed differently. Ms. Beddim wore a pointed hat and carried a small broom. Mr. Creel painted an enormous blue smile on his face. A pumpkin stood on the counter at the nurses' station—someone had carved a face into it. Orange and black words hung on the walls.

Felix hid his face behind his flattened hands. Halloween, he signed. People like to dress up.

In the main room, people scooped stringy white guts out of pumpkins and drew faces on them with markers. Anders and Bernice sat at the table painting people's faces using brushes and a tray of colors.

Let's go, I signed.

We sat down, and Anders painted a skull on Felix's face, and Bernice painted a black cat on mine. We went into the hall, and Ms. Beddim opened a bag full of small objects wrapped in orange, yellow, and red plastic. I reached inside and brought out one. She held the bag higher. *More!* I took out a handful of wrappers. Ms. Beddim offered Felix the bag and he took a few.

What are these? I signed.

Felix tore one of the wrappers and held up what looked like a small piece of shit. It smelled sweet. He put it in his mouth.

I tore open a wrapper, smelled the piece, put it in my mouth. I held it on my tongue and let it dissolve slowly. I never chewed.

You've never had candy? Felix signed.

Not like this.

Felix slid his right C-hand across the back of his flat left hand.

Church?

Chocolate.

I tore open two more pieces and put them both in my mouth. I bit through them, releasing more sweetness. I pushed the chocolate around with my tongue, painting the walls and ceiling and floor of my mouth with it, staining all my teeth with it. I did that with all the pieces until they were gone.

We ate lunch a short time later. The food disappointed.

You need to stop taking your medicine, Felix signed. Swallow the water, not the pill. I don't have a choice—they use a needle with me—but you have a choice.

Ms. Beddim stood along the wall watching us. I smiled a little at her. She aimed the end of her broom at me.

It helps with my bad dreams, I signed.

It's a way for the doctors and nurses to get inside you. They want you to rely on them. Some pills make you sweat, vomit, piss blood, some make your skin dry and crack, make your heart cave in.

Yours does that?

No.

What about Anders? Bernice? Hortense?

It helps some people, but you don't need it.

After lunch Felix told me to wait in the hall outside the dining room. When he came out, he pulled me into the bathroom. He checked the stalls, then brought a handful of raisins out of his pocket.

Pretend this is a pill, he signed.

He put one in his mouth and gave one to me.

This isn't a pill, I signed.

I said pretend.

What's pretend?

Picture this as a pill. See it as white, not brown.

Why?

Felix waved his hands. When the nurse gives you your pill, put it in your mouth and stick it to the roof of your mouth. If they check under your tongue, you'll be fine.

Those are food.

Watch me. He snapped his V-fingers out and trained them on himself.

He opened his mouth, lifted his tongue, and dipped his head forward so the raisin was hidden. Then he tilted his head back and showed me the raisin pasted to the roof of his mouth.

After that, he signed, walk to the bathroom and do this. He bent over and spit the raisin into the toilet and flushed it down. Use the toilet, he signed. Not the sink or garbage.

I nodded and popped the raisin into my mouth and chewed it and swallowed.

Do you understand what I said?

Yes.

What'd I say?

Come to the bathroom, spit it in the toilet.

Swallow the water, not the pill.

I want more color on my face.

Swallow the water, not the pill, Felix signed.

That night most of the young people sat in the main room and watched a story on the TV. Felix and I sat at the back eating more chocolate.

When I looked up at the TV, I jolted. What looked like a huge dog mixed with a man—all thick gray hair and dull blue eyes—stood on two legs and pulled its lips back from its sweaty yellow teeth. I dropped my chocolate.

Felix touched my arm. It's just a movie, he signed.

The dog's face filled the TV. Its bloody teeth snapped; I could smell its breath. I leaned back in my chair.

It's okay, Felix signed. It's not real.

On the TV, people chased the dog through their village as it climbed buildings trying to get away. I stood and shouted. Everyone turned toward me, and I ran out of the room.

I never slept that night. I kept my blanket over my face, too frightened to look out the window and see the dog-man or the men with the body.

That's what we do on Halloween, Felix signed the next morning. We scare each other. It's supposed to be fun.

Being scared isn't fun, I signed. I thought that dog would come get me.

It wasn't a dog. He pointed up the medication line. Remember what to do?

At the head of the line, Ms. Beddim handed out the pills. She didn't have her pointy hat on anymore.

Swallow the water, Felix signed.

Not the pill, I signed.

Ms. Beddim gave me my pill and a paper cup of water. I stuck the pill against the roof of my mouth and swallowed the water. Ms. Beddim nodded. I stepped past her, then turned to Felix. He waved me forward.

I ambled toward the green door of the men's room a short way down the hall—and the pill fell and tumbled down my throat, choking off my breathing. I leaned against the wall, coughing and heaving. I spit the white tablet onto the floor.

Mr. Creel helped me straighten up. He picked up the pill and led me back to the nurses' station. Ms. Beddim was sticking a needle in Felix's arm; Mr. Creel tossed the pill in the garbage.

Ms. Beddim gave me a new pill and a new cup of water. Mr. Creel watched me. I swallowed the water again. As I started to leave, Mr. Creel dropped his hand on my shoulder. He made his flattened hand into a mouth that he opened along with his mouth.

I lifted my tongue, then as I set it back down, the pill dropped onto my tongue. I snapped my mouth shut but Mr. Creel pointed. *Ey.*

What do I do? I signed.

Felix shook his head. Mr. Creel glanced at him. Ms. Beddim gave me another cup of water and pointed to my throat. *Zwalloh.* Mr. Creel grinned and spoke to Felix, nodding toward me. Felix turned red.

Later, at breakfast, he told me what Mr. Creel had said. *Shouldn't have any trouble swallowing, should he?*

The next day, I started receiving injections.

THICK WHITE BITS of what looked like dust began falling from the sky, like it was collapsing bit by bit. It whitened everything, erasing the line between ground and sky, providing extra cover to whatever bubbled under the prairie. I still saw the burial each night, the men digging into the frozen white ground with ease.

The green hallways and pink rooms became cold as metal. I struggled to find warm clothes that fit me. They kept the clothes in gray plastic bins—everything was too big or too small or too holey or too itchy. Felix told me all the clothes were laundered downstairs and donated by strangers or left behind by dead patients.

I asked him about the room where people fed clothes into machines.

They make curtains and other things, he signed. They're not allowed to make clothes for us—they have a contract or something. I once asked for a new shirt. They told me to go to the bins. They sell everything they make here. They make it cheap.

George left the day after the first heavy snow. He stood at the double doors hugging Bernice and Hortense and Ms. Beddim and shaking Dr. O's hand. He looked much thinner. I gave him a small wave.

George approached me, reached into his bag, and pulled out a black shirt with a bird drawn on it. The bird had wide yellow eyes and pointed ears. It spread its wings across the chest. He unfolded it and held it up against my chest, then pressed it into my hands.

Thank you, I signed.

His eyes narrowed, like he was disappointed. He turned and stepped through the doors.

I put the shirt on. It was stiff, like new, and much too big. Yet it hugged me.

New people kept coming into the institution. Different faces. Different ways of moving through the world. Each morning the medication line stretched from the nurses' station all the way down the hall; everyone waited longer for their food trays at mealtimes.

Two young men whose names I didn't know worked with Marvin to build houses out of their mattresses and pillows and posed like the people in Marvin's comic books. A girl with red hair kept watching Felix and I signing. I asked her if she was Deaf. She said something I didn't understand and shook her head.

Felix said the third floor was full. All the doctors and nurses were busy.

Dr. Pearl might really start killing people now, he signed, if he hasn't already. The more people are here, the less they can help them. We have to stay strong until we get a chance to leave.

One morning Felix wasn't in the medication line. I asked Ms. Beddim where he was. She shrugged as she injected me.

I walked down the hall rubbing my shoulder. The two boys who played with Marvin stood along the wall hunched over a comic. They had the same brown eyes and freckles. They might've been brothers.

I peered inside the main room. Felix and a man with blond hair and a mustache sat across from each other, signing to each other. Both their hands moved stiffly but quickly, much quicker than when Felix and I conversed with each other. I tucked myself out of sight and hid along the wall outside the door.

The man's fingers whirled and whipped. It took me a moment to adjust to his speed.

Seems okay here, he signed. They treat you well?

Felix shook his head.

It was here or jail. You'd never survive jail.

What took you so long? Felix signed. You never come to see me.

I got a new job. Did Father Hoff tell you?

Stop sending him here. I don't want to see him.

I thought you'd like to see a familiar face.

Felix pointed at a large gold band on the man's wrist. Where'd you get that watch?

Bought it for myself. Birthday gift. You like it? I got a new car, too. I finally sold grandpa's shop. A little something to celebrate.

You know what they've done to me? Felix signed. What they do to others here?

The man tapped his F-hand twice on his heart.

That's not my name anymore, Felix signed. With his F-hand Felix drew a halo around his head.

The man smiled but his eyes blackened. The air between them hardened as they signed.

I'm not calling you that, his father signed.

Where's Mom?

I don't know. We're not together anymore.

Does she know I'm here?

I don't know where she is.

You know I don't belong here.

I'm selling the house, his father signed.

Felix sat up. The space between him and his father began to churn; a storm seemed to rise between them. I leaned toward them, then pulled myself back. They didn't see me. A wide barred window stood behind them and their fingers chewed up the empty space lit by the white prairie.

Where will I live?

If you want to come home, you have to— His father made a sign that looked a lot like my name.

Felix shook his head. Confess what? he signed.

The fire. The murder. Tell the police everything.

Felix slid his eyes away from his father.

You were walking back from the river, his father signed. You were shaking. You didn't say why.

I was cold.

Did you push him into the river?

Why don't you support me? I'm your son.

Your doctor says you admitted to the school fire. Says you're controlling another kid in here.

Did you ever think of talking to me? Asking how I am? What I'm feeling?

Doctor says you're gay, too. Is that true?

No, not true.

His father leaned back and pulled at his mustache. You always preferred your mother, he signed. That explains it.

Felix opened and closed his fists. His head tilted. What'd you tell the police when they picked me up? That your Deaf son is insane? Do they know you're Deaf, too?

His father sat still for a moment. You got a letter from the Vatican, he signed.

What'd they say?

You, a saint? Only great people become saints.

Show me the letter.

Do you think God would allow a killer to speak for him? A bent killer?

Felix's eyes flashed with water. Why won't you let me explain? he signed. I'm just trying to love people, but I get punished for it. They inject me and put me into comas and drive me into seizures. I almost died.

His father shrugged, lifted his eyebrows.

The truth of what happened is between me and God, Felix signed. God has heard me and forgiven me for it. Why can't you?

Man up, his father signed. Take responsibility. Confess.

I thought of stepping into the room, since they seemed to be saying my name, but the way they said it made it look like they meant something else. I stayed put.

You take responsibility, Felix signed. You didn't look after me. You're not a father. You're not even a man.

Felix's father leaned forward like he wanted to slap Felix, then he sat back. You're sick, he signed. You're an animal. You're not my son anymore.

Felix smiled. A stiff smile. He wiped his eyes.

Once you turn eighteen next year, his father signed, you're done. You get nothing of mine when I die, nothing of Grandpa's or Grandma's, either. You're out of the family.

Felix balled up his fists, then flexed his fingers. I want nothing of yours, he signed. I hate that I have your blood.

I'm giving you a week, his father signed. If you don't tell the police by then, I'm telling them.

Felix smiled. It took you this long to figure it all out? You're a lazy, selfish fuck-up. Grandma and Grandpa would be ashamed.

His father bit his lip. His face contorted as he forced blankness into his eyes. Grandma and Grandpa never saw what you're really like, you little Satanist.

I don't need you, Felix signed. I've left the past behind and washed everything away. I've started a new church, and when I leave here, I'll spread my gospel throughout the land. You mean nothing to me anymore.

His father smiled. You're worse than I thought, he signed.

He stood from the table and pulled on his coat. Then he sat back down.

Listen to me, he signed. There's no God, no devil, no Jesus. We take care of ourselves. That's what your mother did, and now it's my turn. There's no promised land, no divine plan, no saints watching over us. We just do our best.

Felix stared. You call this your best? he signed. Why did you and Mom have me?

His father shrugged. He tapped his chin with his Y-hand. It was a mistake, he signed. He stood again and zipped his coat. One week, he signed. Merry Christmas, son.

His father kept his eyes on the floor as he passed me.

Felix remained sitting at the table. Alone in the big room, he looked smaller than I'd ever seen him. I sat beside him. His face clenched like he was holding in a scream. Then he made a face like he wanted to smile but couldn't. He signed, All I have now are you and God. God will never leave me. Neither will you, right?

I nodded and rubbed his back as he covered his head and sobbed into the table.

◉

I DIDN'T SEE Dr. O again until all the windows had white U-shapes of frost at the bottom and the hallway was full of red and white striped hooks and green tree shapes. When I sat in his office, his face had new lines. His lips were flaky like he hadn't had a drink in a long time.

A man sat beside him. Short with soft curly hair and pink cheeks.

Good morning, Dr. O said. We have a new interpreter today.

The man signed for him. I couldn't believe how long his fingers were in contrast to his body. The overhead light flashed off his glasses and hid his eyes.

How are you? Dr. O said.

Where's the woman? I signed.

She wasn't— The man signed something unclear.

What?

She couldn't come. She had other things to do.

I liked her signs.

Dr. O nodded. I'm sorry that it's been so long since we last met.

The interpreter signed quickly. I found it hard to pay attention to him.

Slow down, I signed. Again, please.

Our budget for interpreters isn't that high, he signed, plus the hospital's over capacity right now.

Over what?

There are too many people here. We're not giving you and your peers the attention you deserve.

Why not let them go? Build a house for them?

Dr. O licked his lips. I wish we could, he said. Are you still having dreams? Still seeing the child being buried at night?

The medicine helped for a while, but not anymore. Sometimes it's a bigger body, like me.

Just remind yourself it's not real. Shut your eyes and count to ten.

I'm not good with numbers.

I've been here at night—nobody ever goes out there at night-time. Okay?

I stayed still for a moment, wrestling with that thought.

I understand you had to switch to injections, Dr. O said. There was a problem with you taking pills?

I didn't have a problem.

The interpreter spelled something too quick for me to understand.

What?

The interpreter signed slower. I still had a hard time understanding. Something about his gentleness bothered me.

Did Felix tell you to stop taking them?

No.

We need to nip this in the bud.

Bud?

Out of all the people on this floor, you might have the best chance at recovering. Felix is holding you back. He's affecting you negatively, so we need to separate you. I realize things will be more difficult, as you won't be able to communicate as well, but it's the best thing for you.

The bottom fell out of my stomach. We won't be together anymore? I signed. Don't send him upstairs. He hates it—that doctor is brutal.

I can't share that with you, but I can say that he'll be taken care of. I do have some good news.

What news?

We've found a placement for you in a group home in Saskatoon. It's a safe facility run by good people. You'll be transferred on January second.

I blinked. My breath hitched in my chest. The interpreter's hands seemed to melt together, his fingers like dancing sticks.

I'm moving?

You can go to school, you can learn to read and pursue your own interests, find out what you want to do.

How will I understand without Felix?

They'll find a way to help you, and in time you'll be able to understand for yourself. You're observant. You're young. You deserve a chance at a better life.

Where's Felix moving?

I can't tell you.

I slapped at the interpreter's hands. He backed away from me in his chair and held his hands up. I shouted at him and stood with my fist raised. Dr. O stepped between us.

I love him, I signed. I don't want to leave.

Dr. O dabbed his hands on the air, trying to get me to sit down.

I don't want to leave, I signed.

You have to. We're over capacity, and you don't need to be here.

Felix can come with me.

What's good for Felix is not good for you. We'll have a plan in place for you to follow. We won't send you out there unprepared.

What about my father?

He won't be able to find you. I read in the newspaper that he's either dead or he's long gone.

Don't take Felix away from me.

I understand that you two have a strong connection, but it's not healthy. We need to focus on you, preparing you to leave. You'll be able to shop for yourself, buy your own clothes.

I paid no more attention to the man's signs. I stood up and turned to the door. Dr. O tapped me and said something; the interpreter's fingers churned over his shoulder.

We're not done, he said.

I started to open the door. Dr. O shut it. He signed to me. Sit down, please.

I yanked the door open. When I'd gone into the office, Felix had been sitting on the bench across the hall writing in his book. Now Irene sat there, crouched over and flexing her body, trying to calm her rattling limbs.

Something flicked at the corner of my eye. Down the hall Mr. Creel and another uniformed man were carrying Felix toward the double doors. Ms. Beddim walked in front of them. Felix thrashed, kicked, bucked, screamed. I ran toward him, but Dr. O seized me by my shoulders. The hallway was full of people, but I saw only Felix. Even from all the way down the hall and in the midst of his skirmish, he locked his eyes onto me. We cried out for each other. Dr. O held me in place with a hard hug. Though he was slender, he was also strong. I couldn't break his grip.

Felix disappeared behind the double doors, then Ms. Beddim closed and locked them. When Dr. O let me go, I ran to the doors and tried to see Felix through their thin windows, but he was gone.

I collapsed to the floor. Ms. Beddim hugged me; I pushed away from her. Further down the hall, one of the young men who'd been playing with Marvin held Felix's gospel book in his hand and was flipping through the pages. He smiled at me. I snapped to my feet and surged down the hall. The smile dropped from his face. He held the book out for me and started to back away. I tackled him and landed on top of him, pinning his arms down with my knees, and punched him in the face. I hit him so hard the sound of my fist bashing his cheek echoed up my arm and filled my head. Someone kicked me in the back, probably his brother. I gripped the young man's hair and kept punching. His face turned bloody. I was aware of Irene on the bench a few feet away. She slid to the end of the bench and made herself as small as possible.

Several hands grabbed me and hauled me off the young man. Dr. O, Ms. Beddim, and two or three of the uniformed men. Mrs. Koepp stuck a needle into my shoulder, and my body became rope—I hung off their arms and could barely lift my head. The young man's brother helped him sit up. He looked as though all the holes in his face had been mashed shut.

I searched for the book. Ms. Beddim picked it up and walked away as the others carried me to my room.

ROYAL SASKATCHEWAN PSYCHIATRIC
HOSPITAL—WAKAW, SK

PATIENT PROGRESS REPORT

Patient Name:	DOB:
Felix Jimson	30 Oct 1963
Admitting Psychiatrist:	Admittance Date:
Dr. Harrison Pearl	2 March 1980
Reporting Psychiatrist:	Report Date:
Dr. Harrison Pearl	21 December 1980

ACTIVE MEDICATION(S)

Serentil—200 mg injection (increased dosage)

PROBLEMS AND PROGRESS

—Diagnosis: paranoid-type schizophrenia & sexual deviation

Patient has shown little progress due to persistent insular attitude. Increasing evidence of sexual deviance ("sexual orientation disturbance" as per DSM II). Shows some intelligence but still refuses to abide basic rules. Therapy sessions and group talk have had little impact, even after several months, suggesting lack of efficacy. Anger and delusions of persecution appear to persist; he has recruited another patient into his fantasies/ deviance. Insulin and hydrotherapy had proved effective in curbing misbehavior but appear to be short-term solutions; deterrent effects are weaker than hoped for.

In conference, Dr. Okimasis suggested outdated therapies are exacerbating patient's symptoms. Suggestion was soon dismissed.

Patient now secured in Ward 3. Remittance to prison an option though am not ready to admit failure. Chemical castration (or surgical, depending on available surgeons) to follow, along with psychosurgery. Long-term corporeal correction best option for peace of mind.

RECOMMENDATION(S)

Continued constant supervision of patient and companion; inquire about available urological surgeons; check stores of medroxyprogesterone acetate and restock if necessary.

BURN

FELIX'S BOOKS AND clothes were gone from his room the next day. A new man lay in his bed. I signed to all the nurses, When is Felix coming back? They didn't answer. I searched for Dr. O but couldn't find him. I asked to send a message to Felix; nobody understood. I tried to get through the double doors a few times, but no one would let me through. No one went outside anyway—it was too cold. The wind spurting through the crack beneath my window had become frigid. I saw my breath at all times. Marvin and I wore as many shirts and pants as we could. We fought over blankets. Mr. Creel brought a man to fix the crack in the window, and when I came back a splotchy white patch covered it. I felt no wind, yet the cold hung in the air.

One day everyone woke up to find small boxes of chocolate outside their doors. Family members gathered in the main room, and Bernice, Hortense, Irene, Marvin, and a few other young people stood in front of everyone in the main room swaying back and forth and speaking in slow unison. Mr. Creel played the piano. Ms. Beddim gave me a brand-new sweater, red and scratchy and warm.

On my way to the dining hall, I stopped at Anders's room and peered inside. The pink walls were completely covered in drawings. The fluttering colorful pages had transformed the room; stepping inside was like stepping into another country. Anders stood up off his bed and gave me a drawing of Felix sitting in the dining room, his face soft and sad but on his way to happy.

I searched the shadows behind Felix for eyes or faces but found none. I pulled a folded drawing from my pocket and handed it to Anders. He shook my hand and lay back on his bed.

I folded Anders's drawing and put it in my pocket.

Just before dinner that night, Dr. Pearl walked through our hallways. I hadn't seen him since I'd been strapped to the bed upstairs. His hands were stuffed in his white pockets, and he smiled stiffly as he walked.

Where's Felix? I signed.

Dr. Pearl said something and kept smiling.

Don't hurt him, I signed.

He said something else. His smile opened—his gray teeth flashed at me. He tapped the side of his nose with his finger, then walked away down the hall.

A FEW NIGHTS later as I walked back to my room, I saw Marvin with the two young men. They'd stacked several chairs in the main room to make a house or castle with walls as high as my chin. They crawled through the narrow passages, and Ms. Beddim laughed and spoke to them as they crawled.

Just as I dropped to my knees and started crawling to one of the openings, Mr. Creel stepped into the room. He started toward the rickety castle, then stopped. His nose wrinkled. He said something; his face tensed. I stood back up; everyone stiffened and glanced at the ceiling, all of them reacting to something I couldn't see.

As we all stepped into the hall, a nurse came running, shouting, her face red. Mr. Creel turned and dashed toward the ward's main entrance, and everyone began to scatter. Ms. Beddim waved to me; her eyebrows were flatter than usual. I followed her and Marvin toward our room.

What's happening? I signed.

When we got to our room, Ms. Beddim threw our coats and hats at us and pointed us down the hallway, then she ran off, shouting at people as she went.

I clutched my coat. I smelled something bitter. Smoke. Fire. Marvin grabbed my hand, and we ran down the hall.

The double doors were wide open. Everyone was rushing through them and putting on their coats and gloves. A box of gloves and scarves stood by the doors. I grabbed a pair of gloves and put on my coat. As we passed through the doors, I felt a soft thrill beneath my panic. I was among a group of people, not separate but running together.

People crammed into the narrow hall. Marvin lagged behind. He kept trying to stop and move toward the wall. People crowded between us. I peered back and saw him fall and disappear. More people fell in front of me. I kneed some-one in the head by accident—I think it was Irene.

We packed into the outside hallway, spread out, and ran down the two sets of stairs. People from the third floor joined us, smoke following them and curling down on top of us as they descended. I couldn't see Felix. I turned back and tried to push through everyone to get to the third floor, but the rushing river of bodies stopped me and forced me toward the building's front door.

With each step, I kept looking for Felix's shiny blond head. Elbows jutted into my ribs. Hands closed over mine on the stair railing. People stepped on my heels—my shoes nearly slipped off. Everyone's odd smells ganged together to make a collective anxious smell that made me lightheaded.

The cold slapped me in the face before I reached the front door. I hiked my coat as high as it could go. I slipped on the icy steps but clapped my feet down on the hard stone before I could fall. I pulled on my gloves. Both of them were right hands: one blue, one black—I had to hold my thumb at an odd angle.

Everyone gathered and huddled away from the building. A bright orange light stretched across the grounds. I glanced up. The whole corner of the third floor was on fire. Enormous flames roiled and trembled upward from the broken windows. I backed into the crowd. Two women with thicker coats pressed their bodies against me, but I pulled away from them.

The staff stood near the doors waving everyone out. Ms. Beddim and Mrs. Koepp walked up and down the line of people while Mr. Creel gave people blankets. Marvin stumbled out of the door, his nose bleeding, his coat halfway on.

I searched for Felix. Everyone's faces were tucked in shadow or lit up orange. They all looked different. I had to stare at a girl for a long time to recognize she was Bernice. She and Hortense and Irene huddled together, wrapping their arms around each other. Bernice and Hortense held their hands out toward me. I walked past them.

A uniformed man waved from a third-floor window, a flailing shadow against the yellow and orange dancing behind him. He coughed and banged on the window. He ducked away for a moment, then returned with a chair. He shattered the window and began beating the outside bars. Smoke rushed up from behind him. He rammed the chair against the bars, hunched over and coughing, each hit of the chair weaker than the last. He coughed so hard he folded in two and sank down beneath the window.

People screamed, hurling their voices at the building and at each other. Mr. Creel handed a blanket to a woman, and a man standing behind her grabbed the blanket and yanked it away. Two other uniformed men started shoving each other, their feet kicking up dirty snow. One man lunged forward trying to punch the other, but he slipped on the ice and fell hard on his elbow. The other man jumped on top of him. Many people jumped up and down or huddled together to keep warm. The clouds from our breath rose together and joined the thick smoke coursing over our heads. I couldn't see the sky.

The fire crawled across the third floor, snagging on curtains, blackening the bricks and the white bars. I tucked my hands under my arms and shivered as I searched the crowd. I saw someone about Felix's height wearing a hat. I pushed the hat off the person's head and saw a swirl of long black hair. The woman shouted at me and hit me on the shoulder.

The ground shook, and a spurt of heat raked along the back of my head. I turned. Something had exploded on the third floor. Fists of flame punched through two windows, and glass shot out at the crowd. Everyone shielded their faces and moved further back.

I stooped to pull my shoe back into place. Someone threw a blanket over my head and began leading me away from the crowd. I tried to stop, but they dug their nails into my arm and pulled me along.

We rounded the corner of the building. From under the blanket, I spotted the brick near my feet. I yanked the blanket away. The fire shone bright on a blond head.

I made a noise and hugged Felix. He pushed back from me.

Let's go, he signed.

Felix huddled with me under the blanket. We ran around the back of the building toward a line of thick green trees. Our shoes sank into the hardened snow, the crusty edges jutting into our ankles.

We ran until the orange glow of the fire could no longer touch us and ice prickled and hardened in our chests and we could see the sky again, our breath making hard white clouds.

What are we doing? I signed, my hands cramped by the gloves.

We'll find a place, he signed. There are houses over there.

He pointed toward a blank field. I saw nothing but snow.

It's cold, I signed.

Felix pulled a hat over his head and started running through the field, taking hopping strides through the snow, his blanket puffing out behind him. I followed. About halfway through the field, I caught up and we began running together, nestled under the blanket. But that was too slow, and we started running separately again.

We crossed the field. A long way behind us, the building burned orange and gray. Black smoke rushed up from the windows, the yellow from the fire playing on it like light on a screen.

It climbed and hung over our heads. The cold air gnawed on my cheeks. Before us were more fields and wire fences and in the distance the road leading away from the building.

Give me your gloves, Felix signed.

I gave them to him and jammed my hands under my arms. He fit his hands into both gloves, shaking his head at the second right-hand.

There are no houses here, I signed. My signs suffered—my hands shook.

Red lights whipped across the field. Felix grabbed my arm and dropped to his knees, pulling me down with him. Two long red trucks steered up the road toward the building. A few minutes later, more red lights appeared. A white van, followed by another red truck. Their lights didn't reach us. The darkness hid us.

We stood and walked along the fence. The smoke followed us, a gray spill forming a puddle in the sky.

Eventually, the moon emerged, covering us in white light, our blue shadows hardened shapes on the snow. I shivered and touched my nose, flicked it. I couldn't feel it. My feet felt emptied. Snow and ice clung to my thin shoes. I no longer felt the hard edge of the snow against my ankles.

Hot wind brushed against my neck. I stopped and turned around, shaking, rubbing my hands. I saw only our footprints in the snow.

Felix came back and wrapped the blanket around me. We can't stop, he signed.

Go away! I signed to the field. It's following us.

There's nothing there.

Felix gave me back the gloves. I pulled them on and felt something sticky in the fingers. I pulled one hand out. Blood had smeared all over my fingers.

I looked closer at Felix. Blood soaked his hands, and a trickle of blood zigged down his face, shining black in the moonlight.

I pointed at him. What? I signed.

He shook his head and blew into his hands. I did the same.

The doctor hurt you? I signed.

He smiled. He won't hurt anyone anymore, he signed.

He stooped down and rubbed the blood on the snow. I did the same, then put the glove back on. It was still sticky.

We kept following the fence, sometimes leaning on the cold wire for balance, until it ended at a road. We stepped out of the snow; the hardness of the road slapped against the bottoms of my feet. My chest tightened. It stung to breathe, and I coughed. My eyelashes kept sticking together. We saw no lights, no houses, no vehicles. Felix asked for the gloves again. My fingers stuck inside the gloves, and it took me a few minutes to get them off. I tried to sign but it was too cold. Even with the gloves on I couldn't feel my fingers.

We started running, trying to stay under the blanket. We soon pulled further apart and stretched the blanket until I dropped it, and it flapped behind Felix. I ran closer to him and pulled the blanket back over my shoulders. I tried to time our strides so we both had some of the blanket, but I had to keep slowing down. His legs were shorter.

The road rose over a small hill, and when we reached the top we spotted a thin white light sprouting through the darkness a long way away. We ran toward the light. Felix slipped on the ice, and I caught him before he fell.

As we got closer a square shape began to form under the light, rising up out of the white and blue prairie. We ran harder. Felix tugged the blanket under his arm, and I swiped the ice from my eyelashes.

At last we reached a small gray building that stood at the base of a tall metal tower. A white light jutted out of the building's wall. Felix tried the door, but it didn't open. A red metal sign with a jagged shape in the middle had been screwed into the door. He took a few steps back, then ran and jammed his shoulder against the door, but it didn't move. I tried kicking it—the impact spiked up my leg. We took turns kicking and throwing our bodies into it, shivering and stamping our feet between each attempt. Felix backed up all the way to the tower, then ran at the door and kicked it, but his foot slid sideways, and he fell against the door. I stood fixed in place and kicked the door multiple times. Finally, it skidded inward a little. I yelled and kicked the door again, and it swung open into the darkened building. We dodged inside and shut the door.

There were no windows. We stood in pure darkness, our backs against the wall. Something poked into my back. I felt Felix move, his hands patting my chest then the wall.

A light snapped on, a flat yellow glow that stretched through the small room and slackened toward the corners. Rows of red buttons and silver switches lined the walls. Black rods that looked like dozens of bowls stacked on top of each other jutted out from white panels with fans embedded in them. A chair balanced on small wheels stood tucked beneath a table.

Felix pulled out the chair and sat down, blowing hard into his hands, his face a shiny white. Clumps of ice clung to his eyebrows and eyelashes. I sat on the floor beside him, brushing the ice from my eyes. I shucked off my shoes and rubbed my feet. Our breath had stopped forming clouds.

Felix walked to the bucket in the corner and pissed in it. I had to piss too, but memories of pissing in a bucket blocked me.

What is this? I signed.

He butted his two hooked index fingers together. Electricity.

He circled two of the red buttons with his pointed finger. I bet we could turn off all the lights in this area if we wanted, he signed.

A block of drawers and cupboards stood along one wall. Felix pulled on all of them. Most were locked but a few skidded open. Felix scooped out pens and tools and silver clips and dropped them on the floor.

They gave us soup, he signed. It was like water. Everyone could smell what you were eating downstairs. A few people cried. They wanted Christmas food. Chocolate, turkey, potatoes.

What's Christmas?

Never mind. Felix rubbed his hands together. I knelt down close to the black rods, but he waved me away. Not there, he signed.

I haven't seen you, I signed.

Felix shook his hands out. Christmas celebrates the birth of Christ, he signed. People give presents to each other and eat good food. Maybe one day you and I will have days named after us. Feast of Felix.

Aren't all the days named? Wednesday, Monday.

Not like that. Thursday was also Christmas. Some days are more special than others.

Felix picked up a metal tool and jammed it into one of the cupboard doors. He pushed on the tool, leaning forward with all his weight. The door didn't move.

I stood and put my hands over top of his on the tool. We took a breath and shoved together, and the door snapped open, wood splintering off the side.

Tall plastic books stood inside the cupboard. Felix hauled them out—blue and white and yellow pages flapped open. He swept his hand across the bare shelf. *Fugg*, Felix said.

In the far corner stood a metal closet. Felix tried opening it. Beside the closet a red metal cylinder with a black hose hung on the wall. Felix picked it up and slammed it into the closet doorknob, slammed it again and again until it broke off and the closet jarred open.

Heavy coats and gloves hung like empty bodies in the closet. Large boots stood on the floor. Felix jerked the coats and gloves off the wires, and I picked up a coat and pulled it over myself.

No fucking food, Felix signed.

He kicked the closet, then sat beside me and tried on one of the coats. His hands were like small searching balls inside the long loose sleeves.

We sat still for a moment. I kept looking at him, waiting for him to sign again. His lips moved a few times. I don't know what he said.

I stuck my hands just outside my coat. They trembled, felt brittle. I rubbed them together.

Once the fire's over, he signed, they'll be looking for us. They'll send the police.

Police?

They put people in jail. They have guns. They cuff your hands behind your back. We should leave—they'll see us during the day.

Go back out?

Let's go.

It's cold. I want to sleep here.

We need food.

Felix buttoned up his coat and tossed me a pair of gloves. We'll find a house or a shed, he signed. He kicked off his shoes and stepped into a pair of boots way too big for his feet. I did the same, the heavy boots cradling my feet.

Before we stepped back outside, Felix took his hands out of his gloves. We're not free yet, he signed. We're almost there. This is our exodus. Remember I said we have a path to follow.

Outside? The road?

The path to freedom and beauty. Felix's eyes glimmered. Did you miss me?

Yes. I tried to go upstairs, but they didn't let me. They injected me.

He hugged me hard, pressing his chest into me. Through his jacket and pants, I felt his dick harden against mine. He kissed me and pulled me down to the floor, his icy hands sliding under my sleeves. He pushed his pants down—I did the same. We kissed again, and I could feel the small dent in his tongue sliding along my tongue, and he pressed his forehead against mine like he did during the ceremony, then he eased me around by my shoulders, so he knelt behind me. I tried to turn to see his hands, but he kept me facing forward. He rubbed my back, then gripped my hips. The hot blush roared up in my crotch, and I blew warm breath into my hand and reached down and began stroking myself. Felix pushed himself into me with an urgent thrust like a man twice his size. I gasped. My back arched. He pushed and pulled, back and forth, digging his cold fingers into my hips. I held myself up with one arm and used the other to stroke myself. He reached down and put his hand on mine and helped me stroke. His cold hands thrilled me.

We clenched together as we finished. He tucked his arms across my chest, holding me tight. He leaned down and put all his weight on me. He kissed my back, then pulled away and got dressed, wiping his eyes, smiling.

You okay? I signed.

You can't imagine, he signed. You can't imagine. My apostle. My love.

He bounced to his feet. Words and symbols were written in black on the wall beneath the buttons and switches, and with his two jabbing fingers he pushed all the buttons and flipped all the switches back and forth, sliding his feet along the floor so they never left his boots, his eyes black and enormous. He grinned. The yellow light above us faded to black, then slowly came on again. We pulled on our coats and heavy gloves and stepped back into the cold.

The white light outside was out. The wind pressed on us but didn't seep through our coats.

I wagged my gloved finger on the air. Where?

Felix beckoned for me to follow, strode down the path, and turned onto the road.

We walked, warmer but more awkward, Felix dragging his oversized shoes over the ice, our shadows ghoulish hulks that hid how skinny we were. A few times I felt warm breath on my neck, and each time I ignored it.

I peered back once to see a narrow line of smoke edged with orange spilling up into the sky. I wondered about everyone we'd left behind. I was glad George left when he did.

The wind kept pressing. I hid my chin and nose under my coat. Soon I smelled metal. Something loosened inside my nose, and I touched my nose with my sleeve. Blood slipped down past my lips and off my chin.

I tapped Felix.

What happened? he signed.

I don't know.

Did someone hit you?

No.

Must be the cold. My grandpa used to get nosebleeds in winter.

I wiped my nose with my sleeve again—the blood spread in a thick smear. I kept my nose under my coat, pinching my nostrils and breathing through my mouth. If blood dripped onto my tongue, I swallowed it.

I scanned the white fields. Several shapes rose from them, large and small, all covered in white, and I started thinking that dogs and ghosts hid beneath the snow, and if we stepped into the snow again, a hundred jaws would chomp on our legs and dig in their teeth and pull us down into Hell. The moonlight shifted—our shadows crowded around our feet. I thought I saw the snow move, and I made a noise, but Felix kept walking.

I hurried to stay close to him, focusing on his back, trusting his direction.

See that? Felix signed.

In the distance, the hard edges of a building stuck out past the trees, black and blocky against the white prairie.

We ran, or waddled, our sleeves slapping against each other, our feet skidding over the road and knocking rocks loose from the ice. The building inched out from the trees as we got closer. A short building, only one level, but wider than the last one. Older looking. No lights on outside. In the front was a wooden door with tall windows on either side of it. Tire marks in the snow curled toward and away from the building.

An old car with no windows or tires stood in the back. At the top of the building was a sign with thick white writing.

What's that say? I signed.

Felix pulled on the front door. It didn't budge. He peered through one of the windows, then strode around the back, past the old car. He found another door with a small window beside it. He picked up a cement block from under the car, tucked both hands beneath it, and hurled the block through the glass, shattering it.

He reached through the broken window and opened the door.

A sour smell like old rot flared up at us. He turned on the light. In the corner stood a table with papers and a machine with numbers on the buttons; on the wall was a large piece of paper divided into blocks with a number in each. A large white box stood in the far corner, and along another wall, cans were piled on top of each other: red and orange and purple and green.

Felix grabbed one of the red cans, opened it, and took a long drink. He handed me one.

I studied it. One word written in white, a white swirl underneath it. I tilted it back and forth and felt the liquid inside shifting. I popped the top. Brown liquid spurted out. Felix smiled.

I drank the warm sweet drink, bubbles crowding in my throat. Felix finished his, threw his can away, and stepped through a doorway into the next room. I put my can down. It was too sweet. I found pieces of paper towel and wiped my nose. Crusty blood broke off my face in tiny black flakes.

I followed Felix into the next room. It was all shelves and glass doors, all of them full of food and drink. The light was soft whitish blue—I could barely see the labels. Cracks trailed along the dirty brown floor.

What is this? I signed.

Felix tore open a shiny green bag and shoved a handful of small pieces into his mouth.

I missed these, he signed. Potato chips.

He tossed a bag to me. I opened it and put a few chips in my mouth. My head filled with salt and crunching.

Felix dumped the bag into his mouth, then opened another.

Whose food is this? Does someone live here?

No.

You broke the window.

Felix finished another bag of chips. As he chewed, he signed, I'm hungry. I need to eat.

We ate more chips. Felix made us sandwiches with bread and a round kind of meat. I drank a carton of milk, and Felix ate a box of cookies, then opened a metal box on the front counter and pulled small pieces of colored paper out of it.

The wall near the front of the store had black glasses and tools and gloves and hats and knives. Felix took a large knife from the wall and weighed it in his hand, pressing his finger against the blade.

You pick one, he signed.

Felix lifted a smaller knife from the wall and held it out for me. I shook my head.

We'll need them, he signed. He set the knife down, and his fingers blurred in the shadows. I caught only a few things. After us. Not. Back there. They think. Dangerous. Can't thumb car. Need take.

Can you slow? I signed.

Felix backed into the dim light. I still had to squint.

I have to go home, he signed. There's a great demon inside me, and I need to get rid of it. I need your help.

I pointed at the knife. Why do you need that?

I want to help you, too—remove all your pain so you can be free for the rest of your life. We have the same pain, and we can heal each other together. Understand? All your bad dreams, the dogs and the bodies at night, they'll go away if you help me.

I don't want mind pictures anymore, I signed. No bodies or dead dogs or father.

No more father. Just love, peace, and light.

We can love now?

Yes.

I'm glad you're with me, I signed.

Felix smiled.

I'm not by myself this time, I signed.

Your love is magnificent, he signed.

His fingers danced strong and clear, weaving a spell even in the dim light. He stood solid as a statue, smiling wide, like nothing or no one could touch him.

He handed me the knife. I took it.

I DREAMT THAT I walked the prairies, my bare feet brushing over the grass, the air full of dirt. I knew any minute the ground would open, and they'd finally pull me under. I walked slowly. It was useless to run.

The ground shook, and I stopped walking. At the distant edge of the horizon the prairie began to split. A deep jagged fracture that reminded me of broken crackers formed on the horizon's edge. I stood still as the crack rushed toward me like a starving mouth.

Something knocked against my foot. I opened my eyes. The floor shook as a woman collapsed to the floor in front of me, mouth and eyes wide open, her face landing near my feet, her white hair flaring up from under her green hat. I cried out and scrambled behind a shelf. Felix stood over her gripping the handle of a tall metal drink container. The woman started to push up off the floor—Felix hit her on the head. The woman's head bounced once, then went still. For a moment, I saw the big white dog and its tired eyes, looking up at me.

Felix watched the woman, his face long, his eyes bright and disbelieving. His lips and teeth kept shaping the word *Sawry* over and over.

A round dent had formed in the silver container. Felix dropped the container and gently tucked his hands into the woman's coat pockets. He searched her yellow purse and plucked out a set of keys. I leaned on the shelf—my legs felt emptied from sleeping on the hard floor. The woman's tongue rolled out of her mouth.

Let's go, he signed.

Who's she?

Come on!

I picked my coat and gloves up off the floor where I'd wadded them into a pillow. Felix grabbed more chips and cookies and cans of drink and put them into a bag. He reached back into the woman's purse and pulled out a small fabric pouch with flowers on it. He took a few green pieces of paper from the pouch and shoved them in his pocket, then pulled me through the front door before I could get my coat on.

The cold pinched our cheeks. The sun was just a pink possibility at the edge of the distant fields. The prairie, to my surprise, was still intact.

Felix opened the door to a small blue car, and I got in beside him. He started the car and turned one of the dials so hot air fogged up the window and blew onto us. He stared at the wheel, his hands hovering.

What's wrong? I signed.

My dad never took me to do my driving test, he signed. I think I remember, though.

He put his hand on the black knob between us and pressed his leg down and pulled back on the knob. The car lurched forward into the snow pile in front of us. *Shid,* Felix said. He pushed forward on the knob. The car jerked back a little, and then the tires turned back and forth on the ice beneath us.

Lights flashed in the mirror. Felix peered behind us, then stomped on one of the pedals. The car trembled but didn't move.

Go out, he signed. Push it back. Go, go!

I dashed out to the front of the car. A truck had pulled in front of the store, and a man was stepping out of the truck. He wore a red and black plaid coat and had a tremendous gut. He said something to me. I leaned down and shoved the car as hard as I could, my boots slipping on the ice. The man ran toward me. The tires spun, flicking snow onto my pants. I slammed my shoulder into the car. The car backed up toward the man, and the man dodged out of the way, rolling sideways.

Felix wiped the fog off the window and waved at me and twisted the wheel. The man stood up, pointing at me. I jumped into my open door and yanked it shut.

Felix drove onto the road. I glanced behind us—the man was running after us. The car swayed from one side to the other, and Felix spun the wheel hard, his hand working the knob until finally the car chugged onward.

When we got far enough away, Felix slowed a little. The road was all ice and gravel. The car smelled like cigarette smoke, and for a moment I missed my mother. I hadn't thought of her in a long time.

I peered around at the fields and trees. To our left, pink sunlight reached over the edge of the fields. A few houses stood behind wooden fences. I kept looking for a metal fence topped with loops of bristling wire but found none. The white plains looked sleepy and harmless in the soft light.

Felix opened the small cupboard in front of me. Look, he signed. Anything?

I rummaged and pulled out large folded pieces of paper with tiny words and smudged pictures. A little flashlight. A few tools. A small empty cardboard box. A metal box full of ashes and cigarettes extended out from below the dials, and in the backseat were more large papers and the bag full of food and drink cans.

Where are we going? I signed.

Felix bit his lip.

Why did you hit her?

He shut his eyes.

She was hurt, I signed.

Felix's face had hardened. He stared at the road like he saw a destination a long way beyond it.

We passed a few signs. Felix turned onto a new road, and our backs faced the rising sun.

I touched everything, spinning all the dials and opening anything that would open, finally having the freedom to move around and see where I was being taken. I kept asking, What's this? but Felix didn't answer. I cranked a plastic knob in the door. The window cracked open.

Felix tapped my arm. Cold! he signed.

I rolled it back up. The road slipped beneath us like someone was always pulling it from behind us. The prairie slid past, revealing more prairie. A few buildings rose from the snow like frozen boils.

Felix kept watching the mirror. A short while later he pulled the car into a small spot just off the road. He reached into the back and opened a bag of chips. He offered me the bag, and I took a few.

They're looking for us, he signed. He tilted his right thumb down into the hole at the top of his left fist. Hope we have enough gas, he signed.

I was supposed to go to someone's house, I signed.

Felix finished the chips and threw the bag in the back. I'm sorry, he signed. I hate hurting that woman and stealing her car.

I wasn't sure what to say, so I repeated myself: I was supposed to go to someone's house.

There's so much they don't tell you, he signed. They took you
there tied up in the back of a van, like a creature. They bring us out
here so they can do what they want, so people don't have to care.
There never was a house. They weren't going to give you a family.
It was all a lie. They were going to keep you in that place until your
eyes stopped seeing and your tongue hung out of your mouth and
your body was nothing but bones, then they were going to kill
you and bury you along with all those other bodies. And no one
would know, and the world would forget you, because that's what
the world does. The world wants to forget us.

I sat still for a moment, still unsure what to say.

Why don't you understand yet? he signed. You need to see
outside yourself. Or do you not believe me? If you don't believe
me, you can leave. Walk back to the store, see what happens.

Felix reached across my body and shoved open my door. His
face looked more hurt than it ever had.

The air outside was cold yet gentle. No wind blew. Golden
sunlight unfolded across the white fields. In the sky, the blue
stretched thin toward the sun until it became white like a
threadbare sheet.

Hurry, Felix signed. It's cold.

I didn't move. My head was full of memories of the last time
I wandered alone. The blank fields. The empty house. My
broken arm and torn ear. My sickening loneliness.

I pulled the door shut. His face softened; his face could
change so easily. He reached into the back and grabbed a green
drinking can and gave me a red one.

It's New Year's Eve, he signed. It's perfect. Tomorrow will be
a fresh start for both of us.

He finished the can and pointed behind us at the sun.
Grandpa said the sun is Deaf, he signed. Same with the moon.

He worked the knob backward and steered the car back onto
the road.

In my pocket I felt the knife he'd given me—the knife we'd
stolen. I slowly wrapped each finger around its handle and

thought of its blade sinking into skin and ripping through muscle. My stomach clenched. I brushed the knife's handle until it fell out of my pocket onto the floor, then I tucked it further beneath my seat.

FELIX TURNED ONTO another, much wider road, and the pebbles fell away and the ride became smoother. He straightened in his seat, shedding his gloves and tightening his grip on the wheel.

The trees thickened and crowded closer to the road. Then they fell away and the buildings appeared, small and scattered at first, but soon growing taller and closer together, all brick and glass. When we stopped at a red light, I saw our reflection in a building window. In our heavy coats, we looked like other people.

Where are we? I signed.

Prince Albert.

Are we staying here?

Felix snapped his N-hand. No, I hate this place.

He stopped the car beside a white metal box with a hose leading out of it. Stay here, he signed. He stepped out and tucked the end of the hose into the back of the car. Black and white numbers started ticking upward on the metal box.

He pulled out the hose and went into the nearby store. Through the window I watched him give the man behind the counter the pieces of paper he took from the woman. Then he walked to the back hallway and disappeared.

I waited. A white car with brown stains all over it stopped on the other side of the metal box. A man with a beard got out and stuck the hose into his car. He looked at me in my heavy coat and gloves and cocked his eyebrow and smiled a little. *Thefugg*, he said, shaking his head. He removed the hose and went into the store to give some paper to the man behind the counter.

My hand started tapping my leg. Two kids walked past on the sidewalk, laughing and throwing snow at each other. My chest tightened. I sweated. The man returned to his car and drove away. I still couldn't see Felix.

I shoved open my door and ran into the store and down the hallway, knocking over a wire stand full of small plastic boxes. There were three doors in the hallway. I tried the first one. It opened onto an empty bathroom. The next was locked; I knocked on it, threw my shoulder into it. The man from behind the counter came around. *Dehelloodoon.* He pointed me away from the door. I hit it again. The man grabbed my coat, and I swung my elbow back and caught him in the chin. He stumbled back, cupping his hand under his mouth. Blood fell from his lips. He pointed at me and ran back to the counter.

I kicked the door. It started to give way. I shouldered it once more, and the door broke open into a dark room full of brooms and bottles and big rolls of paper.

Someone tapped me. I turned.

What are you doing? Felix signed.

I grabbed his hands and held them with relief. Felix peered toward the counter. The man at the counter held a phone to his ear. He spit blood onto the floor. Felix yanked on my arm, and we ran out of the store, the man yelling and pointing at us, spitting blood onto the counter and everything near it.

Felix turned on the car and we drove away. When he was able to free his hand from the knob, he balled his fist and hit me on the arm several times.

He steered the car off the street into a short narrow path between two buildings. Shadows filled the car; sunlight curdled in the street behind us. He stopped the car and faced me, his eyes completely black, his hands a flurry in the shadows.

What were you doing? he signed. Why didn't you stay in the car?

I'm sorry, I signed.

He hit me again. With my heavy coat it was like being hit by pillows.

I thought you left me, I signed.

I was taking a piss. You ignorant fuck. You're like a dog. Doesn't know how to stay.

I'm not a dog.

Did you hit that guy? In the store?

I said nothing.

Felix shut his eyes and rubbed his forehead like he was in pain. He called the cops, I bet, he signed. They'll know where we are. They'll look for this car, and when they find us they'll take us back, or to prison.

Felix leaned forward and rested his head on the steering wheel. He took several long breaths, then snapped upright and hit the wheel. He reached across and squeezed my hand.

I need you, he signed. You're the center of my gospel, the vision of redemption. I can't build my church without you. But you can't do anything unless I say so. If I tell you to stay, you stay. If I tell you to run, you run. To keep you safe. Understand?

I understand.

What did I say?

If you tell me to run, I run.

Tonight's the most important night of your life, he signed. Think of your father. Picture his face. Think of all the horrible things he did to you, how sad and angry and helpless it made you feel. Think of the dogs, their teeth in your skin, their claws ripping at you, all the blood you've shed to get where you are now. Tonight, you will get rid of all those thoughts and feelings. I will give you peace. But to do that, you must listen to me.

I don't want to think about his face.

Soon that's all he'll be. Just a face in your head. And in time you'll forget that, too.

Okay.

Stay here. Felix pulled on his gloves. I'll be back. Don't leave the car. His signs were much wider with the gloves on.

Where you going?

Stay here. Leave the car on to keep warm.

Felix left the car and walked back to the bright street. He glanced around, then turned around the corner, his boots dragging over the ice.

I kept my eyes on the side mirror and ate a bag of chips and a handful of cookies and finished my drink from earlier. My teeth felt rusty after.

I held my father's face in my head. His beard, his eyes, his tight mouth. I could smell him. He smelled like anger, sweaty and bitter. I made faces in the mirror, scrunching up my eyebrows and flashing my crooked teeth, trying to will my father away from my eyes and the shape of my face and find my own eyes, my own face.

The shadows between the buildings deepened. People walked past on the street, but no one approached the car. Smoke kept chugging out from behind the car, and I wondered if they put the fire out at the institution.

A small itch arose between my legs. Then a quick lurch. I had to piss. I pinched my legs together and squeezed my pants. I rummaged through the car for a bucket or container, then searched outside for a place, but Felix had told me to stay in the car.

I opened my door a little and put one knee on the car floor and one on my seat. I checked no one was looking, then pissed onto the ground, melting away the ice and splashing a little onto the door.

I shut the door and sat back. I twirled the knobs back and forth and waved my hand over the warm air coming up through the holes in front of me and drew shapes on the fogged-up windows. I thought that cars were amazing with all these wheels and dials and rods working together and that people were amazing to create something that goes so fast while we can sit in comfort. I thought about Dr. O asking me what I'd like to do and how one day I might create something that people can use.

I'd just started falling asleep when Felix tapped my shoulder. He shut the car off. He now wore a black coat with black gloves and black shoes. He carried his rubber coat in a bag.

Let's go, he signed.

He threw the keys ahead of the car, leaving his door open. I got out and followed him onto the bright street.

Felix got into another car. Wide. Brown. Smelling of trees. As he turned the car on, I saw blood slipping from his lip.

Never mind, he signed.

We drove past more buildings, then turned onto a street with rows of houses on both sides. Kids played in the snow; a few of them had dogs. I tensed, thinking the dogs would snap through the kids' small limbs. But the dogs didn't bite them. They jumped and spun and rolled onto their backs as the kids laughed.

Felix stopped the car. He focused on a house up the street that had two cars with blue and red lights parked outside.

Fugg, Felix said.

Is that your house? I signed.

Felix turned to me, biting his lip.

Three men came out of the house, all of them tall with brown shirts and black coats and round black hats with yellow bands. Felix's father stood at the door.

Felix pulled on the silver stick above the steering wheel, and we rolled away.

We parked in another alley and went to a restaurant that was empty except for us. We sat in the corner near the window. A woman came over to us, and Felix pointed at words on a piece of paper. Soon she brought us sandwiches and fries.

Stellan's, Felix said. I used to come here a lot when I was little. When my mom was here.

We ate two sandwiches each. Felix played with his fries and his ketchup.

I went to use the toilet and came back to see the sun had shrunk away from the street outside. The light over his head made him look tired.

Maybe Jesus wasn't a miracle birth, he signed as I sat back down. Maybe he was just a man who loved people and wanted the best for them, and his love for his father distracted from his true journey and got him crucified.

Maybe, I signed.

Felix's mouth drooped, like he wanted to talk to someone who understood what he meant.

What's the new year? I signed.

That's how we tell time.

Like a clock?

A clock measures minutes and hours. A year is thousands of hours. It's 1980 right now, but later tonight it'll be 1981.

Big numbers.

Felix's fingers skittered, making the table hum beneath my hand. He breathed slow and deep as though trying to calm something struggling inside his body.

Human beings have been around a long time, he signed. A lot of beauty, a lot of death, a lot of pain. We keep going in circles, thinking the same ideas and hating the same people, ignoring the bright sparks of light, killing people who help us love better. That's our greatest tragedy, that all this time we could've done better.

Are you okay? I signed.

Tell me you believe in me, he signed.

I believe in you.

Tell me you love me.

I love you, Felix.

Felix sat straight. Do you have your knife? he signed.

No.

My father stands in the way of our journey. So does your father. They swim in our blood. They want us gone. We can't be free unless we get rid of them, so we need to open a door that I told myself I'd never open again.

What do you mean?

Felix glanced toward the kitchen. I need you to help me kill my father, he signed.

Why?

Because.

I don't want to. I don't like hurting people. Or anything else.

It'll be over before you know it. People die all the time. It's as simple as walking from one room to the next.

Won't we get in trouble?

If people don't understand when we act with love, we need to speak their language and send a message. We need new rules. Understand?

I've never killed anyone.

All that anger you have, everything wrong that was done to you, we're healing that tonight. We'll pull it out of your head and throw it all into the world through the knife. You have the right to get rid of your pain.

Why don't you kill him yourself?

This is the next part of your baptism, a show of devotion. Your pain is greater than mine. You have the chance to exorcise it. Forgiveness doesn't work. Forgiveness makes that pain stay still. There's no relief. Those faces never go away.

I don't know forgiveness.

Letting people get away with hurting you. Do you think that's good?

I don't have a knife.

Use mine.

I picked Felix's butter knife off the table. He smiled and took it back.

My other knife, the sharp knife. I'll give it to you later.

I don't want to kill him.

You're my apostle. If you love me, I need you to show it. I will love you forever.

Felix stood from the table and pulled on his coat and took a few pieces of colored paper from his pocket. He left them on the table.

I followed him outside. The street was even colder in the dark. The green light from the restaurant's sign stuck to Felix's back until he stepped around the corner. He walked slow for a moment, then sped up, like he was excited.

FELIX PARKED THE car on the edge of a cluster of trees. A mess of metal objects stood in strange formations nearby: L-shaped bars sprouted out of a large metal disc, a long metal beam tilted over another bar, and half a globe made of criss-crossing silver rods rose up from the snow, its other half seemingly buried under the ground. The moonlight and frost coated them blue. I pointed to them.

Playground, Felix signed. Kid stuff.

Can we play on them?

Not now.

He returned his hands to the wheel and turned off the car lights, and we sat in darkness. He stared at the trees, through the trees. I blinked and tried to focus. The metal objects tilted a little and seemed to move closer even though I sat still.

My head, I signed.

Me too. We didn't have our medicine today. Pray with me.

He squeezed my hand, then bowed his head and shut his eyes. I bowed mine too. I kept looking sideways at him to see if his head was still down.

A red light burst in the air above the car. Felix snapped straight up, his head jarring against the seat. More red lights blinked and quivered, lighting up the snow and the metal playground objects and the car and the wall of trees. A green light burst, then blue. The sky filled with blossoms of light, long drooping strings of red and glittering bushels of yellow and flowering bursts of blue and green.

What's that? I signed.

Felix kept his eyes on the trees. I watched the lights. Forceful, brilliant, like worlds coming into being then immediately dying out.

The lights stopped. The darkness seemed even darker without them.

Felix signed to me, his hands like a colorless flame: Happy New Year. Time for a new beginning.

He kissed my hand, then held it open and placed his knife into it, closing my fingers around its handle. He stepped out his door and walked slowly into the trees.

I followed him; he quickly became a shadow, a soft shape on the snow. I strained to see him. He walked with certainty, knowing where to put his feet. I tried to put my feet in the same place, but I slipped on the ice a few times and had to hold myself up using the trees.

The trees started thinning, and soft lights began to glow. Houses stood in a long row, their windows lit up, the lights above their doors stretching into the yards. I lost Felix for a moment then found him off to the side. He stood still. Before I joined him, something pressed on my back. I glanced behind me. No one was there. The shadows seemed to bend like someone had left their shape on the air.

We stayed within the trees, working our way down the row of houses. In one of the windows people drank and hugged and smiled and laughed. I stopped to watch them.

What's happening?

Felix pulled me after him, and we soon came to a house with no lights on. Felix stepped over the short fence and approached the back door. He took his knife out of his coat pocket and handed it to me.

Stay there, he signed.

I backed up against the wall near the door. Felix crept to the corner of the house and peered around the corner toward the front, then he darted over to a small wooden building in the backyard and reached under the roof's overhanging part. I studied the trees just past the yard, searching for faces between the thin trunks. I felt dizzy. My stomach ached like I'd swallowed a rock, and I struggled to focus. Sharp teeth and black holes and my father's grinning gray face all swam and collided in my head. I didn't understand what Felix and I were doing or why we were there. My only anchor was his promise that my father would no longer be in my head.

I gripped the knife hard, pressing its handle into my palm and waving it at the trees. I missed George and Bernice.

Something silver flashed in the moonlight, and Felix came back holding a key. He stuck it in the door and turned it, slowly pushing the door open. He licked his lips, his eyes narrow and glittering.

His gloved hands flickered in the moonlight. Hold all your pain in front of you, he signed.

He waved me along, and I stepped inside. My boots knocked shoes over. Felix shut the door behind us, took my hand, and led me up a short set of stairs. My toes stubbed against each one as my eyes settled in the darkness.

I tapped him. Where's the light? I signed.

No. His fingers like a crow's beak in the shadows. No light.

We reached the top of the stairs and entered a kitchen. Felix went to the counter and broke a small piece off a loaf resting there. He put it in his mouth, then handed me a piece. I ate it and hardly tasted it—the room smelled like shit and piss.

Felix stepped into a small square of moonlight coming in from the window and held up his hands, his face barely visible. His room's down the hall, he signed. I'll open the door, and you take that knife, and you stab him for every time your father hurt you. For every scar you have.

I nodded toward the back door. Someone's watching me, I signed. I feel sick.

As I signed to Felix, whatever had followed me outside and all across the prairie rushed into the house, surrounding me, thickening the air like rubber, gripping my shoulders as though prepared at last to swallow me. Something like a knife edge rang up my spine. I cringed and shuddered and took a step toward the door. Felix pulled me back. I could hardly focus on what he said.

You've survived so much, he signed. You can survive this. It's almost over.

Don't you feel the air? There's something here.

There's nothing here. It's just you and me. Simple. I'll push open the door, you run to his bed and get him. His bed's three steps from the door.

Felix ate another bigger piece of the bread and offered another piece to me. He hasn't made this since I was a kid, he signed.

He stood on his tiptoes and kissed my forehead, then led me out of the kitchen, gripping my hand.

We inched our way down the hall, deeper into the darkness, our feet scuffing along the carpet. The shadows were so dark they seemed like entries to other places. My stomach lurched. The taste of the bread bubbled up. The thing hovering around me had wrapped itself around my neck. My heartbeat filled my head, and I could see it on the air, a thin gray pulse. I made a noise and rubbed my eyes; I forgot I'd been holding the knife, and I almost cut my cheek. Felix stopped. The shadow of his face turned, and his hand reached out to touch the wall. My hand shook. My whole body shook. He seized my wrist and jerked me forward.

We stood outside the door at the end of the hall. I could just see the outline of the door. He squeezed my wrist hard. I raised the knife, swallowing to keep my stomach quiet. My head filled with dogs and small rooms and sickness, screaming men and thick blood and walls full of monsters. The disgusting reek of the basement room blared through my nostrils.

Felix put his hand on the doorknob. My body clenched. I shook my head. Felix nodded and shoved the door. I didn't move, didn't breathe. I couldn't tell if it was actually open. Felix grabbed my coat and hauled me into the room. I slashed the knife back and forth, more protecting than attacking. I hit my leg on the bed and started swinging the knife down like a stick, beating the blankets and pillows.

The light came on. The room was empty.

Felix's shoulders sagged. He must be out, he signed. He rocked his fists up and down: You hesitated.

I what?

You didn't walk in.

I couldn't see. My head feels weird.

I sat on the bed and put my hand on my chest and tried to control my breathing. The thing clinging to my body had relaxed.

Felix bowed his head and touched his forehead with his clenched hands. Give me the knife, he signed. He was right. We're just alone. You don't love me.

I love you.

Give me the knife.

I couldn't see!

His head turned, like he saw something down the hall. *Shid*, he said. He stepped into the bedroom and swiped off the light and shut the door.

What? I signed.

He's here.

I stood up. A light glowed under the door. Felix's fingers whipped through the darkness. I caught shreds of what he said: Wait. Open door. He get you. Kill him you. Love me you. Last chance.

My father's face swelled up into my head like pus, blocking out everything else. My stomach hardened.

Ready?

I felt a grim presence on the other side of the door. The thing, the ghost, was there now—had become flesh and blood. I raised the knife over my head. Felix stood against the wall. Everything I'd ever felt balled up in my heart and coursed up my arm into the knife.

I love you.

I love you.

Under the door a shadow stepped into view. The door opened. Felix slunk away. The shape of a man stepped into the room, and shadows and light blended together and for a second I saw my father's grinning face. I screamed and ran at the shape and started stabbing, my arm whipping downward, the knife thunking into skin. I kept my head down. Didn't want those eyes settling on me. I stabbed randomly, in the arm, in the chest, in the shoulder. Once I looked at the holes I made and saw blood seeping through. I thought the holes were too thin. They had to be bigger, more blood had to come out. The shape had to die. The shape fell onto its stomach and tried to crawl away. I stabbed its back. Its blood became my need; I needed more of it. My hand and arm grew sore. I thrust the knife into the back of its head. The knife scraped bone. It stopped moving, then it moved only when I stabbed it.

I stopped, holding the knife still. I looked at the shape. The knife was sunk halfway into its back, and the skin on its back had turned to shreds. Parts of its spine and ribs poked up. The knife and my fist were completely soaked. My hand shook.

I stood up quickly. The shape's body gripped the knife, and I jerked it out. Splotches of blood arced onto the walls and carpet. The shape was now a glistening hunk of torn clothing and hair and meat.

I dropped the knife. Felix touched my shoulder and eased me away from the body, lowering his head against my back. My legs lost their strength—I slumped down against the wall. I couldn't think. It seemed I'd been knocked out of my body and was now hovering in the air looking down at myself and Felix and the dead man. My language and memories had all been scraped away. Blackness completely filled my head.

Felix knelt beside the body, his eyes sweeping over it. He touched the blood on the wall and stared at the blood on his fingers, then stood up and wiped it on his leg and remained still, staring, getting used to the body, its non-movement.

I wanted to cry, scream, react somehow. But I couldn't react. Not in any way that felt right. The ghost had quieted, as though satisfied after a meal.

I snapped back into my own head when I noticed Felix had left. I braced myself on the wall to stand up and then ran to the back. The door was open, and I stumbled down the stairs, searching for him in the darkness. The moonlight caught his white-blond head bouncing toward the trees. He'd tossed his hat. His jaw moved—I couldn't tell if he was laughing or crying.

I sprinted through the trees, slipping on the ice but never stopping. I caught him just before he opened his car door. He smiled, his eyes full of tears.

We did it! he signed. We're free! Let's do the priest now.

What?

Come on. You and me!

No!

I reached for him. He shoved me away. I grabbed him by the coat, and he spun and slapped me. I held onto his coat and grabbed his hair and slammed his head into the window. He went limp. He stared at me, his face innocent and questioning.

I slammed him against the car, his small body like twigs. My body boiled with everything that had chased me, my arms and legs and hands crammed full and charged with ghosts. I tried to sign, but my fingers shook too much; the only way I could speak was by hitting him. As I raised my fist again, he snapped straight and clawed my cheek and kicked my knee. I buckled. He drove his knee up into my face and knocked me backwards, then got into the car and backed it away. I ran toward him. Hot blood spurted from my nose and spilled onto my chest. He aimed the car at me, the lights filling my skull. I tried to move but my foot slipped. The car slammed into my hip and threw me into the spindly stick globe. The car's lights swung away and in the mirror I saw him smile and spit words through his teeth. He held up his tightened fist, his eyes wide and totally black. Soon the car faded into the darkness and became part of the road, its back lights like two faceless red eyes.

GOSPEL OF THE NEW PROMETHEUS

Pastor Felix Jimson

31 DECEMBER 1980

Some people are designated to feel more than others, they feel all the emotions think all the thoughts absorb all the pain scream all the rage embrace all the joy. Normal society can't or won't listen to them so they have to be put away in horrible places even though these people share more truth than anyone. A mental ward is the most truthful place in the world—they try to hide truth but it always escapes.

I carry my truth, my gospel, always in my heart, I wish the world nothing but love—

If the body is language then our every act is a way of speaking. Breathing, eating, sleeping, sex, nothing speaks clearer than the body.

I am again and always a holy ghost among the unenlightened. I carry light in my hands.

God is an absent father who forsook his only son; thus, I achieve my final form upon severance of blood ties.

To love is to lift others.

[EXCERPT FROM VOIR DIRE HEARING, SASKATCHEWAN COURT OF THE QUEEN'S BENCH— PRINCE ALBERT, SASKATCHEWAN—3 JUNE 1988]

PRESENT ARE:

ACCUSED: Mr. Kellan Gray

JUSTICE: Judge Dominique Bourque

CROWN: Mr. Benedict Berg, Esq.

DEFENSE COUNSEL: Mr. Michael Pysyk

CLERK: Mrs. Nancy Quill

CROWN: Mr. Gray, can you describe your role within the Prairie Nettles enterprise? Mr. Gray?

ACCUSED: Fuck you. I'm saying nothing.

JUSTICE: Answer the question, Mr. Gray, and watch your mouth, please.

ACCUSED: I got a right to silence. I'm not a fuckin' criminal. You're all staring at me like I fucked up.

JUSTICE: You were sworn today, Mr. Gray. Answer Mr. Berg's question.

ACCUSED: [chuckles] I get a cigarette, at least?

JUSTICE: No smoking in here, Mr. Gray.

ACCUSED: [unintelligible] What was the question?

CROWN: Your role within Prairie Nettles.

ADAM POTTLE

ACCUSED: Transportation. Low on the ladder. Someone had an order, I made sure that order went out and arrived on time.

CROWN: How long did you work there?

ACCUSED: You all probably got the records.

CROWN: Can you give an estimate?

ACCUSED: I was in my early twenties. Twenty-one, twenty-two.

CROWN: You have an office? A base of operations?

ACCUSED: You got the records, man.

CROWN: We're here for your perspective, Mr. Gray.

ACCUSED: My perspective is this is fucked.

JUSTICE: Civil language, Mr. Gray. This is not a bar. Start answering the questions directly.

CROWN: Where was your office?

ACCUSED: Here in PA.

CROWN: What about in Saint Louis?

ACCUSED: No.

CROWN: That's where you live, though, correct?

ACCUSED: Not anymore, thanks to you cocksuckers.

JUSTICE: Getting impatient, Mr. Gray.

CROWN: Where are you based now?

ACCUSED: BC. Fort Nelson.

CROWN: May I ask what you were doing in BC?

ACCUSED: I moved when the company expanded. They made me supervisor.

CROWN: When was that?

ACCUSED: Seventy-nine or eighty.

CROWN: So, you never worked at home? You took no business home with you?

ACCUSED: Always left it at the office. Man's got to play in the evenings.

CROWN: Can you explain why you had a tall fence with razor wire across the top? Makes your property look almost like a prison. If you didn't work at home, why have a fence like that?

ACCUSED: Security. Peace of mind.

CROWN: For your family?

ACCUSED: Didn't have a family.

CROWN: You were married, no?

ACCUSED: For a few years, then we broke up.

CROWN: Can you tell me about your marriage?

ACCUSED: Not much to tell. We were together, then we weren't. Young and restless, as they say.

CROWN: How long were you together?

ACCUSED: Six, seven, eight years. A fucking lifetime.

JUSTICE: Do I need to wash your mouth out with Ivory, Mr. Gray?

ACCUSED: I'm more a Palmolive man, your honor.

CROWN: Was your relationship amicable?

ACCUSED: [chuckles] She once broke a vase over my head.

CROWN: You divorced in 1972, is that correct?

ACCUSED: [unintelligible]

CROWN: Can you say that again, please?

ACCUSED: That was messy.

CROWN: Why was it messy?

ACCUSED: She hated me. I hated her. Always kept pressing me for money. Fucking courts always love the wife, never the husband.

CROWN: How much did she know about your criminal enterprise?

DEFENSE: Objection. The accusation's yet to be proven in court.

CROWN: Withdrawn. I'll rephrase. How close would you say you were?

ACCUSED: I don't know. She was my wife.

CROWN: Can you elaborate?

ACCUSED: We liked to share smokes. She always asked me to stay home and watch TV or listen to Joni Mitchell or Guess Who. She never had a job, just sat around on the couch all day smoking and doing nothing. She liked fuck—screw—she was a great lay. Even after we divorced, we met up a few times.

CROWN: She passed away in March 1976, correct?

ACCUSED: If that's the date.

CROWN: You remember how she passed?

ACCUSED: Yeah, police came to tell me. Was sad to hear it.

CROWN: Drug overdose. Coroner found a massive amount of heroin in her body.

ACCUSED: She did love the needle.

CROWN: How old was your son when she passed away?

DEFENSE: Objection. Again, this hasn't been proven.

ACCUSED: I don't have a son.

CROWN: The DNA test says otherwise, your honor. Do you have any brothers or sisters, Mr. Gray?

ACCUSED: No.

CROWN: Are your parents still living? Does deafness run in your family?

ACCUSED: Do I look like the kind of man who'd have a mongrel for a kid? I'm not fuckin' defective.

JUSTICE: Language, Mr. Gray.

CROWN: Are you ashamed of your son, Mr. Gray?

ACCUSED: Are you deaf or what?

CROWN: According to multiple sources, your ex-wife, Bethany Nariman, had not only kicked her drug habit but was trying to get your son back just before she died, isn't that correct? Visiting your property, calling you? She'd found a job, but you were holding your son hostage.

ACCUSED: I don't have a fucking son. She kept calling 'cause she wanted money, or to bust my balls. Like I said, she didn't work. Expected me to pay all her bills, like I was responsible for her misery.

CROWN: Aren't you, in a way, responsible for her misery?

ACCUSED: She was miserable before I ever met her.

CROWN: She ran into legal complications when she realized your son's birth had never been registered. Legally speaking, your son didn't exist.

ACCUSED: He doesn't exist, no matter how you slice it.

CROWN: And how do you explain the dead bodies found on your property in April 1980? Or the gunshots neighbors heard? Or the bullet holes in your house? Or the grave dug in your backyard? Or the room found in your basement? Or the dead dogs found buried in the woods nearby?

ACCUSED: I don't know what the fuck you're talking about. You just said he doesn't exist.

JUSTICE: Last warning, Mr. Gray.

CROWN: But that's why we're here, Mr. Gray, to bring your son into existence—

ACCUSED: Nope. Horseshit.

CROWN: —and to bring him justice for all the harm you caused him, in addition to proving your role in the Prairie Nettles enterprise. Rest assured, we will hear your son's story, Mr. Gray, and should—

ACCUSED: I said—

[Whereupon the Accused leapt from the witness box and tackled Mr. Berg. The Accused was soon restrained and removed from the courtroom.]

[END OF EXCERPT]

TESTIMONY

THE COURTHOUSE LOOKS a lot like the institution, all brick and small windows. They could be brothers. Every room has a stiff rhythm that makes me stand up straight. I can never get comfortable.

Out in front is a stone woman standing on a white block. She holds a wreath. I wanted to ask my lawyer who she was, but my hands were in cuffs and my lawyer and the interpreter were behind me. My interpreter had combed back his sparse black hair and wore a suit and tie instead of his usual jeans and sweatshirt.

Two policemen held me by my arms, and we walked up the steep steps together. Ahead of us, someone walked backwards up the steps aiming a black glass eye at me. It was hot, and when we got to the top I had to catch my breath. I wasn't used to walking so much.

I'd woken up feeling sick, so I didn't eat much for breakfast. I'd been thinking of my mother each day. My lawyer told me she'd gotten a job and had been trying to get me back when she died, and I couldn't shake the image of my father holding her down and filling her full of drugs. As we walked into the large room with all the seats and shining brown wood on the walls, my stomach started churning, and I flexed my body, clamping down on myself.

We sat at a table and waited for others to come in. A tall man with a long face was already waiting for us, and a man in soft brown clothing stood near the high table at the front. A woman with short hair and a bright blue dress sat behind a small machine and spread her fingers above it.

I pointed at her. Court reporter, the interpreter signed.

I flexed my hands within my cuffs. I tell her what happened? You tell the judge. He's not here yet.

Does he know Sign?

No, I'm going to interpret for you.

I pointed at the man with the long face, who frowned at my finger. Who's he?

You met him before. He's the prosecutor, the Crown.

A tall man with fading hair and a mustache sat down at the table across from us. He said a few words to my lawyer. My lawyer's face was stiff. I always have a hard time measuring her mood.

A side door opened, and two policemen led my father into the room. His eyes immediately gripped onto me. I looked away.

A man in a black robe entered and sat in the high chair at the front of the room.

Who's that? I signed.

Get up.

We all stood up. The man in soft brown clothing spoke, and we all sat down again. The interpreter stood up and walked around to the front of the room where I could see him.

Watch me, he signed.

Behind him, the judge began speaking, and he turned the judge's words into signs.

Mr. Berg, the judge said, how are you today?

The interpreter pointed to the Crown man sitting beside my lawyer. Fine, Your Honor, he said.

The judge turned over a few papers on his table. Voir dire again, he said. We're focusing on charges brought from a specific witness today, along with the amsiliby of those charges, is that correct?

That's correct, Your Honor.

What's amsiliby? I signed.

The interpreter's fingers slowed. Admissibility, he signed.

Is that his name, Your Honor?

Charges before the court today, the Crown man said, in addition to the trafficking, possession, and murder charges already listed, include kidnapping, forcible confinement, attempted murder, criminal negligence causing bodily harm, and assault causing bodily harm.

The interpreter's fingers flew, spelling out long words. I could barely keep up.

He's talking about me? I signed. Who was murdered?

The judge looked at my father. Mr. Gray, he said, will we be better behaved today?

The man with the mustache stood. My client understands the stakes, Your Honor, he said, and he's assured me he will not repeat his outburst.

I turned to look at my father, then turned away. Even though he didn't face me I could feel his hatred. It baked the air around us.

Good morning, Mrs. Holstadt, the judge said. Is your client prepared to speak today?

My lawyer stood up. Good morning, Your Honor, she said. Yes, he is. I'd like to remind everyone present that my client is still feeling—and will likely continue to feel—the effects of the trauma he has endured, and that being here today is an incredibly difficult and courageous act for him, especially since Mr. Gray has already tried to harm him in prison.

My father's lawyer raised his hand. Objection, he said. That hasn't been proven yet. Everything is alleged at this point.

What's alleged? I signed.

The judge spoke. The interpreter continued. His knobby hands became a blur. I caught only a few words. Communication. Ask. Proper. My stomach turned watery. I flexed my body harder.

Slow down, I signed. You're going too fast.

My hands chafed in the cuffs. I couldn't pull them apart enough to make certain signs. I raised my hands and made a noise. The judge looked at me. I turned to my lawyer, my hands still raised.

My lawyer nodded and lowered her hand onto my arm. Your Honor, she said, may we please remove the handcuffs from my client's hands? He's Deaf and his hands must be free to communicate.

Objection, my father's lawyer said. Mr. Smith is a convicted murderer, so for the safety of everyone in the court, we ask that his hands remain bound.

We're here for his story, the judge said, and he can't tell his story properly if he's gagged. Please remove the cuffs.

One of the policemen sitting behind us pulled out a key and took the cuffs off my hands.

Thank you, I signed to the judge.

The judge nodded at then glared at my father. You're not on the stand, Mr. Gray, he said. You'll speak when you're spoken to.

I looked at my father. Beneath his table, he raised his middle finger at me. Sweat started pooling down my back and beneath my arms and knees. I hunched forward to quiet my stomach.

The Crown man stood up. Your Honor, he said, I'd like to invite Mr. Smith to the witness stand. He waved at me.

I looked at my lawyer, who nodded at me.

My father shook his head and smiled. *Thizzbullshid*, he said.

I stood up and walked to the chair just below the judge. The interpreter faced me as the man in brown clothing raised his hand.

Raise your hand, the man said, raising his own.

Me?

Yes.

I imitated his gesture.

Do you swear the evidence you give shall be the truth, the whole truth, and nothing but the truth, so help you God?

I lowered my hand. Is evidence my story? I signed.

Say yes, the interpreter signed.

I raised my hand again and curled it into a fist. Yes.

You can sit, the interpreter signed.

I sat down. I could see the fingers of the woman in the blue dress flying over rows of small tabs.

Her fingers are fast, I signed.

The Crown man approached me. Mr. Smith, how are you today?

My name isn't Smith, I signed. My name is— I dragged my fist up chest and spread my fingers.

The interpreter spoke to the judge. My father shrugged and threw up his hands.

I understand, the Crown man said, but for our purposes here in court, may I call you Mr. Smith?

Yes.

Do you understand why you're here today?

My father yelled at the judge. The interpreter pointed at him and signed, This is bullshit. That hand shit doesn't mean anything.

Be quiet, the judge said.

I stared at the floor. My stomach had begun to bubble. Through the corner of my eye, I saw the interpreter waving at me.

May I ask why we're wasting the court's time with this, Your Honor? my father's lawyer said. While Mr. Smith's hand gestures may be surprisingly clear, he is not only Deaf and unable to hear any incriminating statements, he's been institutionalized, and that was prior to his conviction.

My lawyer stood up. My interpreter shook his hands loose like they were getting sore.

My client's mental state has been evaluated several times, Your Honor, she said. The psychiatric testimony is in his file, and it's wrong to confuse mental incompetence with Deafness.

If the witness has information involving your client, the judge said, we need to hear it, however that information may come. The judge glared at my father. You and your client will therefore treat the witness with respect. He turned to the Crown man and said, Please continue.

The Crown man nodded. Thank you, Your Honor. He walked toward me. Mr. Smith, can you tell me about the first time you remember seeing that man? He pointed at my father.

My father's beard fluttered as he spit more words at me. *Oolilfugg.* I swallowed and rubbed my stomach. The room began to tilt. I felt like I'd been given the red drink.

When did you first see him? the Crown man said.

I raised my hand to point at my father. My hand shook. He stopped at my mom's house a few times, I signed. They yelled at each other. One night he woke me up and took me out of my mom's house and put me in a truck and dragged me into his house and threw me into a room under the ground.

I stopped. Pointing at him felt like jabbing a wolf.

Tried to kill me, I signed. Made me fight dogs. Had to kill them or I'd be dead. Dug a hole—

The Crown man and the interpreter held up their hands. Mr. Smith, please slow down, the Crown man said. I appreciate you being so open, but we need to go over it step by step.

I shuddered. Shifted in my chair.

He wants to kill me right now, I signed. I can feel it.

The Crown man spoke. The interpreter's hands fluttered. I couldn't tell what he was signing. The room swayed. My stomach lurched. As the Crown man stepped toward me, I leaned away from him and vomited onto the floor. The reporter stood from her seat and backed away as orange juice and small bits of bread splattered on the tile.

The interpreter approached me, signing, You okay, you okay? I didn't have to look up to know my father was grinning.

Break, the judge said. Fifteen minutes.

I stepped away from the chair, averting my eyes from my father, as though looking at him would cause me to melt. I started to walk toward the door, but the two policemen stood in front of me. One of them put the handcuffs back on. My lawyer and the interpreter approached.

Let's go into the hall, she said to the policemen. Let him calm down.

We all went out into the hall, leaving my father and his lawyer in the room. I stood against the wall and hunched over, taking deep breaths and waiting for the world to stop tilting.

The interpreter brought me a paper cup of water. I swallowed it.

I'm sorry, I signed.

My lawyer and the interpreter spoke, both to me and to each other. I didn't know what they were saying. I focused on my breathing. I thought of Felix, wondering where he was.

When we went back in a man with a long stick pushed a rolling yellow bucket out the door. Brown water sloshed inside the bucket. The tile was wet and clean. My father stuck his tongue out at me, mimicking me vomiting.

The judge came back in. We all had to stand up.

How are you feeling, Mr. Smith? he said. Are you able to continue?

I'll try, I signed.

The policemen removed my cuffs again, and I stood at the front and raised my hand to the man in the brown clothes and sat down. The Crown man walked toward me, slower this time, like he thought I might vomit again.

Can you please tell us about the basement room Mr. Gray put you in?

I made fists then stretched them out. It had a dirty mattress, I signed. I was always alone. The light was always on. People were upstairs; I could feel their footsteps. I had to pee in a bucket.

Did they feed you? Bathe you?

They used a hose. Outside. It was cold.

Do you know how long you were kept in that room?

I shrugged. Years.

The Crown man came a bit closer. How many years?

I don't know.

Can you guess?

My father's lawyer stood. We're not here to guess, Your Honor, he said. If the witness can't remember dates, how can we rely on his testimony?

The Crown man faced the judge. Your Honor, he said, Mr. Smith was not only a young child when he was taken, he had the ability to tell time taken away from him. He should've been taught by his parents—namely, his father—but he wasn't, so he has to do his best and estimate.

How do we know he was a young child? my father's lawyer said. He can't even say.

Overruled, the judge said. Please work toward concrete details, Mr. Berg.

What's overruled mean? I signed to the interpreter.

The Crown man turned back to me. How many years do you estimate you were kept in that underground room, Mr. Smith?

I was short when I went in. I was tall when I went out.

So, from child to teenager?

Okay.

Can you roll up your sleeves, please, and explain how you got those scars on your arms?

I pulled my sleeves back. My arms glinted in the courtroom's soft light. From the dogs, I signed.

What dogs?

I lifted my eyes to my father. Now that my stomach was empty I could point at him. He put me in a cage and made me fight dogs, I signed. They gave me a red drink before I fought. I always felt angry. I couldn't stop.

They drugged you?

There was a bottle in the kitchen. He and many other men watched. They shouted at me. They hit the cage walls. The dogs bit my arms, and I had to kill them or he'd shoot me.

My father glanced around the room, tapping his fingers on the table.

How do you know that? Did he threaten you?

He pointed a gun at me.

How many times did you have to fight the dogs?

I don't know.

Every day? Every few days?

I stared at my father, at Kellan. The interpreter's hands flickered at the edge of my vision.

Mr. Smith?

It kept changing, I signed. I fought a lot.

How'd you escape?

He took me outside. Someone was digging a hole by the fence. He made me stand by the hole, and he put his gun to the back of my head. My arm was broken. I couldn't fight.

How'd you break your arm?

One of his men pushed me down the stairs.

That same day?

A different day. Someone put a stick and tape on it. The man digging the hole got shot and fell into the hole, and everyone started running around. Trucks came through the fence in the front and back, people shooting everywhere.

The Crown man went back to the table and picked up a photograph and held it up for me. I cringed at the face of the bigger man.

Did this man get shot?

Yes.

You saw him get shot?

Yes.

Where was he shot?

In the head. And the chest.

He lowered the photograph and pointed at Kellan. Did he do any shooting?

Yes.

Did he shoot at you?

I looked at everyone in the room and swallowed back tears. I wished Felix was there. I had no family or friends to support me. I shrank a little in my seat.

I didn't see, I signed. I ran.

Where'd you run?

Through the fence, into the woods. I found a house. There was no one there.

An empty house?

Yes.

What happened there?

I saw people drive to the house at night. I wanted help, but they drove away. I followed the road they took and found more houses. I fell asleep on the road, and they put me in a hospital.

The Crown man put the photograph back on the table and picked up a piece of paper and gave it to the judge.

Let the record show, he said, that there is an entry from Victoria Hospital dated sixteen April 1980, three days after the gunfight, describing a young man with no identification of

unknown age and matching a description of Mr. Smith's physical state at that time: scarring on his arms, a broken left arm,
a circle-shaped tear in his right ear, powder burns on his neck,
and a laceration on his right leg. Mr. Smith, may I ask what
happened to your ear and your leg?

I don't know about my ear. I didn't feel it until later. I hurt
my leg in the dark—a piece of wire from a fence.

The Crown man pointed at my father again. Did you know
who this man was while you were in his house?

Are we almost done? I signed.

Not yet. Did you know who he was?

No, but I felt we were related somehow. We have the same
eyes.

My father sprang up from his seat and jabbed his finger at
me. *Fuggoo!* he said. *Oolilshid!*

The interpreter's hands went still. The judge spoke, and the
policeman sitting behind my father pushed him back into his
seat. My father gritted his teeth.

The DNA test agrees with you, Mr. Smith, the Crown man
said. Or should I say Mr. Gray? You are family; he is your
father. How do you feel about that?

I don't feel like family, I signed.

Did you see him at any other time after that? Before you
entered prison?

I bit my lip. He hugged me one time, I signed. He sat in my
room and hugged me, then he gave me to the dogs.

My father waved me toward him. *C'mon,* he said. *Chiggenshid.*

Mr. Smith? Did you see him after?

I saw him outside sometimes, digging holes and burying
children.

Where was this?

The institution. He always went out at night.

You had dreams—nightmares—about him?

I saw him, like I'm seeing him now.

Objection, my father's lawyer said.

Is there anything else you'd like to say, Mr. Smith? Anything
you'd like to say to him?

I kept staring at my father. I let my tears fall. My hands shook. I'm sorry, I signed. I'm sorry you don't feel love. I'm sorry everything you see is black and horrible.

I glanced around the courtroom. At the reporter. My lawyer. The judge.

I fixed my eyes on Kellan. He raised his eyebrows. Challenging me. I whipped my words at him. The interpreter tensed as he delivered my words.

I know you killed my mother, I signed. We may be family, but I'm not your son. You tried to kill me. You tried to take everything from me. But I escaped. I don't care what happens to you.

I wiped away tears and leaned into my signs. I never looked away from him. All my life I've felt like a ghost, I signed. I'm tired of people not seeing me, not feeling me. I want to reach out to people. I'm full of love, and I have no one to give it to, but someday I'll find someone. I'm done hurting people. I'm never hurting anyone again. I don't know what my path is in life, but I'm going to do good and bring light to the world.

The interpreter winced as he translated my father's words. You and me, Kellan said. I'm going to get you, you lousy little fuck.

The judge flicked a finger at Kellan, and the two policemen took him out of the courtroom. He kept jabbing his finger at me, and I kept staring at him until he was out of sight.

The Crown man sat down. Kellan's lawyer stood and asked me questions. About my crimes. About my time at the institution. About my Deafness. About my relationship with Felix. I answered all his questions simply.

At the end, Kellan's lawyer said, Mr. Smith saw a fellow teenager as a Christlike figure and did so without question. The way Mr. Smith sees the world is, I'm sorry to say, fundamentally flawed and completely unreliable. His narrative neither supports nor coheres with any idea of justice or normalcy, so I ask that you remove his story from this case and clear Mr. Gray of the charges.

The judge dismissed us.

I asked my lawyer what happens next. We wait, she said.

As we went down the courthouse steps into the hot sun, my body felt strangely empty. I breathed deep, the deepest breath I'd taken in a long time. I was empty but also stronger, more together, ready to be filled.

SKY

LIGHT PRESSED SOFT and pink on my eyelids. I opened my eyes—I lay on my side. The blanket twisted off me. The soft blue morning light made the walls of the empty house look furry. The world seemed new. No ghosts clung to me.

My neck hurt. My knuckle bled. It hurt to close my hand.

Across the room was a square metal skeleton. All rusted ribs and thick limbs. A stained mattress slumped off the skeleton onto the floor beside it. The floor was old dirty wood. I could feel the whole house's emptiness from that room.

My throat was dry as the paper curling off the walls. I stood and walked down the hall. The boards in the floor bent upward up in places. My arm hurt; my hand below the break felt heavy, like it had turned to stone. I searched for whatever creature had pattered past me in the night then stepped carefully down the stairs.

Every room was full of furry blue light. My feet were cool, and I watched where I placed them on the splintered floor. The whole house smelled like dirt, like it had been buried. Many of the walls had holes punched into them. A few had drawings of dicks and silly faces in pink and green paint. The cupboards held dust and empty bowls. I tried the faucets again but nothing came out. On the main floor the front window had been shattered. The remaining glass had browned.

I sat on a chair along the wall. I hadn't sat in a chair in years, and I felt uneasy so I stood again.

One of the windows in the front room was intact. I walked over to it. Saw myself approaching the glass. I hadn't seen myself in years either.

I was expecting a child, not the tall thin dirty ghoul I saw. I recoiled. Blood ran down the side of my face. Black spatters spread from my jaw to my neck. My hair hung off my head in snarled red-brown clumps. Whiskers sprouted above my lip. My skin was grubby, and my teeth were gray and jagged. My father's eyes stared back at me.

I made a noise, a small ant of a sound that skittered up my throat. I touched my face. Pulled at my whiskers. Threw my hair back and forth. I grew dizzy and turned away from my reflection and sank to the floor.

I was alone. No one knew where I was. No one knew who I was. I didn't know who I was. Looking in the mirror solved nothing. The light slowly filling the house shone only on more galling emptiness. I didn't know where I was supposed to be or what I was supposed to do. The prairie outside the window was green and gold and open, but I couldn't go. I had nothing. I was nothing. In a vague way I knew all of this. The thought sat in me. That's what happens with thoughts you can't say. They sit. They sink into you.

I felt sleepy again, so I lay flat on the floor. I was hungry and thirsty but had no energy. Dirt clung to my hair and skin. I touched the rip in my ear; I wanted to vomit but I had nothing in my stomach.

The house was empty, yet every room had weight, a crouching fury waiting to lash out. The faces and dicks and broken walls and splintered floors poked at me, tried to dig into me.

Something flashed. Quick and white. I thought it was a gun. The house trembled. Outside there was another flash—white filled the air. The house shook again. I cringed and hugged the wall. The rumbling worked through my body. The walls shook. I thought the house might cave in, so I ran outside. The sky was a ceiling of thick gray muscle. Flashes lit up the fields with hot white stabs that cracked the air. The ground rumbled but didn't shift, didn't open. The rumbles came right after the flashes. They had a rhythm. They had power bigger than any person. They started to hold me instead of frighten me.

I raised my hand, reaching for the sky. More flashes dropped into the fields, and I felt the rumbling from my backbone outward. My blood thrilled. I wanted to touch that power the way I touched grass. Multiple flashes surged. Some fell from the sky, and some looked like they shot up from the fields. I yelled. More white stabs tore down into the fields. The rumbles held me. My hand fluttered. I screamed with joy, full and free. The light and the rumbles and my voice were all the same. The pebbles under my feet shook. I stretched my eyes wide open to let in the light, staring at the places where it cracked the air. I yearned to live in such light—within those cracks it seemed there was space for me. The white light soaked into my eyeballs. My torn ear and my bloody leg and my broken arm glowed. My pain was not just pain. It was more. The rumbles came down on me and my muscles quivered and my mind emptied. The air tasted new, like fresh rocks. I screamed again, emptying my lungs at the sky.

Drops of water fell. Light, then heavy. I turned, thinking someone had spit on me like they did in the cage. The flashes and rumbles continued. Water fell hard onto me—the sky sweated. I opened my mouth. Cupped my hand and slurped up the water. I ran into the house and grabbed a dirty bowl and filled it and drank. The blood on my leg and neck washed away. My hair became thick. My clothes clung to my body like a second skin. I got another bowl and set it on the ground and laughed as it filled up.

Soon the flashes and rumbles faded. Then the water stopped. The air turned sweet.

I took both bowls inside and sat by the window sipping from them. The gray muscle slackened and emptied out of the sky like it was tired.

The light continued to blare throughout my body, as though my blood was made of sky.

ACKNOWLEDGMENTS

IT TOOK ME ten months to write the first draft of this book and even longer to find a home for it. It was by far my most difficult project to date, and I couldn't have completed it without the love and support of a village worth of beautiful people.

First and foremost: thank you to Sadie Hartmann and Rob Carroll at Dark Matter INK for welcoming this problem child of a novel into the warm and cozy nest they've built. Thank you also to my Dark Matter siblings: Tracy Cross, Steph Nelson, R. L. Meza, Ai Jiang, Izzy Lee, and Catherine McCarthy. And thank you to Marissa van Uden, who performed laser-focused surgery on the manuscript. The story is clear because of her efforts.

Diann Block of the Saskatoon Correctional Centre helped me understand the Saskatchewan prison system and was instrumental to this story, as were Sue Delanoy and Laura Baker. Talila A. Lewis pointed me to research surrounding Deaf inmates. Charity Blanc guided me through the narrator's story and eventually introduced me to the narrator. Lisa Long of the Saskatchewan Archives helped me find police documents, court records, and psychiatric reports. The Saskatchewan Arts Board graciously granted me funding that allowed me to complete the first draft.

Endless thanks to my literary community, especially Amanda Rheaume, Amanda Leduc, Alicia Elliott, Jenny Ferguson, Brad Fraser, Erin Soros, Jael Richardson, Gary Barwin, David Demchuk, Niko Stratis, Kai Cheng Thom, Amber Dawn, and Ann Y.K. Choi. Your friendship and encouragement sustained me as I worked on this novel.

Applause to my Deaf community in Saskatoon and beyond, namely Janet Dittrich, Ebony Gooden, Chris Dodd, Torrie Ironstar, Sage Ravenwood, Ross Showalter, Sara Nović, Kelly Andrew, Maryam Hafizirad, and my fellow Signed Ink members. You all give me hope.

Chocolate-filled Lament Configurations to the magnificent coalition of demons and werewolves that is the horror community. Your work gave me the courage to leap from literary fiction to genre fiction. I am all the better for it.

Thank you to my agent Ron Eckel and the brilliant team at CookeMcDermid. I'm lucky to work with you all.

Love to my mother, who believes in me even when I don't.

My goldendoodle Valkyrie was and is by my side every single day, filling me with warmth and joy and lifting me up when I need it most.

The prairies of Saskatchewan—Treaty Two, Four, Five, Six, Eight, and Ten territory—haunt me everyday. They are loaded with beauty and deserve our everlasting reverence.

I thank the narrator for trusting me with his story and for reminding me that, even when we endure the ugliest, most gruesome horrors, we can still find small pockets of beauty in this world.

Lastly, I thank my wife, Deborah, who held me and told me everything would be okay and steered me toward the light in more ways than anyone ever has.

—Adam Pottle

ABOUT THE AUTHOR

ADAM POTTLE IS a Deaf author whose works span multiple genres. His groundbreaking horror fantasy play *The Black Drum*, billed as the world's first all-Deaf musical, was produced in 2019 and will be published in Spring 2024. He was a 2022 Warner Bros. Discovery Access screenwriting fellow, developing a supernatural horror feature script during his tenure. His historical suspense novella *The Bus* won the 2015 Ken Klonsky Award and was shortlisted for two Saskatchewan Book Awards. He lives in Saskatoon, Canada, where he can often be spotted walking his goldendoodle, Valkyrie.

Chopping Spree by Angela Sylvaine
ISBN 978-1-958598-31-3

The Bleed by Stephen S. Schreffler
ISBN 978-1-958598-11-5

Free Burn by Drew Huff
ISBN 978-1-958598-26-9

The House at the End of Lacelean Street
by Catherine McCarthy
ISBN 978-1-958598-23-8

The Off-Season: An Anthology of Coastal New Weird
Edited by Marissa van Uden
ISBN 978-1-958598-24-5

The Dead Spot: Stories of Lost Girls
by Angela Sylvaine
ISBN 978-1-958598-27-6

When the Gods Are Away by Robert E. Harpold
ISBN 978-1-958598-47-4

Grim Root by Bonnie Jo Stufflebeam
ISBN 978-1-958598-36-8

Voracious by Belicia Rhea
ISBN 978-1-958598-25-2

Abducted by Patrick Barb
ISBN 978-1-958598-37-5

Darkly Through the Glass Place by Kirk Bueckert
ISBN 978-1-958598-48-1

The *Threshing Floor* by Steph Nelson
ISBN 978-1-958598-49-8

Club Contango by Eliane Boey
ISBN 978-1-958598-57-3

Psychopomp by Maria Dong
ISBN 978-1-958598-52-8

Little Red Flags: Stories of Cults, Cons, and Control
Edited by Noelle W. Ihli & Steph Nelson
ISBN 978-1-958598-54-2

Frost Bite 2 by Angela Sylvaine
ISBN 978-1-958598-55-9

Other Books in The Dark Hart Collection

Rootwork by Tracy Cross
ISBN 978-1-958598-01-6

Mosaic by Catherine McCarthy
ISBN 978-1-958598-06-1

I Can See Your Lies by Izzy Lee
ISBN 978-1-958598-28-3

A Gathering of Weapons by Tracy Cross
ISBN 978-1-958598-38-2

Milton Keynes UK
Ingram Content Group UK Ltd.
UKHW040110290624
444859UK00004B/255